Once a lady resolves to b[...]
she must be prepared to [...]

Kindred Spirits

"*I* wonder if it is dependent on me," she said, pulling her hand from his, "or on something else. Forces already set in motion."

"You mean fate?" he asked. "Destiny, the ordination of the stars, something like that?"

"Actually, I was thinking more in terms of desire, need. Unadulterated lust."

"Lust?" He nodded slowly, ignoring a moment of surprise at her words. He had flirted with any number of women in his life. Yet he wasn't certain he had ever met a woman whose nature was quite as direct as Lady Chester's. It was most intriguing. "Lust can indeed be a powerful influence."

"And dangerous as well."

"I would certainly never force my attentions upon you." He leaned close and lowered his voice. "Or drag you into my arms and kiss you until you begged for more, unless I was confident you wished to be kissed."

"That is not the danger that concerns me," she said.

By Victoria Alexander

A LITTLE BIT WICKED
LET IT BE LOVE
WHEN WE MEET AGAIN
A VISIT FROM SIR NICHOLAS
THE PURSUIT OF MARRIAGE
THE LADY IN QUESTION
LOVE WITH THE PROPER HUSBAND
HER HIGHNESS, MY WIFE
THE PRINCE'S BRIDE
THE MARRIAGE LESSON
THE HUSBAND LIST
THE WEDDING BARGAIN

Coming Soon

WHAT A LADY WANTS

VICTORIA ALEXANDER

A Little Bit Wicked

AVON BOOKS
An Imprint of HarperCollinsPublishers

This is a work of fiction. Names, characters, places, and incidents are products of the author's imagination or are used fictitiously and are not to be construed as real. Any resemblance to actual events, locales, organizations, or persons, living or dead, is entirely coincidental.

AVON BOOKS
An Imprint of HarperCollins*Publishers*
10 East 53rd Street
New York, New York 10022-5299

Copyright © 2007 by Cheryl Griffin
ISBN: 978-0-06-088262-4
ISBN-10: 0-06-088262-X
www.avonromance.com

First Avon Books paperback printing: January 2007

Avon Trademark Reg. U.S. Pat. Off. and in Other Countries, Marca Registrada, Hecho en U.S.A.
HarperCollins® is a registered trademark of HarperCollins Publishers.

Printed in the U.S.A.

10 9 8 7 6 5 4 3 2 1

This book is dedicated to all those nameless librarians through the years who helped me discover worlds I never dreamed existed.

To Rivka Sass and the librarians of the Omaha Library system for their commitment, enthusiasm and humor.

And to my favorite librarian, Jeanne Hauser, because she can find anything, and she makes a wicked peanut butter ball.

Prologue

London
February 1854

"Very well then." The Honorable Nigel Cavendish, the only son of Viscount Cavendish, who seemed in excellent health and was expected to live for many, many years, raised his glass a little higher. "Here's to love."

"To love," Oliver Leighton, the Earl of Norcroft, seconded.

The toast echoed around the circle of four men who had gathered at their favorite club to privately mark the wedding of their friend Jonathon Effington, the Marquess of Helmsley, and Oliver's cousin, Fiona, a scant few hours ago. In spite of the fact that each and every man raised his glass to love, there was a distinct variance in degrees of enthusiasm. It wasn't that any of them was particularly opposed to the emotion, indeed, Oliver would have wagered every man here was at heart a romantic, with the possible exception of Daniel Sinclair. The American was new to their number and was an interesting addition to their group. He was, as well, their mutual hope for turning a tidy profit in a railroad development venture in America.

"And to the ever-present desire that love, as opposed to mere duty, will accompany the inevitable," Gideon Pearsall, Viscount Warton added.

Sinclair raised a brow. "The inevitable being marriage?"

Warton shrugged. "What else?"

Although Warton might be an exception as well since he alone had experienced a taste of marriage and, given the circumstances, one would assume had experienced love as well. It was not far-fetched to further assume, due to the brevity of both the marriage and, no doubt, the love, neither had gone well, although he had never spoken of it and his friends had never asked.

"Hear, hear." Cavendish nodded.

And then there was Cavendish who was far and away too busy having a grand time with any number of ladies to concentrate on one in particular. Love, for Cavendish at the present time, would be most inconvenient.

As for Oliver himself, he was certainly not opposed to either love or marriage even though he was not hurtling headlong toward either at the moment.

The men settled back in their chairs, and Oliver glanced around the circle. "So, I gather there are no questions as to the terms of the wager?"

"The tontine," Sinclair amended.

"This tontine." Cavendish pulled his brows together. "I hate to appear dim—"

"And yet," Warton murmured.

Cavendish ignored him. "We all put in a certain sum—"

"In this case a mere shilling," Oliver said.

"Which I still think is remarkably insignificant given the stakes," Cavendish continued. "However, that is neither here nor there at the moment. And the winner, that is the last man among us to evade the bond of holy wedlock—"

"*Bondage* being a more appropriate word than *bond*," Warton said wryly.

Sinclair grinned. "And I thought the most important word was *evade*."

"Well said." Warton smiled and clinked his glass with the American.

Cavendish narrowed his eyes in annoyance. "As I was saying, the last of us to survive, the last man standing as it were, wins the four shillings." Cavendish shook his head. "Although I still don't think four shillings is enough."

"It's not the money." Oliver shrugged. "The money is merely a symbol."

"Still," Sinclair said thoughtfully, "he does have a valid point. Symbolism aside, four shillings does not seem a worthy prize for managing to avoid marriage for however long the tontine remains unclaimed."

"Perhaps not." Warton considered the matter. "Depending on the fortitude of our respective natures, the last man standing might well have to use a cane to do so and a nurse to bring his whisky to his lips."

"Brandy," Oliver said without thinking, then looked at the others. "Better still, Cognac. If I am the last one left, I should much prefer to celebrate the newfound fortune of four shillings with Cognac rather than anything else. We should add Cognac to the tontine."

"A very fine Cognac will age for a century or longer." Admiration sounded in Warton's voice. "Excellent idea."

"Much better than a mere four shillings." Cavendish nodded with satisfaction. "Are we agreed then? We will add the bottle of the club's finest Cognac to the tontine so that the last man will be able to celebrate."

"Or console himself," Sinclair said with a smile.

"Nonsense." Cavendish grinned. "When that day comes, if the rest of you are nice to me and can escape from your wives, I shall share my Cognac with you."

"Unless, of course, it becomes my Cognac." Oliver chuckled. "And I may or may not share."

Warton smiled in a dry manner. "Well, I, for one, have absolutely no intention of sharing."

If it had been a straightforward wager, Oliver would have put his money on Warton as the one most likely to remain unmarried the longest. Certainly, duty would compel them all to wed eventually, to produce an heir to their respective fortunes and titles. Even the American was under continued familial pressure to marry. But Warton was entirely too cynical to succumb to anything as frivolous as love. When he at last wed, Oliver was confident the decision would be well thought out, the bride a suitable young lady of good family and equally good fortune. No, Warton would indeed be the last to go.

The question was, who would be the first?

Chapter 1

It was far and away the perfect opportunity, and only a fool would let it slip away. Gideon Pearsall, Viscount Warton, was no fool.

He suspected no one else in the overcrowded parlor at Lady Dinsmore's monthly evening of Musical and Literary Entertainments had noted the lovely Lady Chester discreetly leave the room. But then he doubted anyone else had been watching the charming widow with as close an eye as he had. No, all eyes were on the hostess's insipid nephew, who even now, with a spritz or two of something into his mouth and numerous clearings of his throat, prepared to regale the gathering with his poetry of youthful passion and dubious quality. Gideon was confident therefore that no one would notice as well when he followed Lady Chester's example. He sent a quick nod of thanks heavenward that he had had the foresight to plan his own escape and had positioned himself in the back of the room.

He slipped out a side door and glanced down the corridor to catch a flash of blue silk skirt as the lady turned the corner. Access to Lady Dinsmore's terrace lay in that direction, as he, and anyone else who had ever attempted to flee their hostess's endless and not especially talented relations' attempts at music or literature or whatever, well knew. Perhaps Lady Chester was in need of a breath of fresh air; it was extraordinarily stuffy in the parlor. It was possible as well that she could be meeting someone. Lady Dinsmore's terrace was as well known as a trysting spot as it was as a refuge. Still, Gideon doubted it. Widows were not as encumbered by the strictures placed on society as nevermarried women; therefore Lady Chester had no particular need of secrecy. Beyond that, given everything he had heard about her, he suspected the lady rather liked being the center of gossip. And gossip, usually remarkably accurate, indicated the lady was not currently involved with anyone. Excellent. He grinned to himself. He too could use a bit of fresh air.

Gideon had known Lady Chester for years, although he did not, in truth, know her at all. She was a passing acquaintance, someone to nod a greeting to on the street or exchange idle pleasantries with at a social gathering, nothing more than that. It was not until the Twelfth Night Ball she had hosted more than a month ago that what should have been little more than a few casual words between the two of them had without warning been fraught with something more significant and completely indefinable. It struck him with a force akin to a lightning bolt, an abrupt awareness of sorts, perhaps of a kindred spirit or the possibility of adventure or a heretofore unsuspected and unimagined attraction. One of his friends had said at the time that there was something in the air that night. Something of a magical nature. It was nonsense, of course. Still, the moment had dwelled in the back of Gideon's mind, lingered just beneath the surface of his well-ordered life. Under other circumstances, he would not have hesitated to call on the widow. But there had been something in that moment that had urged caution as well. That too was extremely odd. Gideon was nothing if not cautious, yet he'd never before experienced a sense of caution in connection with a woman, even when he should have. It was damn near irresistible.

He pushed open the glass door to the terrace, and his breath hitched at the cold of the February night. Still, it scarcely mattered at the moment. The night was unusually clear given the season, and Lady Chester's figure was silhouetted against the star-laden sky. She stood a scant dozen feet or so away, gazing into the night. He started toward her, then paused, for the first time in years not entirely certain of himself.

"Did you find it as stifling as I did or do you simply dislike poorly written poetry as much as I do?" Lady Chester said without turning around, a definite note of amusement in her voice.

"Both I should think." Gideon chuckled. "But is

it wise to comment on either the atmosphere or the entertainment without first looking to see who has joined you? For all you know I could be Lady Dinsmore come to herd you back into the fold."

She laughed, a lovely rich sound as clear as the night itself. "I knew precisely who had joined me, my lord."

"Did you?" He stepped toward her, the beat of his heart quickening with his step. "How?"

"Anyone who stations himself near the most discreet exit instead of sitting by the side of his aunt, who has probably insisted on his accompaniment to begin with, is obviously waiting to escape at the first opportunity. Beyond that"—she turned toward him—"you have been watching me all evening."

"Have I?"

"Indeed you have."

"And you were aware of my perusal?"

"Very much so."

"Because you were watching me as well?"

"Absolutely." She laughed. "But I think I was much more subtle."

"Oh?"

"You did not notice me watching you whereas I—"

He laughed. "Your point is well taken."

She studied him for a moment, the features of her face faintly illuminated by the light from the door and windows behind him. "Why have you not called on me?"

His grin widened. "Did you expect me to do so?"

"I did."

"Alas, I found I did not have the courage." He adopted a mournful air. "I am not nearly as daring as I appear."

"I doubt that. Am I so intimidating then?"

"Yes." The word was out of his mouth before he knew it. He shook his head. "*Intimidating* is not the right word."

She tilted her head and gazed up at him. "What is the right word?"

"Intriguing. Enticing. Fascinating. Terrifying." He paused. "Mysterious."

"Mysterious?" She laughed. "I shall let *terrifying* pass for the moment, but do tell me why I am mysterious. It seems to me my life is very much an open book that no one has hesitated to read. I daresay, everyone knows virtually everything about me."

"Everything?"

"Perhaps not everything but nearly so. I do have some secrets; every woman should, you know. Come now, my lord, I have been discreet in the decade of my widowhood but I have not spent those years"—she searched for the right word—"*alone*, as it were."

"I am aware of that," he said simply. He was indeed aware that Lady Chester's life since the death of her husband had not been lived in a despondent state of celibacy. One of his oldest friends had had a liaison with her several years ago and, to his credit or hers, even now considered her a friend.

"I would wager so is everyone else in London. As I said, my life is a well-read book." She spread her hands wide before her. "Why then would you call me mysterious?"

"Perhaps because I have never met a woman I would call terrifying before either."

His words hung in the air between them, abruptly fraught with far more significance than he had intended. As well as entirely too much honesty.

She drew a deep breath. "May I confess something to you?"

"Is it something I wish to hear?" He stepped toward her. "Or will it put me firmly in my place? Send me packing to nurse the remains of my shattered heart?" He forced a light note to his voice.

"I doubt any woman has the power to shatter your heart," she said wryly. "You are the estimable Viscount Warton. You are well known for your wit and your dry sarcasm and your cutting manner. You are considered both aloof and arrogant—"

"Arrogant?" He gasped in mock dismay.

She nodded. "Most certainly arrogant. Superior, as it were, to those of us who are mere ordinary mortals."

"It is entirely without conscious effort on my part, I assure you." He grinned. "Some of it."

"You do not deny, then, your arrogant manner or superior attitude?"

"I should very much like to, but"—he shrugged—"no. I am as well aware of my flaws as I am of the more desirable aspects of my character. Aspects that are far too numerous to mention, I might add."

Amusement sounded in her voice. "Oh?"

"Modesty forbids my discussing them at the moment." He grinned in a manner that was not the least bit modest. "However, I should be more than happy to provide you with an itemized list of my sterling qualities at a later date."

She laughed.

"Although I should warn you now that I count persistence among those qualities." He paused. "I believe you mentioned a confession?"

"Did I?" She shrugged. "It must have slipped my mind. For the life of me I cannot recall what I wish to confess to you."

"There is nothing then?" He stepped closer. "Nothing at all?"

"Not a thing."

He took her hand and raised it to his lips. "Surely there is something? Some secret perhaps you wish to unburden to a sympathetic ear?"

"Regardless of the sympathetic nature of your ear, I scarcely think I know you well enough to unburden myself of anything to you."

He brushed his lips across her gloved hand and wished he could see into her eyes. But even with the light behind him, it was far and away too dark. Pity. They were blue, as he recalled, a deep, rich color. "Still, isn't it much easier to unburden oneself to a stranger?"

"Only if one is certain that stranger shall remain a stranger." There was an interesting note in her voice, of challenge perhaps or invitation or simply amusement.

"My dear Lady Chester." He turned her hand

over and kissed her palm. "I have absolutely no intention of remaining a stranger."

"What do you intend?"

"That is entirely dependent on you." He wondered what she would do if he were to pull her into his arms. It would be highly improper. They were indeed very much strangers at the moment.

"Is it?" she said thoughtfully. "I wonder."

"What?" He couldn't recall ever having kissed a stranger before. It held a great deal of appeal. Especially in regard to this particular stranger.

"If it is dependent on me." She pulled her hand from his. "Or on something else. Forces already set in motion."

He raised a brow. "You mean fate, destiny, the ordination of the stars, something like that?"

"Actually I was thinking more in terms of desire, need, unadulterated lust." A grin sounded in her voice.

"Lust?" He nodded slowly, ignoring a moment of surprise at her words. He had flirted with any number of women in his life, often with the explicit goal of eventually sharing their beds, yet he wasn't certain he had ever met a woman whose nature was quite as direct as Lady Chester's. It was most intriguing. "Lust can indeed be a powerful influence."

"And dangerous as well."

"I would certainly never force my attentions upon you."

"That is not the danger that concerns me."

"Or call on you if my presence was not wanted."

"I never thought—"

He leaned close and lowered his voice. "Or drag you into my arms and kiss you until you begged for more unless I was confident you wished to be kissed."

"A wish prompted, no doubt, by lust." She heaved a heartfelt sigh and trailed her fingers lightly over the lapels of his coat. "As I said, a very dangerous emotion."

"And yet"—he caught her hand—"not especially unwelcome."

"No, my dear Lord Warton." She reached upward and brushed her lips across his so lightly, he wasn't sure they had touched at all, then stepped away before he could react. "Not at all unwelcome. Besides, it is the element of danger that makes it all so much fun. Don't you agree?"

"I do." He resisted the urge to make good on his threat to kiss her. He wanted nothing more than to feel her lips pressed against his and was confident she wanted the same. But there was something altogether too exciting about this game played between them on a darkened terrace in the cold of a winter night to allow it to end too soon. It was a tantalizing first course, an enticing prologue, a promise. And as such far too tasty to rush. "In that case"—he chose his words with care—"if indeed you and I choose to fall prey to the demands of lust or fate or whatever else we wish to call it, do I have your permission to call on you? Would you do me the honor of joining me for supper? The day after tomorrow perhaps?"

"I fear I am otherwise engaged the day after to-morrow."

"The day following that then?"

She shook her head. "I have a previous commitment."

"Four days from now then. Or five. Or next week if it suits you better."

"Is this the persistence you mentioned earlier?"

He flashed her a grin. "Do you like it?"

"It is most impressive. Very well then, shall we say five days from now?"

"Excellent. I shall send a carriage—"

"Oh, no. You shall join me for supper. At my home."

"Your home?"

"On the field of play of any sport it is always best to have the home court advantage."

He laughed. "And I have always relished a good game. I shall count the days. Now." He offered his arm. "It is entirely too cold for us to linger here any longer. I fear we shall soon lose all feeling in various appendages."

"Odd, I had not noticed the cold until now."

"You were no doubt basking in the warmth of my presence," he said, a feigned note of humility in his voice.

"Yes, I'm certain that was it," she said lightly, then paused. "You're not at all as I expected."

"Is that good?"

"I haven't decided. Besides, if I said yes it would go straight to your head, and I fear that would only exacerbate an already serious flaw in your character."

"We can't have that." He chuckled. "May I escort you back to the festivities now before we both freeze to death?"

"*Festivities* might not be quite as appropriate a word as *sentence*, although bearing up under the offerings of Susanna's—Lady Dinsmore's—assorted nieces and nephews is a small enough price to pay for the privilege of her friendship. She entertains a great deal, and the diverse nature of the company she gathers is always interesting, even if the entertainment itself leaves something to be desired. I would never tell her that, of course. However"—she shook her head—"I think it's best if we each returned as we left. Alone, that is."

"Surely you are not afraid of what people might say if we appeared together?"

She laughed. "I am not the least bit afraid of what people might say. Goodness, I am often disappointed that they do not say nearly enough, although admittedly the tales of my exploits are somewhat exaggerated."

"And that does not bother you?"

"Not at all." She waved off his question. "If one is going to have a reputation, it might as well be as interesting as possible. Besides, I have not completely fallen off the edge of respectability."

"Ah yes, you are discreet."

"Indeed I am. I enjoy my position in society and I should hate to forfeit it with unduly scandalous behavior."

"Unduly scandalous?" He laughed. "As opposed to simply scandalous? Or ordinarily scandalous? Or merely scandalous?"

"Precisely. It's remarkable how forgiving society can be when one has a tidy fortune as long as one is not too outrageous." Her voice carried an almost prim note, but he suspected she was holding back a laugh. "I have the wealth left to me by my parents and my husband. I have as well the freedom to do exactly as I please and the intelligence to understand what will be overlooked and what will not." She paused. "I freely confess there are certain boundaries I have never, nor will I ever, cross."

"Aha! At last. Confession." He chuckled in a conspiratorial manner. "It feels good, doesn't it? The unburdening, that is."

"A great weight has been lifted from my shoulders," she said wryly. "As I was saying, I am not afraid of the talk that will ensue if we are seen in one another's company, but rather the commitment such an appearance would imply."

"Commitment?"

She shrugged. "The moment we are linked together by gossip, well, we are linked together. There is an implied commitment of sorts in our appearing together that I am not yet prepared to make."

"I see," he said, even though he wasn't sure he saw at all. "Then you do not wish to . . . that is to say . . . I had the impression—"

"I shall look forward to our evening together, my lord," she said brightly in a manner that made him wonder if she would now pat his head as one did to appease an annoying child. "Now, if you will excuse me." Lady Chester turned and started toward the door.

"One moment if you please," he said quickly.

She paused and glanced at him over her shoulder.

"You do understand, I fully intend to seduce you."

"Do you?" Her laugh was rich with delight and anticipation.

"Indeed I do. Furthermore, I suspect—no, I am confident—that thought does not displease you."

"Are you certain your confidence is not misplaced?"

He flashed her a wicked grin. "My confidence is never misplaced."

"Still, if I were to confirm your suspicion, it would take away any sense of challenge you might feel, and it is *my* suspicion that you are a man who quite likes a challenge. No"—she paused to emphasize the word—"a mystery."

"Challenges perhaps, but I've never been overly fond of mysteries."

"Then I shall take some of it away for you. Consider it, oh, say, a gift of sorts." She opened the door, then looked back at him. "The appropriate word is not *if*, my lord, but *when*. Good evening." She nodded, stepped into the house, and closed the door behind her.

He stared for a confused moment, then realized exactly what she was saying. He smiled slowly.

Lady Chester would indeed be a challenge. Not in the bedding, that was a foregone conclusion. But whereas with other women that was the end of the pursuit, he had the oddest feeling that, with this particular lady, it would be merely the beginning.

* * *

". . . 'twas for her alone his ardor raged . . ."

Judith slipped back into the parlor and for once was grateful for the endless length of Susanna's nephew's recitation. She took her seat with an apologetic murmur to the older lady beside her, who blinked several times in response, then smiled absently. Judith bit back a smile of her own. She had apparently awakened the woman.

Out of the corner of her eye Judith noted Lord Warton's circumspect return. He stood now in the back of the room: cool and collected, an observer of life, aloof and unaffected by the world around him. Still, it appeared he was not quite as cynical as he looked. A brief conversation on a terrace was far too little upon which to judge a man's nature, but he was not exactly what she'd expected, given everything she'd heard about him as well as her own observances in the past. She'd been surprised to find he was a great deal more amusing than she'd suspected. She had fully expected to feel desire, but she hadn't for a moment expected to laugh.

And she had certainly never expected to now feel butterflies fluttering in the pit of her stomach. No, not butterflies. Butterflies were delicate, fragile creatures. Whatever was tumbling about in her stomach was much more significant than mere insects. More like geese than butterflies. An entire flock of geese. Flapping and squawking and knocking about inside her. Why, if she dared to open her mouth at the wrong moment, no doubt a honk would sound and a feather would shoot from her lips. The image popped unbidden into her mind, and she choked back a laugh.

The lady beside her leaned closer, her voice barely more than a whisper. "There, there, dear, it will be over soon and then we shall surely have a moment to compose ourselves before the next round of "— she heaved a resigned sigh— "entertainments."

"Perhaps it will be quite wonderful," Judith said with a forced note of optimism.

The older woman raised a skeptical brow, then turned her attention back to Susanna's nephew.

". . . where the posies nod their graceful heads in a fond bid of adieu . . ."

Judith smiled weakly and attempted to pay attention to the recitation. Or rather to look as if she were paying attention. Her mind was anywhere but on passionately delivered, yet nonetheless poorly written poetry.

There wasn't a doubt in her mind that she and Lord Warton would soon share a bed. She had known that with an unerring certainty at her Twelfth Night Ball. There had been the strangest moment between them as if the air itself was alive with excitement. With promise. It would have been most disconcerting if it hadn't been so exhilarating and just the tiniest bit dangerous. She wasn't sure she had ever felt anything quite like it before. Although perhaps once, a long time ago, when she was very young and substantially more foolish than she was now. Oh, certainly, there was always a sense of anticipation when she embarked on a new adventure with a gentleman. Not that there had been that many gentlemen through the years. She was both discriminating and selective. Judith had to like a man before she joined him in his bed. Her lovers were first and foremost her friends in the beginning as well as at the end. And she could count on the fingers of one hand the number of *friends* she'd had in the years of her widowhood. Why, if one strictly defined both *friend* and *adventure,* it would not be necessary to include the thumb, and one finger would as yet be unused.

She slanted a discreet glance at Lord Warton. He stared at Susanna's nephew with an expression that was just a shade too polite to be truly called bored. The vaguest hint of a satisfied smile quirked up the corners of his mouth as if he knew she was watching. Judith jerked her gaze back to the poet, and an annoying flash of heat washed up her face. Good Lord, she was blushing. She couldn't remember the last time that had happened either. At the advanced age of thirty she should be immune to blushing. It implied a loss of control that she rarely if ever experienced. Her position as a widowed baroness as well as her fortune and an innate sense of her own worth meant she seldom, if ever, and never if she had her way, was at anyone's mercy. Blushing definitely put one under influences that could not be easily managed. It was most annoying.

And the blame could be placed firmly on the arrogant, self-satisfied, undeniably attractive Viscount Warton.

Still, Judith allowed a slight satisfied smile of

her own, it was quite exciting and would no doubt become more so with every step toward each other they took. Indeed, one could argue there was something about an annoying man that made him practically irresistible. Judith had never found it so before, but then she wasn't sure she'd run into the likes of Lord Warton before. There was much about the man yet to be determined, but it struck Judith that this was a man who was very much her equal. That too was unusual. Oh, certainly there was nothing *unequal* about the men she had chosen to be with in the past, although her previous adventures had always been very much on her terms. Lord Warton did not appear to be the kind of man to live by any terms other than his own. All in all, he was annoying, arrogant, and amusing. Oh, this held a great deal of promise indeed. Let the adventure begin.

Chapter 2

Lord Warton was annoyingly prompt but then she knew he would be. At this very moment he was awaiting her in her parlor although it was entirely too soon to greet him yet.

Judith glanced at the clock on the ladies' desk in her boudoir. Seven minutes more would make his wait an even quarter of an hour, an absolutely perfect amount of time for a gentleman to wait for a lady to appear. Less than that and she would seem far too enthusiastic for his company. Longer would be, well, rude.

She drew a deep breath and assessed the image in her mirror yet again and acknowledged, yet again, that her reflection was practically perfect, at as least as far as those things she could control. Not a blond hair was out of place. The gown she had carefully selected for the evening had not rumpled or shifted since she had donned it in some defiant show of fashion rebellion to reveal more than she had intended or—God forbid—to conceal more than she had planned. In regard to an evening such as the one that lay ahead, what a lady revealed was every bit as important as the time she kept a gentleman waiting. A gown that concealed too much of a lady's assets indicated to a gentleman she was not especially interested in anything beyond supper, while displaying too much would be interpreted to mean she was not merely willing but eager. Regardless of how she truly felt about whatever gentleman was at hand, Judith would allow him to see a certain amount of enthusiasm, but eagerness? She shuddered. That wouldn't be at all proper. The absurdity of the thought struck her, and she grinned at the Judith in the mirror. Proper? There was nothing the least bit proper about inviting a man to join you for supper with the distinct—if unstated—intention of having him join you in your bed sometime after dessert was served. Or possibly even before. Which might well verge on improper but not substantially so, all things considered.

Still, Judith did have certain rules she abided by, including what was and was not proper for the evening ahead. Certainly, those ladies of English society who blindly adhered to the regulations of appropriate behavior endorsed by Her Royal Majesty would not see anything whatsoever proper about an unchaperoned woman, widow or not, entertaining a handsome, dashing bachelor. However, to Judith's way of thinking, in her younger days she had behaved exactly as expected for a young lady of good breeding and background and had, therefore, fulfilled any responsibility she'd had to continue to abide by standards she'd had no say in setting. She had married quite properly and respectably, if a bit young, to a nearly as young gentleman of good family and wealth who was, as well, she had thought, the love of her life. But he had died, and as she had not died with him, well, she saw no reason to spend the rest of her days behaving as if she had.

What would Lucian think if he could see me now?

The smile in the mirror faded just a touch. It was not the first time in the decade since Lucian's death that the thought had occurred to her. Usually it arose unbidden, as it did tonight, and as always the answer was the same. Her husband might well laugh with the sheer, unadulterated delight that had underscored so much of their life together and applaud her efforts and encourage her to live as fully as he had now that he was gone. Or he might become thoughtful, even appear sullen to someone who did not realize his melancholy was the hallmark of genius, and heralded his vanishing into the library to compose poetry she had loyally thought brilliant at the time and might think so now as well, although she had not read his poems for years. Or he might rage with a towering fury fueled by unwarranted jealousy, all the more terrifying for its rarity and its suddenness, and he would call her a whore and show her what men did with women like her.

She shook her head to clear it of the memory. It was very long ago and scarcely worth remembering now. Besides, in the three brief years of their marriage she had seen his anger no more than a handful of times. He had laughed far more than anything else and had lived life with a fire she had not seen before or since. No, she thought firmly as she always did when these memories intruded, Lucian would have laughed and approved of her life and her choices. It served no useful purpose to think otherwise, and it was pointless to consider him now. Now she had the intriguing Lord Warton to consider.

And what would he think when he saw her tonight?

She wrinkled her nose at the question. A nose a bit too sharp to be truly considered pert, but a nice nose nonetheless, situated on a face with even features, wide, appropriately spaced blue eyes; and a blush in her cheek only slightly augmented by a dash of powder. Up to this point in her life the combination of those features had been such that she was considered quite pretty. Indeed, she had on occasion been described as the epitome of English beauty. In truth, she noted little change in the mirror yet, although one couldn't help but wonder how long she still had before *pretty* turned to *handsome* and eventually to "one wouldn't know it to look at her now but she was considered quite a beauty in her youth." There would come a day when she would glance into the mirror and note a wrinkle or two or twenty. There was nothing to be done about it, of course. She was thirty, after all. One simply had to accept aging as one did everything else in life that was inevitable: with a certain grace and humor. Besides, interesting women simply became more interesting with age. And while even as a child Judith had been pretty, *interesting* had come only with experience and maturity. As a quality, she thought it considerably more valuable than appearance. Still, it would be nice to retain a fetching appearance along with an interesting character.

Her figure would serve as well, although she had never been overly fond of it. She was far and away too short and her bosom rather too full for her liking. Still, her waist was proportionately small and her neck graceful and her skin unblemished. All in all, she was holding up nicely. At least for the moment.

Would he think so?

It was rather absurd that she was this apprehensive about tonight. Or was it anticipation that knotted her stomach? She hadn't seen him since Susanna's gathering, five full days ago. While she certainly hadn't sought him out, she'd made no effort to make herself scarce either. Why, one night she'd attended a dinner hosted by Mrs. Windham that might have been considered a small, private affair save that there were easily two hundred of the lady's closest friends in attendance. Another evening had brought her attendance at Lord and Lady Carlyle's musicale, where the entertainment was considerably more polished than at Susanna's. On yet another night she'd joined a small group of friends at the theater for an eminently forgettable performance of an equally forgettable play. However, it featured an actress she rather liked, and by that virtue alone redeemed itself somewhat. Admittedly, one of the reasons she might not recall details of the play was that she had spent a great deal of the evening casually searching the theater for His Lordship.

Still, to be entirely fair, she had been the one to dictate when and where they would dine. Therefore, it wasn't at all reasonable to blame him for the fact that they had not seen each other, although it did bring up all sorts of unpleasant thoughts. Was he anywhere near as eager to see her as she was to see him? To give the man his due, even without appearing in person, he had made his presence felt. The day after the evening at Susanna's, a book of Keats's work was delivered with a note expressing His Lordship's hope that this poetry would prove more palatable than that at Lady Dinsmore's. Two days later there had been a simple note, no more than a few lines, expressing how much he was looking forward to seeing her again. Very polite, nothing whatsoever improper, yet it did seem to her that there was a distinct undercurrent that sent a thrill of anticipation racing up her spine. Of course it could well be that that thrill had nothing whatsoever to do with either his words or his intentions and everything to do with hers. Yesterday two dozen roses had arrived, yellow, which Judith found somewhat surprising. She would have thought Lord Warton was more of a red rose type of fellow, but then it was probably best to set aside any assumptions she had previously made about the dashing viscount.

Blast it all. She stared into the mirror. There had been nothing whatsoever between them up to now, save a moment at a ball and a conversation on a winter night, and the man had her heart thudding and her mind thinking all sorts of unreasonable thoughts based on nothing but conjecture. In addition, those annoying geese had taken up permanent residence in her stomach. How much worse would it be when they had actually spent some time together? When she was in his arms. Or . . . She smiled slowly. How much better?

She glanced at the clock. It was time. She could, of course, make him wait a bit longer, but that would be playing a game she had no wish to play. She drew a deep breath. In spite of the candid manner they'd adopted thus far, it was inevitable that between men and women there would be some games played.

She cast a confident grin at the Judith in the mirror. Making him wait was simply not one of them.

Gideon resisted the urge to pull out his watch and check the time. He steadfastly refused to glance at the French gilded clock perched on the mantel although the timepiece with its ornate golden figures and matching candelabra was almost impossible to ignore. Nor would he act in any way as if he was aware of the minutes ticking by. He was not about to give in to the restlessness prompted by nerves that currently held him in its grip. He didn't like it one bit and could not remember the last time he had experienced anything remotely similar. It was very much an exercise in self-control, and Gideon was, as usual, pleased with his ability to rule his own impulses. Aside from that, neither clock nor watch was necessary. Gideon had always had the unique ability to accurately judge the passage of time. He knew he had been waiting for Lady Chester for precisely six minutes thus far and fully expected to wait for at least six more. She was a woman, after all. Besides, if she had been awaiting his arrival he would have been somewhat taken aback. While he hadn't a doubt in the world that she was as eager to see him again as he was to see her, for her to have greeted him personally upon his arrival would have been unseemly. There was a proper way to do this sort of thing.

Unless, of course, she had changed her mind about seeing him again.

Nonsense. He brushed the thought aside. He was, after all, wealthy, attractive, witty, and in considerable demand with the fairer sex. He was considered quite a catch, not that marriage had anything to do with this. In addition, while he didn't know Lady Chester well—indeed, he didn't know her at all—she was obviously the type of woman who would have let him know she had decided against furthering their acquaintance long before he had arrived at her door. She was not a shy, retiring maiden but rather an experienced woman who knew her own mind. If she did not want him, in her home or her bed, he was confident she would make her feelings known. He liked that. There would be no foolish games with Lady Chester. Everything would be aboveboard and honest between them.

Gideon clasped his hands behind his back and strolled around the perimeter of the parlor. The house itself was large, in a fashionable part of the city. Like most formal parlors, this was a room that was used primarily for the entertainment of guests. Still, one could learn a lot about a person from the manner in which she decorated her home. All in all, it was not an unpleasant room. While not overtly feminine it was still a bit cluttered to his way of thinking, with statuary and vases and the assorted odds and ends that ladies were so fond of. It was the current fashion and as such unavoidable. His own home was considerably fuller than his well-ordered nature preferred, thanks to the influence of his aunt. But then she was his only living relative and he was willing to humor her in those things that were of little consequence, including the decoration of his home—or rather their home. Besides, it was no doubt the very temperament of women that led them to feather their nests in such a manner. That too was unavoidable.

Paintings covered the walls, landscapes and portraits primarily. English works for the most part, although he did note a significant number of French artists. On one side of the fireplace was the unmistakable style of Boucher, while a Fragonard graced the far wall and a David hung on another. The selection was an interesting mix of the frivolity of pre-Revolution France and much darker, more somber later works.

The furniture was intricately carved, again in the style of the times. Heavy drapes covered the tall windows, and he wondered if Lady Chester kept them drawn during the day against the fading effects of the sun. He rather hoped not. She struck him as a creature of light, and he would hate to be wrong about that. A creature of light? He smiled to himself. What an odd, whimsical notion. Not at all the sort of thing he usually thought about a woman.

"I do hope I haven't kept you waiting too long." Lady Chester swept into the room and reached out her hand to him. Her blue eyes sparkled in the gaslight, her skin glowed, her blond hair shone like pale gold. *A creature of light.* How had he managed to wait five full days?

"Indeed you have." He took her hand and lifted it to his lips. "Every moment not spent in your presence is an eternity."

She raised an amused brow. "Very good, my lord. Very good indeed."

His gaze met hers directly. "Yes, I am."

She laughed and pulled her hand from his. "I meant your words, and you knew exactly what I meant."

"Ah, yes, but can one really separate the man from his words?"

"I should think so."

"What, or rather who would Keats be without his words? Or Byron or Shakespeare?"

"I have no idea."

"Neither would anyone else." He cast her an overly smug smile. "My point exactly."

She studied him for a moment. "You are very clever, my lord."

"And good." He wagged his brows at her in a decidedly wicked manner. "Don't forget *good*."

"I daresay you won't allow me to forget *good*."

"No," he said in a low voice, "I won't."

His gaze met hers, and for a long moment neither of them said a word. Nonetheless, there was an exchange between them. An acknowledgment of sorts, of shared desire and mutual curiosity and anticipation. Delightful and exciting.

She drew a deep breath, and the moment was lost. Pity. It was the sort of moment when a man could take a woman—even a woman he scarcely knew—into his arms and she would go willingly. Although it was probably for the best. His own breath was oddly unsteady as well, and who knew what loss of self-control that might lead to.

Her gaze slipped to the unwieldy, brown paper–wrapped package he had left on a nearby side table. "Is that for me?"

"Direct and to the point. No coy pretense with you as if you weren't aware of the large, bulky package that could, in fact, be nothing but a gift." He nodded in a mock serious manner. "You dispense with the playing of games, my lady. I like that."

"Not at all." She laughed. "I quite enjoy playing games and I have every intention of playing games with you. Unless it has to do with gifts."

He winced. "Rather mercenary of you, isn't it?"

"I don't think so. I would term it . . ." She paused to find the right word. "Practical. Yes, that's it. If you have brought me a present and placed it in plain sight, which indicates it is not meant to be a surprise, then it's nothing short of impractical to pretend I haven't seen it. *Mercenary* implies greed, and your gifts thus far have not been extravagant enough to provoke greed."

"I did not wish to offend you with extravagance," he said slowly. Gideon had thought, with this particular woman at this particular time, extravagance would be an error in, well, tactics. "I hope I was not mistaken."

"Of course not, although extravagance is rarely offensive." She cast him a brilliant smile. "However, it has been my experience that men give women expensive gifts as a lure to entice them into their beds. An advance on the position of mistress, as it were. As I do not intend to be your mistress, your gifts were entirely appropriate and quite, quite perfect."

"They were?"

"Most certainly."

"But you do not . . . that is to say . . . what I mean is . . ." Words, at this particular moment, failed him completely. But then he had never been in this position before. Nor was he entirely certain what his position was.

"Absolutely not." She shook her head firmly.

"Then I fear you have me confused and"—he smiled wryly—"more than a little disappointed."

"My dear Lord Warton." She laughed again, and he noticed what a lovely laugh it was. Honest and direct, as if it came from somewhere deep inside. And deep inside, she obviously found him rather more amusing than he would prefer. "You and I are dealing with a difference in perception or perhaps definition. Mistresses are supported in a financial manner by gentlemen in exchange for their favors and possibly their affection as well, I would imagine. I have no need of financial support from a gentleman, therefore I find the very term *mistress*"—she wrinkled her nose—"inaccurate and inappropriate and rather subservient as well. I have no intention of being subservient. Ever."

"I see," he said, although he really didn't. Best then perhaps to keep his mouth shut. Still . . . "Then in regard to you and me—"

"I am confident you shall not be the least bit disappointed. Now then." She nodded pointedly at the package. "May I?"

"Please do." He hadn't the vaguest idea what had just occurred here, yet he was fairly certain an understanding had been reached. Damned if he knew what it was.

She approached the package and studied it curiously. It was rather obvious, at least to him, that it was a plant of some sort. He grinned in anticipation. But it was the perfect plant.

She tore off the paper carefully to reveal a tall orchid plant sporting a large blossom with pale pink petals, a darker lavender center section, and a few fat leaves. He knew little about plants in general and nothing at all about orchids, but this was an outstanding example. At least that's what he'd been told.

She stepped back and stared. "Oh my."

"It's a cattleya", he said proudly.

"Indeed it is," she murmured, still staring at the plant. "*Cattleya labiata*, to be precise."

He stepped toward her, feigning interest in the orchid. "And a fine specimen too, I understand."

"Very fine indeed." She leaned closer and studied the plant. "And in excellent condition." She glanced at him. "You've taken good care of it."

He shrugged modestly. "I will confess it has not been in my possession long."

She straightened and smiled at him. "How did you know?"

"About your passion for exotic plants, particularly orchids? A mutual friend told me." And wasn't it exceptionally clever of him to have talked to Lord Helmsley about Lady Chester's likes and dislikes?

"A mutual friend?" Her smile remained but her voice held a curious note. "Do you mean Lord Helmsley?"

He nodded. "Yes."

"You discussed my likes and dislikes with Lord Helmsley?"

Rather awkward to tell the woman you hoped would soon become your lover that a former lover of hers had told you how to win her affections. It didn't seem quite as clever now as it had a moment ago. While she did not appear angry, it might be best to be completely candid with her. Still, he chose his words carefully. "I have to confess I did exactly that."

She narrowed her eyes. "Why?"

"Why?" He considered the question. Honesty might well be the only way out even if honesty, in regard to women, was something of a new concept for him. He blew a long breath. "I wished to impress you. To curry your favor. To sweep you off your feet with the thoughtfulness of my manner. I was trying to be—"

"Wonderful?"

He nodded. "Exactly."

"Charming? Dashing?"

"That too." He smiled in a rueful manner. "Dare I ask if I succeeded?"

"That depends on what, beyond my penchant for orchids, you learned from Lord Helmsley," she said pleasantly. He wasn't entirely sure he believed it.

"I can assure you, Lady Chester—"

"Judith." She smiled. "If we are to be"—her blue eyes twinkled—"*friends*, you should call me Judith."

"Are we to be *friends*?"

"You are entirely too impatient, my lord."

"It's a flaw." He shrugged. "I mentioned that I had flaws. And if I am to call you Judith, you must call me Gideon."

"As in the biblical Gideon?"

He chuckled. "As in a grandfather named Gideon who insisted his only son name his only male grandchild after him."

She raised a brow. "In the Bible, Gideon had seventy sons."

"And numerous wives and concubines as well." He grinned. "If I recall he lived to a very ripe old age and died happy."

"I don't doubt it for a moment." She waved at the orchid. "Would you be so kind as to carry this into the conservatory for me?"

"Ah, the famous conservatory." He picked up the pot carefully and followed her. "I am quite looking forward to seeing it."

"Are you interested in plants then?" She led him out of the parlor and down a long corridor.

"I admit to absolutely no knowledge about plants beyond the ability to distinguish a daisy from a rose. However, I am interested in anything that captures your attention," he said smoothly. Very good. Honest and charming at the same time.

She cast a smile over her shoulder. "Did Lord Helmsley tell you about the conservatory as well?"

"It was mentioned in regard to your interest in plants."

"You must have spoken at length."

"Yes. Er, no. Not really," he said quickly, trailing behind her through the endless corridors of the house although he scarcely noticed their progress. "I should tell you Helmsley was most circumspect during our conversation."

"Then that is not the Lord Helmsley I know."

"*Circumspect* is perhaps the wrong word. *Discreet* is a better word." *Discreet?* He groaned to himself. That didn't sound at all as he had intended. It was precisely the sort of thing one might say if one were trying to hide something. And he wasn't. Not really. "Nor did I inquire about anything of a particularly personal nature."

She laughed but didn't comment.

"I'm beginning to feel rather foolish," he said under his breath. "I do hope, Lady Chester—

Judith—that you do realize my intentions in speaking to—"

"Here we are." She pushed open a glass-paned door and stepped inside.

"See here, Judith, I really must insist that you stop for one moment and allow me to ex—" He stepped after her and pulled up short. "Good God, it's a jungle."

"Do you really think so? I've always thought of it as an overly abundant garden." She glanced around. "Or perhaps it is something of a jungle if one can have a civilized, orderly jungle."

"That is the question," he murmured. "I would say the answer is no."

In spite of Helmsley's description, Gideon was not the least bit prepared for Judith's conservatory. He had, of course, visited the Palm House at Kew and had on several occasions been a guest of the Duke of Northumberland at Syon Park and seen the great conservatory there. While this was significantly smaller, it was no less grand in nature.

It was completely made of glass and wrought iron, an addition off the side of the house, the brick wall behind him the only solid wall of the structure. And exactly as in a jungle, there were lush plantings everywhere he looked. Palms and other varieties of exotic tree reached to a high glass ceiling where stars could be seen peeking through the clouds. The conservatory was thick with humidity, precisely as he'd always thought a jungle would indeed be like, and there was the sound of running water in the distance. *The Amazon, no doubt.* Where on earth had that come from? Gideon was not prone to fanciful notions and this was the second tonight.

"I promise it is quite civilized. I assure you there are no wild beasts lurking behind the banana tree, although I do have a few specimens of carnivorous plants which would be most menacing if you were an insect." She cast him a flippant grin, then started down a pathway paved with flagstones, just wide enough to accommodate the width of her skirts. Gas sconces provided a dim but adequate light. "Come along."

"I should hate to be left behind. I would never find my way," he said under his breath.

It was at once overwhelming and most impressive, as if he had stepped from the order of London into the chaos of the tropics. Judith's wealth was obviously greater than he had imagined. She led him along the walkway lined with ferns and more palms and all sort of things blooming in wild and distinctly disorganized profusion. There was the scent of something sweet in the air. Jasmine, he thought, and who knew what else. His offering of the orchid now struck him at the very least as understated. It was like offering a pretty colored stone to the keeper of the crown jewels. He resisted the urge to glance down at the poor plant to see if it was wilting in the embarrassment of its inadequacy.

The path opened up to reveal a white marble fountain. Tall, it reached well above his head, with water splashing from three tiers into a circular basin, but it was not particularly wide, no more than five feet in diameter. Beyond the fountain he could see the flagstones continue. He hadn't noticed before but the path was lined with wood-planked tables, almost completely obscured by the potted plants positioned on the surfaces as well as on the floor.

Judith skirted the fountain and stopped before a table covered with what he assumed were orchids in a startling variety of shapes and sizes and colors. Sympathy stabbed him for the orchid he carried, although he was feeling a bit wilted himself, at least where his confidence was concerned.

She took the pot from him and placed it on the table in a lone empty spot between two similar orchids. He drew his brows together and stared. Two very similar orchids. In fact, if he did not know better, he would swear the three plants were much the same.

"Good God." He gritted his teeth.

She grinned.

"I shall have to kill Helmsley."

Her eyes sparkled with amusement. "I understood he was a very old and very good friend."

"He was. Nonetheless I shall have to kill him." He narrowed his eyes. "I am not only confident he will understand but I would wager he expects it."

She laughed. "Lord Helmsley was here yesterday wishing to purchase one of my orchids, although I have never sold one before, for what he said was an excellent cause. A good deed, as it were. I, of course, being the generous soul that I am, refused to take any compensation. After all, it was for a charitable purpose, and I can always use another good deed to my credit."

"As can we all," he muttered. "Perhaps I shall allow Helmsley to live."

"That would be a good deed, although mine was a significantly greater sacrifice and I am quite pleased to have the plant back." She turned toward the array of orchids. "Of all the curious and fascinating plants I have filled this conservatory with, the orchids are by far my favorites." There was a note in her voice, a look in her eyes when she gazed at the flowers, and the thought struck him how fortunate any man would be to have that note and that look reserved for him and him alone. "They are magnificent, don't you think?"

He stared at her, at the curve of her neck and the creamy smoothness of her skin. "Magnificent."

"I should very much like to see them in their natural habitat. They grow by the thousands in Colombia. I intend to travel there one day to see for myself. It shall be a grand adventure."

"Indeed it shall." His gaze strayed to the low cut of her gown, within the bounds of fashion yet provocative and enticing. "The grandest of adventures."

"They're considered quite erotic, you know." Her voice was low and thoughtful. "Not at all the proper thing for a lady to grow. It's feared that we may become quite overwhelmed by passion at the mere sight of the blossom."

He swallowed hard. "One can only hope."

She glanced at him. "Do you fear I shall become overwhelmed by passion?"

"It is my most fervent prayer." He grinned.

She turned toward him. "What, precisely, did you and Lord Helmsley discuss?"

"Only your likes and dislikes. In regard to an appropriate gift," he added quickly.

"You said there was nothing of a personal nature. By that I assume you mean an intimate nature."

"Indeed there was not," he said staunchly. "Absolutely not."

"Why not?"

"Because that would take all the"—he thought for a moment—"the adventure out of it."

She raised a brow. "The adventure?"

"I have never been a man who has especially sought out adventure, at least not since my youth. But I have never met a woman who, without warning and without reason, has made me feel . . . Yes." He nodded. "An adventure. A grand adventure." Even as he said the words he realized that was exactly how he thought of whatever might happen between the two of them. "My dear Judith." He stepped closer and took her hands in his. His gaze met hers. "I wish to discover your likes and dislikes, those of a personal nature, even an intimate nature, for myself." He drew one hand to his lips and brushed his lips across it. "I shall never hunt orchids in South America or explore the jungles of Africa but I fully intend to explore whatever this is between us." He lifted the other hand and kissed it. "And you."

"I see." Her voice had a seductive, breathless quality. "And when do you intend to begin your . . . your exploration?"

"This"—he pulled her firmly into his arms—"seems like an excellent time." He bent his lips to hers, and she reached up to meet him without hesitation. Her lips were soft beneath his, and warm and every bit as delicious as he had known they would be. For a moment time itself seemed to stop, and he lost himself in the feel of her lips against his.

Without warning the passion that had simmered between them erupted. He pulled her tighter against him. Her mouth opened to his, and his tongue met hers.

She wrenched free and stared at him. "It's only lust between us, sheer, animal lust. You do know that, don't you?"

He nodded. "Indeed I do."

"Good." She grabbed the edges of his coat and jerked his lips back to hers. She tasted of all things exotic and delicious and intoxicating. And kissing her would not be nearly enough.

His lips left hers and trailed along the edge of her jaw and down the curve of her neck. "Nor do I expect anything . . . anything . . ." She shuddered beneath his touch. "More." The word was but a sigh or a breath.

"I can accept that," he said against her skin. Her head dropped back, and she braced her hands on the table behind her. He kissed the hollow of her throat.

She gasped. "This does not imply a . . . a commitment of any sort between us."

"I don't expect one." His mouth traveled lower, toward the invitation of her breasts straining at the confines of her bodice. If he were the type of man to indulge in fantasies, this would certainly be one of them. The scent of the tropics in the air, the warmth of a summer night in the midst of winter, a beautiful woman in his arms. Although in his fantasy she wouldn't be dressed in the latest fashion with voluminous skirts and layers of clothing not even the most skilled of men could easily dispense with in the heat of passion. Why had men ever allowed women to give up the simplicity of the clothing worn by the Greeks? He could probably unfasten a toga with his teeth.

"We scarcely know one another." Her voice was heavy with desire and scarcely more than a whisper.

"I intend to remedy that," he murmured, nuzzling the valley between her breasts.

Still, while he had never especially wished to *know* a woman before he shared her bed this— Judith—was a decidedly different matter. Perhaps his passion was coloring his judgment. He snorted to himself. There was no *perhaps* about it. Reluctantly he raised his head. "Do *you* think we should know one another better before we . . . well . . . first?"

"Undoubtedly. It would be the wise thing to do. However, at this particular moment"—she smiled up at him in a distinctly wicked manner—"we know enough." She threw her arms around his neck and pressed his lips to hers.

Her ardor caught him off guard and he stumbled backward, flaying his arms to regain his balance. He held on to her with one hand and caught an upper tier of the fountain with other. Water cascaded down his arm and splashed over them both with a shocking thoroughness.

Her eyes widened, and she stared up at him. "I daresay I have never had my enthusiasm doused quite like this before."

Still, she didn't pull out of his embrace. "And is it doused?"

"Well, we are rather wet." She reached up to brush her lips against his. "I should think if we don't get out of these wet clothes quickly we shall surely catch nasty colds."

He smiled slowly. "We are not all that wet."

"Nonsense, we've been doused. We are soaked." Her lips against his, the promise of her body through layers of clothing, and any hesitation that might have lingered within him vanished. "And one should never take chances with one's health."

"Then Judith, by all means"—he gazed into her blue eyes and smiled—"let the adventure begin."

Chapter 3

*I*t was shocking. Completely shocking. She would never have believed it possible.

How on earth had they managed to get from the conservatory all the way up the stairs to her rooms without his having had his way with her on the conservatory floor? Or in the endless corridors? Or on the stairway? Or in the library or the ballroom or any number of other rooms they had passed on their way here? Although there had been a moment or two when she had thought, when she had wanted, when she had hoped . . . And even more shocking yet: how had she kept from having her way with him?

Judith's back pressed flat against the door to her rooms and she gasped for breath, not that she particularly cared about breathing. Gideon's lips were everywhere at once: on her mouth, her throat, her shoulders. She twined her fingers through the hair at the nape of his neck and urged him on, her free hand groping for the door handle.

Good God, she'd never known passion like this before. Even with the handful of men she'd taken to her bed it had always been, well, civilized. Intimacy had always followed a prescribed course: flirtations, outings, intimate dinners, and lengthy preliminaries. And while relations had always been satisfying, she had never before felt she would surely die if the gentleman in question did not take her. Right now. This minute. *Take her?* Dear Lord, she'd never wanted to be *taken* before!

She caught the door handle, turned it, and the door gave way behind them. They fell into the room, tumbling onto the lush carpet, their fall cushioned by her skirts and petticoats, and she scarcely noticed. He kicked the door closed with his foot, and a part of her mind not thoroughly fogged with passion admired his skill. His arms wrapped around her, her legs entwined with his. Dimly, she noted a sharp repetitive noise and ignored it. She existed only in the touch of his hands and the heat of his mouth.

Without warning, he wrenched his lips from hers and lifted his head. Confusion shone in eyes dark with passion and absolutely irresistible. "What is that?"

"What?" She pulled his head back to hers.

"That infernal noise." He braced himself on his hands and raised his head again. "Bloody hell, it's a dog."

Only now did the noise she had noted earlier become distinct. So much for passion. "Oh dear, I completely forgot about Arthur." She heaved a frustrated sigh, pushed Gideon aside, and sat up. A small, white, adorable ball of fur leaped into her lap, put his paws on her chest, and swiped a lick at her chin. "Good evening, dearest."

Gideon sat back and stared. "It is a dog, isn't it?"

"Of course it's a dog." She sniffed. "A quite wonderful dog."

"It looks like a furry rat."

"Don't be absurd. It—he—is considerably larger than a rat."

"Not considerably. A dog—a real dog—should stand about, oh"—he held his hand at the level of his shoulder—"this tall at least and have some sort of purpose. Hunting or retrieving or"—he glared at the dog—"ratting."

Arthur's lip curled upward in a slight snarl.

"Arthur has a purpose. He is a faithful companion and provides unconditional affection."

Gideon studied Arthur, and Judith could have sworn Arthur returned his perusal. Neither dog nor man seemed especially impressed with the other. "Are you sure it's not a rat?"

"*He* is not a rat, nor does he look like one. Arthur is a bichon, a very old, very noble breed. Bichons have been owned by kings and painted by the finest artists in history."

"Rat painters no doubt," he muttered.

"I daresay if I needed him, he would defend me with his life," she said staunchly. She hadn't the vaguest idea if Arthur would indeed come to her rescue, although he had on occasion been known to nip at the heels of a newly hired servant.

"I know I would fear for my life if he were aroused," he said solemnly although there was a distinct twinkle in his eyes. "or at least for my ankles."

"You are not the least bit funny." She picked up Arthur and set him firmly on the floor. "Arthur, go to bed at once." Arthur obediently trotted across the room and jumped into his basket. "Gideon—"

"If you are about to command me to bed, I warn you, I shall not be nearly so quick to go alone as your Arthur."

She stared at him. It was astounding how quickly passion could vanish when confronted by a yapping pet. And even more shocking how swiftly it could be reignited with nothing more than the look in a man's eye. *The right man, perhaps?* The right man for the moment, she amended. "Would you be so good as to help me up."

"Certainly." He scrambled to his feet and reached down his hand. His hair was rumpled, his clothing askew, and he might well have been the most desirable man she'd ever seen. She grabbed his hand, and he pulled her up and into his arms.

"Gideon." She sighed his name, drew his mouth down to hers, and closed her eyes. His mouth lingered on hers, but she had the distinct feeling his thoughts were elsewhere. She opened her eyes. "Gideon?"

His lips remained against hers but his gaze shifted. "This room is pink," he said in the same manner one might say, "That horse is brown," a simple observation of fact that nonetheless implied that there was something innately wrong about brown or, in this case, pink.

She drew back and looked at him. "It's not just pink. It's white and gold as well with touches of green, I might add."

"It's primarily pink and it's ... it's ... I don't know." He glanced around the room. "Frilly. Fussy. Overly feminine."

"I am overly feminine," she said firmly. "And I don't see the least bit wrong with it."

Her gaze swept the room, over the chaise with its rose-colored brocade upholstery, the white and gilt Louis XV furnishings, the pastel Aubusson rug, the flowing rose and green drapes, and of course the bed, large and cushy and, in her mind, delightfully decadent, with a brocade coverlet that matched the chaise and a canopy swathed in rose and green silk. Vases filled with fresh flowers from the conservatory were placed strategically around the room. Most of them were neither pink nor white nor gold but a myriad of colors and admittedly not quite in keeping with the room, but she loved them nonetheless. Certainly it had been years since she had had the room decorated, and admittedly there was a *pinkness* about it, but regardless it was quite lovely.

"It looks ... I don't know." He grimaced. "Like a ... a flower in here. I expect to see butterflies or bees or even a fairy flitting about at any moment."

"Nonsense. There are no butterflies or bees or fairies, although one or two might be quite charming." In spite of her words, she conceded, if only to herself, the room was perhaps the tiniest bit extreme. She lifted her chin and met his gaze. "I like it."

He shook his head, turned her around, and started unfastening the hooks on the back of her dress. "This is not a place for a man."

"It's not supposed to be. It's mine. My sanctuary, as it were." She felt her bodice loosen. He was really quite skilled at this, quick and deft.

"Yes, well, your sanctuary is rather intimidating. All this femininity."

"Don't be absurd." What else was he skilled at? Desire pooled in the pit of her stomach.

"How do you expect a man, any man, to perform successfully in here?"

"Perform?" She started to tell him other men had not found it especially difficult, then held her tongue. She knew, although she wasn't sure how she knew, but she knew he was not like other men. Nor would this be at all like anything she'd experienced with other men. "Like an actor?"

"No, not like an actor. More like a . . . " He paused to find the right words. "A thoroughbred. Yes, that's good. Very appropriate."

"A thoroughbred? A race horse?" She tried to force a note of indignation to her voice, but it was difficult to be indignant when one was mentally counting the number of hooks opened and the number yet to go. She thanked whatever stroke of foresight tonight that had prompted her to don less than her usual number of petticoats. "I daresay I have never thought of any activity involving a man in my bedchamber to be even remotely akin to a race."

"Of course it's not a race." He blew an exasperated breath, slipped the dress off her shoulders, and let it fall to the floor. "It's more like a steeplechase in which endurance and skill as well as mastery of the reins is more important than speed." He unfastened her petticoat, and it sank to the floor.

"I should hope so," she murmured.

"However, a room like this encourages speed." He shuddered. "One fears if one doesn't leave as soon as possible, one's, well, *masculinity*, for lack of a better word, will simply shrivel and disappear as some sort of pagan sacrifice to a vengeful goddess."

She laughed. "You're insane."

"Or brilliant. A fine line, you know, between insanity and brilliance." He ran his hands lightly up and down her arms.

She leaned back against him. "And yet you have not crossed it."

"For you, dearest Judith, and no one else, I shall run the risk of sacrificing that which I hold dear."

"I am fortunate." And who wouldn't feel fortunate dressed only in one's corset and chemise and drawers with a dashing man at one's back? Even if he was still fully clothed.

"Indeed you are." He spoke low into her ear. "I am the last of my line, you know. Should anything happen to me before I sire an heir, it would be a great shame." His hands rested lightly on her shoulders, and he nuzzled the side of her neck. "Besides, this is not at all the type of bedchamber for a woman like you."

"It's not?" She closed her eyes. "Why not?"

"It's too expected." His hands drifted lightly over her arms. "The colors are that of an English rose. Pretty enough, but really rather unexceptional. Unexciting. You are not a rose."

"I'm not?" She could feel the long length of his body, solid and warm, behind hers.

"No indeed." His hands skimmed along the sides of her corset and rested on her waist in a manner at once provocative and possessive. "You are an exotic blossom. The rarest of orchids."

She bit her lip to keep from gasping aloud. "I don't recall saying you could take my gown off."

"I was being practical." He kissed the curve between neck and shoulder.

She caught her breath. "Practical?

"In much the same way that it is impractical to pretend one hasn't seen a gift left in plain sight that was clearly not meant to be a surprise." He turned her around to face him and gazed into her eyes. "Although I daresay there are any number of surprises ahead, you, Judith, are a gift."

"Am I?" She rested her hands on his chest and stared up at him. "Are you sure?"

"I have not been certain of anything since I looked into your eyes at the Twelfth Night Ball." He smiled slowly, and her heart leaped. "Since that moment, my life has been . . ."

"What?" She stared up at him. She had no idea what she wanted him to say. Declare his immediate and undying affection? Of course not. They scarcely knew each other, and whatever this was between them had nothing to do with love. Nor did she wish it to. Still, God help her, she didn't know what she wanted. Save him. "What has your life been?"

"A matter of little more than marking time." His smile faded, and there was an intensity in his eyes that took her breath away. "Since that moment, I have felt as if I were holding my breath. As if I were waiting for something quite wonderful. Something just out of reach."

"And why did you not reach for it?"

"Why, my dear Judith." His smile returned and he pulled her closer against him. "I believe I am doing precisely that."

"Past time too." She slipped her arms around his neck. "One might have thought—" His lips crushed hers, and any thoughts she had fled, dashed aside by the unyielding demand of passion. Her mouth opened beneath his and his tongue met hers, insistent and greedy. She met his greed with her own, countered his demand with hers, answered his need and hers.

She pushed his coat over his shoulders and he shrugged it off and let it fall to the floor. She pulled at his cravat, and he yanked it from his neck. They moved in a frenzy of yearning and desire and parted only long enough for him to pull his shirt over his head and for her to unhook the front closure of her corset. His trousers joined his shirt, she shed her drawers and chemise, and then she was back in his arms. Her naked body pressed against the long, hard length of his. She marveled at the heat that radiated from his flesh into hers and reveled in it. His hands roamed over her back. His lips explored her neck, her shoulders, her throat. She dropped her head back and arched upward toward him. His erection prodded against her, and her knees weakened with desire.

She gasped. "It is good to know the nature of the room has not adversely affected your masculinity."

He raised his head and grinned wickedly. "That is good to know." He cupped her buttocks and pulled her tighter to him. "Still, one does wish to be sure."

She ground her hips against his member and delighted in his small gasp of surprise coupled with pleasure.

"You shall pay for that," he growled and scooped her into his arms. He kicked aside the mounds of clothing at their feet and strode to the bed.

"I do hope so," she murmured and nipped at his shoulder.

He deposited her on her feet beside the bed, slid one arm around her back, then cupped a breast in his hand. She arched toward him in anticipation and desire. He bent to take one nipple in his mouth. He sucked and teased, tongue and teeth toying with the sensitive flesh. Waves of pleasure rippled from his touch. She gripped his shoulders and moaned softly. He shifted to lavish attention on her other breast, and she wondered how long she could remain upright, how long before she melted into a puddle at his feet.

He dropped to his knees before her and nuzzled the flat of her stomach. His hands caressed her bottom and skimmed over her hips, and his mouth moved lower. She ran her hands through his hair and wanted to urge him on but knew it would be ever so much better if she allowed him to lead. And wanted him never to stop.

Abruptly he stood and gently pushed her back onto the bed. She smiled up at him and wondered that she could smile at all, wondered that she could breathe. He ran his hands along the insides of her legs and spread them apart. The cool night air drifted over her, every nerve in her body alert to the slightest breath, the merest touch. His hands reached the juncture of her thighs, and anticipation gripped her. She wanted his fingers, his mouth, his cock. He hadn't touched her there and yet she throbbed with yearning and wondered if he knew. And thought surely he must. His fingers drifted over the curls guarding her most private places, so slight she wasn't sure she had been touched at all. So light it was a tease, a promise, nothing more. She arched her hips up slightly. His finger flicked lightly over the point of her pleasure and she gasped and held her breath. She wanted, she needed, more. He touched her again and she moaned with desire. Dear Lord, he was indeed making her pay. And what an exquisite payment. His finger slid over her, slick with her own need, in a slow, easy manner. Her arms stretched out at her sides and her hands clutched the bedcovers in an effort to keep herself still, like an offering to a god of carnal delight. Every fiber of her being was intent on his touch upon her. Intent on the slow, wicked stroke of his finger.

He spread her open with his hands, then leaned forward to replace his finger with his mouth. She sucked in a hard breath and fisted her hands in the bedcovers. All sense of who she was vanished beneath the pleasure of his mouth and his tongue. She existed only as a creature of erotic awareness, of sheer sensation. Dimly she heard an odd, whimpering sound and realized it came from her. The tension inside her tightened, spiraled toward release.

Without warning he stopped, and she cried out in frustration. He climbed on the bed and without pause settled between her legs and plunged into her. She gasped and her hips drove upward in welcome. He was large and hot and hard and filled her with a perfection she had not imagined. She wrapped her legs around his waist and urged him deeper. He thrust into her and then withdrew almost entirely and then thrust again and again. She caught his rhythm and together they moved in a tempo as natural as nature itself, as glorious as the heavens. The bed rocked with their efforts and she wondered if it might collapse around them and didn't care. Nothing mattered save him and her, and the world itself existed only in their joining. Faster he drove into her and harder she pushed against him until the tight, aching sweetness of release exploded within her. Waves of sheer delight coursed through her and she bucked beneath him and screamed with the joy of it. A moment later he thrust again and then shuddered within her and groaned in the way of a man who has been caught unawares by the power of his own release.

He withdrew from her, then gathered her close and rolled to his back, and they lay together as one, her head resting on the warm, hard planes of his chest. She could feel her heart thudding inside her and could feel as well the beat of his against hers. She wanted to do nothing more than lie here in his arms forever. It wasn't merely that he was an excellent lover; he was certainly that and she had expected as much. But there was something in the intensity of their coupling, something beyond mere pleasure of the flesh that struck her as significant even though she wasn't entirely sure what it was. It was probably nothing more than that this man was very, very good and more than a little bit wicked.

There was a great deal to be said for more than a little bit wicked.

"That was quite . . . quite . . ." She giggled with the pure exhilaration of it. "Lovely, I should say."

"Lovely?" he scoffed. "I would call it substantially more than *lovely. Lovely* is such a"—he kissed her nose—"pink sort of word."

"Nonsense. It's not the least bit pink." She laughed. "What would you call it then?"

"I would call it"—he thought for a moment—"delightful."

She raised a brow. "*Lovely* is pink but *delightful* is acceptable? I think *delightful* is almost as pink as *lovely.*"

"Very well then." He adopted a somber expression, surprisingly impressive for a naked man lying on his back with an equally naked woman draped over him. She stifled a giggle. "Incredible, I should think. Nothing pink about *incredible*."

"Definitely not."

"Even magnificent." His gaze met hers. "Yes, that's it. It was magnificent." Without warning he pulled her close and rolled over, to trap her between his body and the bed. "And I suspect it will be magnificent again." He kissed her shoulder. "And again." He kissed the hollow of her throat. "And again."

She shuddered with delight. "And then?"

"And then, dearest Judith." He grinned down at her. "You owe me supper."

"I have never dined in a lady's boudoir before," Gideon said in an idle manner and sipped his wine thoughtfully. "It's a rather unique feeling."

"A bit wicked perhaps?" Judith sat across the table from him, a distinct spark of amusement in her eyes.

"A bit." He grinned. He couldn't help but grin. He might well grin for the rest of his days based on this evening alone. It had indeed been magnificent, every moment. He wasn't entirely sure what had made it magnificent, what made it unique from any other evening he'd spent in the bed of any other delightful woman, but now was not the time for examination. There was still much of the evening left to enjoy.

They dined in a small alcove off her bedchamber. It too was overly pink. Judith had an excellent cook, and the meal was as perfect as the rest of the evening. The only discordant note came from that nasty creature she claimed was a canine who even now glared at him from a beribboned basket. The dog obviously didn't like him and the sentiment was returned.

"Do you like it?"

"Feeling wicked? Most certainly." He took a long sip of a very good wine. "I can't imagine why anyone wouldn't."

"Do you feel wicked . . . frequently?" she said casually.

He resisted the urge to laugh. "Frequently?"

"Yes. Frequently. Often."

"Why do you ask?"

"Curiosity. Nothing more than that." She shrugged. "I don't believe you, you know."

"About the pleasure to be had in feeling wicked?"

"Oh, that I believe, and furthermore, I agree." She leaned her elbows on the table, entwined her fingers, and rested her chin on her hands. "What I don't believe is that you have never dined in a lady's boudoir before."

"You don't?"

"Not for a moment. Your reputation precedes you, Gideon."

"*My* reputation?" He set his glass down, leaned back in his chair, and studied her. If there was nothing else he had learned about women in his thirty-two years of existence, he had learned it was never wise to assume one knew exactly what a woman was talking about. Ever. The best course was usually feigned ignorance followed closely by denial or, as a last resort, cautious confession and guarded honesty. "Would you care to be more specific?"

"I would indeed but the problem with reputations is that they are rarely specific. They are often built on little more than a kernel of truth."

"Even yours?"

"Especially mine. However, we are not discussing my reputation at the moment but yours." A thoughtful light shone in the lady's eyes. "Now then, you are known to be extremely cynical and you have a sharp wit you wield like a sword. You are cool and unruffled, even in your dealings with women, and I am told you are perhaps the most discreet among your friends when it comes to the fairer sex. Which makes it decidedly difficult to find out anything whatsoever about your past liaisons."

He grinned. "That is precisely the purpose of discretion."

"Nonetheless." A smug smile curved the corners of her mouth. "I have it on very good authority that this is not the first time you have had supper in a lady's bedchamber. From what I have heard, you are not unfamiliar with late-night suppers with actresses or opera singers or ballet dancers."

"Ah, but you see, a late-night supper after a theatrical performance is not necessarily in a woman's bedchamber."

She frowned. "It isn't?"

"No."

"I always thought it would be. It is in novels." She narrowed her eyes. "Are you sure?"

"I can only speak to my own experience and in that I am sure."

"And as we were speaking of your experience I shall have to take your word for it." She considered him for a moment. "I understand you were married once."

A muscle tightened in his jaw. His brief, ill-fated marriage was so long ago, he doubted even the most dedicated of gossips remembered it at all, although it was possible his closest friends did even if they had never spoken of it. Perhaps he would have to kill Helmsley after all. He forced a noncommittal note to his voice. "You must have had a long talk with Helmsley yourself."

"Oh my, yes." She laughed, and any irritation he felt at Helmsley's revelation of his past, which, while not common knowledge was not a secret either, vanished at the sound. "I fear I do not have the moral fortitude that you do. While you restrained from asking Lord Helmsley highly personal questions about me, I felt no such hesitation. I asked him everything about you that came to mind." She cast him a brilliant smile.

"Everything?"

"Everything I could think of."

"And did you learn anything of interest?"

She heaved an exaggerated sigh. "Very little, I'm afraid. More than anything, he simply confirmed what I knew. I was aware, if vaguely, of the nature of your character as well as the extent of your fortune and your lineage. I knew as well that your only living relative is an elderly aunt that you have kindly taken in. I did not know about certain . . . oh, what did Lord Helmsley call them?"

"I have no idea what you're talking about," he said coolly but braced himself for whatever incidents from his past Helmsley might have related. While Gideon might well have been both discreet and relatively well behaved in recent years, there was a period before that when he was anything but.

"Escapades. Yes, that's the word he used." She shook her head. "I must say I was shocked."

"Then my past is substantially more interesting than I thought it was. I would have doubted anything would have shocked you."

"You're right." She grinned. "A better word is *amused.*"

"Those days are long past. I am"—he thought for a moment—"reformed."

"Not too reformed, I hope."

"Never too reformed."

She studied him curiously. "You are not revealing a great deal, you know."

"Nor will I."

She straightened in her chair. "Why not?"

"The past is over and done with." He reached across the table and took her hand. "I much prefer to consider what happens next."

She stared at him for a long moment, a bemused smile on her face. Her blue eyes glowed, her cheeks were slightly flushed, a lingering effect of their exertion or the excellent meal or the wine or more likely, all three. She'd loosely pinned her hair on top of her head, but more blond curls had escaped than were confined. The dressing gown she'd donned was trimmed in lace and ruffles, a silly garment, but the memory of what it concealed quickened his blood. "We should discuss that."

"What happens next? In regard to the state of the world as we know it? Politics and the like?" He adopted an innocent tone but he knew full well what she meant.

"No." She withdrew her hand. "In regard to the two of us. If we are to continue beyond tonight—"

"As I fully intend."

"As do I," she said in a prim manner. "Then we need to come to an understanding of the . . . boundaries, as it were, of what we share."

"Boundaries?" He raised a brow.

"Perhaps *boundaries* is the wrong word. *Rules* might be a better term."

"Rules?"

"No, *rules* isn't right either." She thought for a moment. "Expectations then."

"Expectations," he said cautiously. Good God, this was about to become very awkward.

"Yes, expectations." She nodded firmly, rose to her feet, and paced the room. "To begin with, you should know that I do not take a man to my bed lightly."

"That is good to know." Although he had, in truth, known it already. Not from Helmsley but from the snippets of gossip about her he had heard through the years. Even disregarding the exaggeration inherent in gossip, he was fairly certain the number of lovers in Judith's life since her husband's death was not excessive. Not that it mattered. Still, one did like to know one was a member of an exclusive club.

"Did you think I did?" She glanced at him.

"Not for a moment," he said staunchly and watched her move absently around the room. For a woman who exuded confidence, her demeanor now struck him as anything but confident. It was curious and most interesting.

"In the past"—she chose her words with care—"when a gentleman and I have come to this particular point—"

"Dinner?"

She ignored him. "There have always been significant preliminaries. We understood or perhaps established—"

"Boundaries," he said helpfully.

"Yes." She huffed. "Boundaries." She clasped her hands together and stared at him. "However, we were discussing expectations."

"Not rules?" He resisted the urge to smile.

"Expectations," she said firmly.

"Expectations then." He crossed his arms over his chest. "Go on."

"First of all, I expect a certain amount of honesty between us."

"Only a certain amount? Not complete, utter, and unequivocal honesty?"

"Don't be absurd. Men and women can never be completely honest with one another. It would take all the fun out of it."

"Perhaps you're right." He chuckled. "A reasonable amount of honesty then."

"There will come a time, be it a fortnight from now or six months or a year, when you will tire of our relationship, of me—"

"Never," he said without thinking. Still, she was right. The affair they were embarking upon would end one day.

"Or I shall tire of you."

He scoffed, "Also inconceivable."

"When that happens, we are each free to go our separate ways without recrimination. In fact, I do hope we can remain friends." She smiled in a pleasant manner.

"Friends?" He stared in disbelief. She was managing the end of their relationship before it had even begun. "Friends?"

"One can always use another friend."

"You've done this before, haven't you?"

Her glance slid to the bed, then back to him. "As in *this* you mean . . ."

"Define boundaries," he snapped. "Discuss expectations."

"No." She blew a long breath. "I haven't. It's never been necessary before."

"And it's necessary now?"

"Dear Lord, yes." The slightest hint of confusion shone in her eyes. "I have never before leaped into bed with a man with the speed with which I have leaped with you."

"To my undying gratitude."

"I have always thought of myself as, well, *civilized*

for want of a better word. And this, with *you*"—she gestured aimlessly—"is not the least bit civilized."

"Again, to my undying gratitude."

"It's most disconcerting. Even frightening." A frown creased her brow. "To have passion rule your senses, overpower your resistance, wreak havoc with coherent thought. Why, we scarcely know one another."

"I agree." He got to his feet. "It is disconcerting, although I should term it exhilarating more than frightening. And very much an adventure." He stepped toward her. "As for scarcely knowing one another—"

"Do not come another step closer." She thrust out her hand to stop him. "We need to talk and I cannot speak rationally if your very presence makes my knees weaken."

He grinned but held his tongue.

"And do sit down. You're much less . . . compelling when you sit." She shuddered. "I never knew a man dressed only in his trousers and shirt could quite be so irresistible. I wish you had accepted my offer of an appropriate dressing gown."

"I prefer to select my own dressing gowns, thank you." He settled back in his chair, his grin widened. "You find me irresistible?"

"Yes." She cast him a reluctant smile. "You wicked, wicked man, I do indeed."

"Good. Is that it then?"

"Not quite. Now, in regard to marriage—"

"Marriage." He sat upright. "Marriage?"

"You needn't stare at me as if I were speaking a language you don't understand."

"Marriage is a language I don't understand," he said under his breath. "Judith, marriage is not—"

"Oh, do be quiet, Gideon, and hear me out." She rolled her eyes toward the ceiling. "Just because we have shared a bed does not mean we should be shackled together for the rest of our days."

"It doesn't", he said slowly. Certainly he hadn't thought it did, but one never knew what a woman, even a woman as free in spirit as Judith, thought about marriage in the wake of a passionate liaison.

"No, of course not. You should understand from the very beginning, before there are any further entanglements, that I have no desire to marry again. Ever."

"You don't?" Relief coursed through him, tinged with the oddest touch of regret.

"No." She shook her head. "I see no reason to marry. I am financially independent. I have the companionship of good friends. I have the freedom and the wherewithal to do what I please and go where I wish. Why on earth would I sacrifice all that for marriage?"

"Why indeed," he murmured.

"You, however, are an entirely different matter."

He narrowed his gaze. "Am I?"

"You well know you are. You said it yourself, you are the last of your line. You must marry and produce an heir. I would wager, within the next few years you will find a sweet, nondemanding, pliable young thing of good family and equally good fortune who will make your domestic life pleasant and undemanding."

"That sounds rather calculating." A slight note of indignation sounded in his voice although—and he would never admit to her—that was exactly what he planned.

"Perhaps, but such is the way of the world we live in. Marriage is, and always has been, more for purposes of responsibility and duty than anything else. Therefore it's only"—she thought for a moment—"practical to choose one's match with the same care one makes any other type of permanent arrangement."

"But what of affection?" he said without thinking. "Love? Passion?"

"Passion is fleeting. As for affection . . ." She stared at him curiously. "Am I wrong then? Do you wish to marry for love?"

"No, I suppose not. You have me there." He met her gaze and heard the words fall from his lips before he could stop himself. "I did that once."

She smiled slowly. "As did I."

Again he got to his feet. "And doing so has convinced you never to marry again?"

"I see no need to do so." She shrugged. "I believe one's fate is preordained. One's destiny is determined from birth. I believe as well that each of us is meant for one person and one person only. Soul mates, if you will."

"And you married your soul mate?"

Did he imagine it or was there a hesitation so slight it might have been nothing more than a breath before she nodded firmly. "I did. Did you?"

"I thought so at the time." He shook his head in a wry manner. "But then I was something of an idiot at the time as well."

"An admission about the past?" She raised a brow. "Now I really am shocked."

"As well you should be." He moved to her and took her into his arms. "Although it seems only fair since you have revealed so much about yourself."

"Have I?" She wrapped her arms around his neck. "What precisely have I revealed?"

"A practical side of your nature even regarding presents and passion. A desire for adventure. A belief in fate, destiny. And best of all"—he gazed into her eyes and smiled—"you find me irresistible."

"Did I say that?" she murmured.

"You did indeed." He scooped her up and carried her toward the bed. "I make your knees weak."

"Oh, surely I didn't tell you that." Her finger trailed lightly across the back of his neck, and desire rose within him.

"Oh, surely you did." He dropped her on the bed in a heap of pink frills and ruffles, looking every bit as delicious as a decadent dessert.

She propped herself up on her elbows and watched him. "My knees are quite strong at the moment."

He drew his shirt up over his head and tossed it aside. "I doubt that."

"And I don't find you the least bit irresistible." The breathless note in her voice and the look in her eyes belied her words.

He unbuttoned his trousers and dropped them to the floor. Her gaze slipped down his body to his erection, and a distinct blush tinged her cheeks. He grinned. "I don't believe that either."

He moved to the bed, reached out, and slowly pulled free the sash that held the confection she wore closed. Her breathing quickened and she sank back on the bed. He opened the gown, and she lay exposed before him. He trailed his hands lightly over her breasts, and her nipples hardened at his touch. He ran his fingers over her stomach. She sucked in a hard breath. He continued lower and ran his hand between her legs and smiled. She was as ready for him as he was for her.

He straightened abruptly and heaved an exaggerated sigh. "Well, if I'm not irresistible and your knees are fine, you obviously don't want—"

She grabbed his hand, pulled him down on the bed, and wrapped herself around him. "Did I mention that you are a wicked man?"

"I believe you may have." He pulled her closer, and they tangled together in the ruffles and lace and the heat of needy bodies.

"It bears repeating." She arched into him, and her breasts crushed against his chest.

"Judith," he murmured against her neck. "How does one recognize one's soul mate?"

"*Le coup de foudre,*" she whispered and entwined her leg around his.

"*Le coup de foudre,*" he repeated under his breath. It had an erotic ring to it, but then anything whispered into his ear right now would have an erotic ring. Especially anything French. He knew the language fairly well but his mind simply couldn't translate at the moment. Nor did he care.

He buried his mouth in the soft, sweet curve between her neck and her shoulder. Had a woman ever tasted quite so delicious? Had a man ever wanted a woman more? Had two bodies ever fit together so perfectly, as if one was meant only for the other?

In the last rational moment before passion claimed his senses completely and he knew nothing more than the feel of her body against his and the need for her and her alone welling within him, he realized the meaning of *le coup de foudre.*

Bolt of lightning.

Chapter 4

"You and Warton? *Warton*?" Susanna stared at Judith as if she had sprouted feathers and a tail right there in Susanna's own drawing room. "Good God, Judith, are you insane?"

"I could be, I suppose, but I don't think so."

"Whatever *are* you thinking?"

"I'm not sure I am thinking." Judith gestured aimlessly. "And must say I like not thinking for a change."

"Not thinking?" Susanna groaned and rose to her feet. "Oh, that's bad, that's very bad." She crossed the room, opened the doors of a tall chinoise cabinet, grabbed a decanter, and returned to her chair. "I've never known you not to think in matters of this nature. You always give these things a great deal of thought before you—"

"Leap?" Judith said brightly.

"Leap?" Susanna plopped into her chair. "You never leap."

Judith bit back a laugh. "Well, I have leaped this time and I must say I am finding it a great deal of fun."

"Fun?" Susanna shuddered.

"Will you be repeating every word I say in this manner?"

"Yes. And probably every word I say as well," Susanna snapped. "Oh, this is bad." She leaned forward and poured a healthy dollop of whatever was in the decanter into her cup of tea and did the same to Judith's. Susanna firmly believed any kind of problem called for spirits. One could determine how seriously Susanna viewed a situation by the strength of the alcohol she poured into her teacup. Cordials were for minor dilemmas, brandy for something more serious, and whisky, either Scottish or Irish, was required for a true crisis. "This is very, very bad." Judith wagered this decanter held whisky, and no doubt Susanna's best.

"Nonsense." Judith took a cautious sip, confirming her suspicions and noting as well the warming quality of the excellent liquor. "I don't see anything bad about it at all."

"I don't see anything good about it."

"Why on earth not? Warton is charming and attractive but really not terribly different from any other man." Even as she said the words, Judith realized they were a lie. Gideon was unlike any man she'd ever known.

"And that is precisely the problem. Or at least

part of it." Susanna took a long, fortifying sip of her tea. "Like any man in his position, Warton needs to marry. He, and every other idiot man with wealth and a title in this country, wants a simpering virgin he can mold to be the perfect, undemanding sort of wife that you, my dear, were once but could never be again."

"Excellent, as I am not interested in marriage with Warton or anyone else."

"So you claim."

Judith widened her eyes in indignation. "How can you say such a thing? You of all people should know I have no intention of ever marrying again."

Susanna snorted. "It's easy to declare one's disinterest in remarriage when one has never found a man worth marrying."

"Warton is not—"

"Judith." Susanna leaned forward. "The danger lies not with Warton but with you. I fear for your heart."

"My heart?" Judith laughed. "My heart is not the least bit at risk."

"I have never seen you fall into a man's bed this quickly. Why, you scarcely know him."

"I know him better now," Judith murmured.

"You've had what? Three lovers since Lucian died? Four if you count Lord Lovett." Susanna frowned. "Do you count Lord Lovett?"

"That depends on what I'm counting for. In the strictest definition, Lovett would not be included on the list."

"There was that unforeseen problem of the wife that no one knew he had." Susanna shook her head in annoyance. "I do hate it when that happens."

"It was regrettable." Judith let her mind drift back over the handsome blond-haired viscount with the laughing eyes. She was eternally grateful she had learned of his marital state before she had joined him in his bed. Judith had known of far too many women through the years devastated by their husband's infidelities to ever be the woman who caused such unhappiness. "We could have had a lovely time. He was quite charming, you know."

"As is Warton apparently, although I certainly can't see it."

Judith stared at her friend. "Surely you must admit he's extremely handsome with his dark hair and his darker yet eyes. Add to that his cynical air and the knowing way he looks at you, why, you're lucky your knees don't collapse beneath you when you gaze into those eyes and he smiles that delicious wicked smile."

"Dear Lord," Susanna muttered.

"He's tall—"

"You're short. Everyone is tall to you."

"His shoulders are nicely broad . . ." At once she remembered the feel of the hard planes of his chest against hers. The sculpted muscles of his buttocks under her fingers. The feel of him inside her . . .

"Yes, yes, he's attractive enough." Susanna waved off Judith's comment. "But he's not *right* for you."

"You sound as if I am planning on spending the

rest of my days with him. I'm not. This is a temporary arrangement. But do tell." Judith heaved a long-suffering sigh. "What, aside from the fact that he will be seeking a wife at some point, makes him wrong for me?"

"You always choose men who are amusing and entertaining. Like Lord Helmsley. They are . . ." She thought for a moment. "Safe, at least in terms of emotional entanglements, because you do not take them the least bit seriously. I've watched you, Judith, and while the gentlemen in question never seem to realize it, you are always the one calling the tune."

It was true, and Judith had realized it years ago. Still, it was one thing to admit one's controlling nature to oneself and quite another to admit it aloud. "What does that have to do with Lord Warton?"

"Lord Warton is aloof, cold, superior. Arrogant." Susanna wrinkled her nose. "Sarcastic. Overly serious."

Judith stared. "How can you say that? You know nothing about him."

"I most certainly do. I don't know him personally but . . ." She sniffed. "When one has the number of brothers and sisters I do, one hears a great deal about a great many people."

"Do you know about his marriage then?" Judith asked in a casual manner that belied the importance of the question.

"I know he was married for no more than a day. An elopement I believe." Susanna thought for a moment. "It was a long time ago, a decade or so I think. It was all kept very quiet. If I recall correctly the girl involved was already engaged to someone else. She and Lord Warton ran off but were found almost immediately after the ceremony, which was annulled at once. The girl then married her fiancé." Susanna paused. "Her name eludes me at the moment."

"And?"

"And that's all I remember except it seems to me his behavior for a while afterward was quite scandalous."

"He says he's reformed," Judith murmured.

"Perhaps he has. Or perhaps he's simply more discreet, which I suppose does indicate reformation of some sort." Susanna paused for a moment. "I will admit that I don't know the man personally. I daresay there aren't many who do. But I do know that he's far and away too reserved for you. He strikes me as a man who holds the reins on his emotions tightly. Not the type you usually choose and not the least bit amusing. I can't imagine Lord Warton would be the least bit enjoyable to . . . well, to be with."

Judith bit back a grin. "Appearances can be most deceiving."

"Good God." Susanna stared. "Please don't tell me it was wonderful."

"Very well. But it was." Judith grinned in a manner far more restrained than she felt. Susanna's reaction to Judith's involvement with Gideon was unexpected and rather shocking. Susanna had never expressed any sort of reservation regarding Judith's liaisons.

Susanna was a year or so older than Judith and had been married to a cousin of Judith's mother so distant, they could scarcely be called relations. Their husbands had died within six months of each other, neither had children, and their mutual losses had forged a firm friendship that only grew stronger through the years. Both women enjoyed busy social lives, but while Judith's parties tended toward week-long gatherings at her country estate, literary salons, and the occasional ball, Susanna preferred musicales and poetry readings featuring her beloved, and numerous, nieces and nephews. She wanted more than anything to have children of her own. Susanna was from an extremely large and fertile family. Judith quite liked watching them from a distance and found herself at once jealous and grateful that she was without family to speak of. Except, of course, for Susanna herself, who was very much the sister Judith never had.

The two women differed as well in their attitudes toward men. Susanna was determined to marry again, but only when she found someone who could make her toes curl and her stomach flutter the way her late husband, Charles, had. The very moment she met such a man she would wed him and bed him without hesitation and not necessarily in that order. Until then, she had no desire to share any man's bed. Even so, she quite enjoyed watching Judith's flirtations and adventures. And until now had done so with both encouragement and enthusiasm.

Susanna drained the drink in her teacup and refilled it with equal parts of tea and whisky. Apparently she thought this was a crisis of unprecedented proportions. She took a sip, set the cup down on a side table, then moved from her chair to sit beside Judith on the settee.

"Dearest Judith." Susanna took Judith's hands. "Cousin." Judith braced herself. Susanna never called her *cousin* unless the situation was truly dire. "I'm very much afraid that you are not seeing what's right in front of you."

"I'm not?" Judith said slowly.

"No, dear heart, you must face the facts. You entered this relationship—"

"Leaped?" Judith offered.

"Exactly." Susanna nodded. "You leaped without hesitation. You have always given a considerable amount of thought before you have shared any man's bed, and that you have not done so now means a great deal."

"Nonsense." Judith tried to pull her hands free but Susanna held firm.

"Beyond that, you have always made a gentleman, to be blunt, *work* for the privilege of your company. There has always been an appropriate flirtation that led, eventually, to your bed."

"It sounds rather predictable," Judith muttered. She wasn't at all sure she liked the idea that this part of her life was predictable.

"It is predictable inasmuch as any sort of dance is predictable. There are steps you must follow to get to the end. One simply can't go flitting about doing whatever move one fancies or, heaven forbid, skipping over all the steps entirely and going right for the final pirouette."

"One can't?"

"Of course not. Why, people would be stumbling around, knocking into one another. It would be chaos. Anarchy."

Judith raised a brow. "Anarchy?"

"And someone could be hurt." Susanna's gaze met Judith. "Someone's heart could be broken."

Judith laughed. "I have no intention of allowing my heart to be broken."

"One does not allow one's heart to be broken. It happens when one least expects it. When one tosses away all semblance of rational behavior and . . . and leaps!"

"I scarcely think—"

"We've already agreed that you have not been thinking at all. You've been swept along by emotion and excitement and passion and, yes, even lust." Susanna sighed. "I can certainly understand being swept away and I agree he is handsome and dashing, but the very fact that you've been swept away at all is what makes this, and him, so very dangerous."

"I don't believe—"

"You never been swept away before. You've always kept your head."

"Even so I don't—"

"You will fall in love with him and he will break your heart because he will abandon you to marry the aforementioned simpering virgin."

"I shall not be abandoned," Judith said firmly.

"We have agreed that when either of us feels it is time to end our relationship we can do so without recrimination. We have no obligation to one another beyond that. Indeed, we have agreed to remain friends."

Susanna gaze met hers. "One cannot be friends with a man one has loved."

Judith scoffed, "I have no intention of loving him."

"My dear, dear friend. Do not forget I have observed you through four adventures—"

"Lovett doesn't count," Judith said.

"He does for these purposes and I have never seen you as you are now. Your behavior, the look in your eye, the lilt in your voice." Susanna shook her head in a mournful manner. "You have all the symptoms of a woman who is perilously close to falling in love."

"You do realize, I have not given up the idea of killing you." Gideon sat in his usual chair in the lounge at his club with two of his oldest friends and savored the taste of a fine brandy.

"Nonsense." The Marquess of Helmsley, Jonathon Effington, settled deeper in his chair and chuckled. "It was a joke and a damn clever one at that."

"Even you have to admit that much, Warton." Norcroft grinned.

"I needn't admit anything of the sort." Gideon turned his attention back to Helmsley. "I have considered shooting you but I fear that will be too quick and possibly painless. I should much prefer that you suffer." Gideon smiled in a pleasant manner and swirled the brandy in his glass. "Strangulation has a great deal of appeal."

Helmsley laughed. "Come now, it was funny."

Gideon narrowed his eyes. "I felt like an idiot."

"It scarcely matters how you felt." Helmsley grinned. "What did Judith think?"

Gideon heaved a resigned sigh. "She found it most amusing."

"I'm not surprised. It's just the sort of prank Judith would appreciate." Helmsley shook his head. "I do have one regret though."

Gideon raised a brow. "That you made a fool out of me?"

"Not at all," Helmsley scoffed. "I simply regret that I was not there to see it." He took a sip of his brandy and studied Gideon over the rim of the glass. His eyes twinkled wickedly. "Was Judith touched by your thoughtfulness?"

"Indeed she was." Gideon smiled in spite of himself. "She was also very pleased to get her orchid back."

"I thought she would be." Helmsley took a sip of his drink and considered his friend. "Dare I ask how the rest of the evening went?"

"You may ask."

"I see." Norcroft grinned. "You have always been discreet, even with your closest friends."

"Especially with my closest friends," Gideon said firmly.

"You will be seeing her again then?" Helmsley asked casually.

Gideon stifled a grin. Helmsley was obviously curious about exactly what had transpired last night with Judith. And if it was any woman other than Judith he probably would have asked directly. It spoke well of Helmsley, but then that came as no surprise. Helmsley was a good man and a better friend, as was Norcroft. Gideon had never told them, nor did he ever plan to, but he credited his own reformation to the two men. He had known both of them in school but they had not become friends until years later. Precisely when he had needed friends.

Gideon had spent the first year or so after his debacle of a marriage in behavior designed to cut short even the hardiest of lives. He lived in a raucous, drunken blur. He lost huge sums at the gaming tables and neither noted it nor cared. He had more women than any man had a right to, names he never knew, faces he did not remember. The only thing that had saved him from the complete ruination of his name and total destruction of his reputation was that he had abandoned proper London society altogether. He attended no balls, no soirees, no gatherings with eager matrons hoping to marry their daughters to eligible viscounts. He moved in an underworld of London life, in the East End near the docks or Southwark or Seven Dials or any number of disreputable districts that few gentlemen acknowledged existed and fewer still dared to visit after dark. He was robbed and beaten on more than one occasion.

It was in Haymarket that he and Helmsley and Norcroft had resumed their acquaintance. The pair were attempting to win an absurd wager with Cavendish, who, for perhaps the first and last time, was smart enough not to accompany them, and were involved in an altercation with ruffians even more unsavory than usual. In subsequent years, all three would disagree over who had rescued whom, while Cavendish would mourn the fact that he was not in on this particular exploit. Seeing these men of his own station in life had shocked Gideon with the realization of how low he had sunk. He had returned home and wondered why he would allow the mere loss of a woman to destroy his life. He considered the question for three full days, locked in his rooms. When he came out, he was no longer under the influence of alcohol or unrequited love. He picked up precisely where he'd left off his life. If he was considerably more cynical, or a touch more droll in manner, if his tongue was sharper on occasion than it should have been, well, it was to be expected. He was a different man. Two years later he noticed he, Helmsley, Norcroft, and Cavendish frequented the same clubs, the same social events, indeed, the same world. The men became friends and had been friends since.

"I intend to see her as often as possible," Gideon said mildly. Every day if he could and most definitely every night.

"I do consider her my friend, you know," Helmsley said in a matter-of-fact manner.

"I'm well aware of that."

"Which compels me to ask about your intentions." Helmsley's tone was unconcerned but there was a serious look in his eyes.

Norcroft groaned.

Gideon raised a brow. "My intentions?"

Helmsley nodded. "Yes."

"Come now, Helmsley," Norcroft said. "You are her former lover not her father."

Helmsley cast a firm glance at the other man. "I am her friend and I take that responsibility seriously."

"You're my friend as well," Gideon said. "Shouldn't you be asking her what her intentions are toward me?"

"He's never shown the least bit of concern as to what a woman's intentions were toward me." Norcroft shook his head in a mournful manner. "I may well never get over the slight."

Helmsley ignored him. "Should the situation arise—"

"I can tell you what my intentions were before last night." Gideon flashed him a wicked grin. "As well as what they are now."

"Oh?" Helmsley raised a brow.

"We intend to enjoy one another's company for as long as we both wish."

"I see." Helmsley considered him for a moment, then blew a long breath. "There are things about Judith you might wish to know."

"I prefer to learn them for myself," Gideon said. The way her back arched upward in the heat of passion, the way her eyes glazed in the throes of lovemaking, the way her heart beat against his.

"Yes, I understand that," Helmsley said wryly. "I am not speaking of intimate details."

"Thank God," Norcroft murmured.

Helmsley paused as if debating the wisdom of his words. "There is much more to Judith than meets the eye."

"What meets the eyes is more than enough." Gideon chuckled. "Judith Chester is perhaps the most independent, self-sufficient woman I have ever met as well as being delightful and quite lovely." He took a sip of his brandy. "Do you know she set, well, *rules* is the only accurate word for it, for our affair?"

Norcroft snorted back a laugh. "Rules?"

"Rules?" Helmsley frowned. "She never set rules for me."

That's because she did not leap into your bed without thought. Gideon smiled but said nothing.

"Rules?" Helmsley shook his head in disbelief. "I wonder . . . it scarcely matters now I suppose. As I was saying, Judith is not exactly as she appears. She is intensely private and I suspect her lighthearted manner is not entirely her nature. I have seen a glimpse through the years of her true character and I don't think she is as strong as she appears."

"Few of us are," Norcroft murmured.

Helmsley studied Gideon. "What do you know of her marriage?"

Gideon shrugged. "Nothing other than I know she believes her husband was her soul mate."

"I thought as much although she's never spoken of him to me." Helmsley stared. "The fact that she has done so to you—"

"It was an offhand remark." Gideon waved away

the comment. "Nothing of true significance." And yet Judith's admission had been oddly unsettling.

"Yes, well." Helmsley looked mildly unsettled himself. "When Judith and I were . . . together, I made a few inquiries about her husband—"

Norcroft raised a brow. "And she permitted that?"

"She never knew and I have no desire for her to find out now." Helmsley met Gideon's gaze. "Agreed?"

Gideon nodded.

"Judith married Baron Chester when she was no more than seventeen. He was not considerably older but had already come into his title and a significant fortune. The rumor at the time apparently was that they fell in love the moment they met. They were married almost at once." Helmsley sipped his brandy. "Judith's parents died the following year."

Gideon drew his brows together. "Both of them?"

Helmsley nodded. "Smallpox, I think. They left her a great deal of money, but all Judith really had left in the world was her husband." Helmsley thought for a moment. "From what I have heard he was an odd sort, fancied himself a poet. He had no family to speak of, possibly a sister if I recall. They entertained a great deal, grand, extravagant parties, but gossip had it that he was melancholy as often as he was in high spirits. Three years into their marriage, he died."

"How?" Norcroft asked.

"Some sort of accident, I believe, but no one seemed to know anything specific, at least no one I spoke to." Helmsley shrugged. "This all comes from various female members of my family. If there is gossip to be had or a juicy story to be told, Effington women are certain to know it. That they had few details indicates either Chester was extremely private—"

"As is his wife," Gideon murmured.

"Or there was something . . ." Helmsley hesitated. "Wrong."

"Wrong?" Norcroft's brow furrowed. "What do you mean *wrong*?"

"Wrong with Chester?" Gideon leaned forward in his chair. "Was he perhaps ill, do you think?"

"I don't know. It was a feeling, nothing more than that." Helmsley met Gideon's gaze directly. "Judith never speaks of him."

"That alone is rather odd, isn't it." Gideon considered the matter. "One would think a woman deeply in love with her husband would mention his name on occasion."

"Unless she preferred to forget him." Helmsley raised his glass pointedly.

"Or she wishes to preserve memories she has no desire to share," Norcroft added.

"Perhaps." Helmsley shrugged. "She built that conservatory of hers after his death. I have always thought she poured the passion she had for her husband into her plants."

"Probably." Gideon settled back in his chair. "Judith is a woman of great passion. One can see it in every step she takes. But I don't understand why you think she is not the woman she appears."

"I don't know." Helmsley tossed back the brandy in his glass and held it up to a passing waiter, who promptly replaced it with a filled glass. One of the best things about a private gentlemen's club was that the staff knew a member's habits and desires almost before the gentleman himself. "You know, Warton, women generally find me extremely charming."

Gideon laughed. "And modest as well."

"Judith and I are better friends than we are anything else."

"No doubt because you're so charming." Norcroft grinned.

"One would think." Helmsley sighed. "However, when we were *more* than friends, she did not . . . we simply did not . . . that is to say, I did but she obviously didn't . . ."

"Obviously didn't what?" Gideon said slowly.

Helmsley shrugged. "My charming nature aside, my feelings for her were significantly stronger than her feelings for me."

Norcroft raised a brow. "You fell in love with her?"

"Everyone falls in love with Judith in one manner or another." Helmsley waved off the comment. "And I didn't, well, I did but not completely. She realized the potential for what I realize now would have been disaster, and ended it, or so she led me to believe. And she did so in a manner so pleasant, we have remained friends and more on occasion."

Gideon stared at his friend. "Are you still in love with her?"

"In an odd way I suppose I am a little and probably always will be." Helmsley chuckled. "Not something I would want my new wife to know, of course."

"She would not take that at all well." Norcroft grimaced. Helmsley had recently wed Norcroft's cousin in what could only be called a love match, if one believed in such things. God help him.

"So." Gideon chose his words carefully. "Let me see if I understand. You think Judith is not as she appears because she did not succumb to your charms?"

"No. I think Judith is afraid to succumb to any man's charms. I think she is afraid to allow her true feelings to be seen."

"I still don't—"

"You haven't told me what happened last night, and as much as that is quite admirable, the very fact that you have said nothing tells me a great deal. I have never known Judith to become involved with anyone this quickly."

Gideon narrowed his eyes. "And?"

"And I think it's entirely possible"—Helmsley met his gaze directly—"that you could break her heart."

"Nonsense," Gideon scoffed. "I don't break hearts. Besides, Judith was very clear as to the limits of our relationship. Hearts are not involved, nor do I expect them to be."

"Still, you cannot be certain of that." Norcroft

shook his head. "Matters of this nature take on a life of their own."

"Oh, but I am certain, Jonathon." Gideon met his friend's gaze firmly, so there would be no question, no mistake as to his meaning. "I think the fact that you have found whatever passes for love in this life with a wonderful woman and will spend the rest of your days in wedded bliss something of a miracle, and I wish you well. Some of us have not been, nor will we ever be, as lucky. I do not believe I am"—he thought for a moment—"fated, if you will, to find the kind of love you have found. At some point, I will meet a docile, well-behaved woman who will make a suitable wife and provide an heir as is my responsibility.

"As for Judith, she might well be the loveliest thing that has ever happened to me. I thoroughly intend to savor every moment that I am privileged to spend in her company. But this is nothing more than an enjoyable interlude. And when it is over, I shall have what I expect to be extraordinary memories to sustain me through the remainder of a proper and civilized, if perhaps a bit staid and even dull, lifetime."

"Good God I was wrong." Helmsley's eyes widened and he stared at Gideon.

"I daresay you have been wrong about a great many things today and will be wrong about even more tomorrow." Gideon rolled his gaze toward the ceiling. "What in particular are you referring to now?"

Helmsley and Norcroft exchanged knowing glances.

"It's not Judith's heart that is in jeopardy." A slow grin spread across Helmsley's face. "It's yours."

Chapter 5

"S weet Phebe, do not scorn me; do not, Phebe;
Say that you love me not, but say not so."

Shakepeare's words drifted up from the stage below but Judith scarcely noticed. She sat next to Gideon in a private box and cast a surreptitious glance at his profile in the darkened theater. On stage, a nicely done production of *As You Like It* was moving toward intermission. Not that Judith's attention was on the amusing tale of multiple pairs of lovers wandering through a forest.

It had been two days since she'd last seen Gideon. She would have much preferred to spend every hour, day and night, with him, but a cautious voice in the back of her mind, a voice she had never heard before, had kept her from sending him a note or, God forbid, going to him in person. She had needed some time to consider what had passed between them. Perfectly logical as she had given it little thought beforehand. While he had sent flowers and a note asking her to accompany him to the theater tonight, he had not appeared in person. She was at once annoyed and grateful, and wondered if he too had needed time to reflect upon what they had begun. Or perhaps if he regretted it altogether. Of course, her own reflection was colored by Susanna's comments.

"I pray you, do not fall in love with me, for I am falser than vows made in wine."

Judith admitted that whatever this was with Gideon was different from the others. Jonathon had been her first lover, three years after her husband's death. It had not lasted long, nor did the adventures that had followed. She and Jonathon had, on occasion, shared a bed in a friendly sort of way through the subsequent years, although she was hard pressed to remember the last time that had happened. Several years, she thought. Looking back, she realized, as she had not realized before, the preliminaries with the gentlemen she became involved with, the dance, as Susanna had so tactfully put it, had always lasted far longer than the affair itself. In truth, she couldn't recall having shared any man's bed more than a few times before she had pleasantly ended the relationship. Beyond that, it was never, well, serious.

And she never remembered wanting to be with a man day and night.

"Who ever loved that loved not at first sight?"

This, whatever *this* was, was more akin to *at first sight* than anything she'd ever experienced. It was surely lust, admittedly lust of an intensity and power she'd never known before, but lust nonetheless. For whatever reason, Gideon triggered something inside her. Something uncivilized and insatiable and probably more than a little bit wicked. Sheer animal passion, perhaps, or unquenchable desire or voracious hunger, but love?

"Utterly ridiculous," she said to herself.

Gideon leaned close, his gaze still focused on the stage, and spoke softly. "Of course it's ridiculous, it's a comedy."

Horror swept through her. Had she said that aloud?

Gideon glanced at her and chuckled. "It's not that bad really. One simply has to accept the absurdities that Shakespeare so cleverly concocts."

"Yes." She smiled weakly. "One does. How silly of me to have forgotten that."

Gideon narrowed his eyes. "Is something amiss? Are you all right?"

"Fine. Really." She cast him her brightest smile. "I am having a wonderful time."

"As am I." He took her hand and squeezed it gently. Her stomach fluttered at his touch.

A moment later, applause rang from the audience and the curtain dropped, marking an intermission. Gideon was still staring at her with a charmingly bemused smile on his lips.

"Whatever are you thinking?"

"I'm thinking that I have no idea how I came to be here but I am eternally grateful that I am." He raised her hand and bent to brush a kiss across it, but his gaze remained fixed firmly on hers. "I would not want to be anywhere else with anyone else."

She forced a teasing note to her voice. "What a lovely thing to say."

"Oh, I say lovely things all the time. You shall have to get used to that."

She resisted the urge to pull her hand free. "You do realize everyone in the theater is staring at us?"

He straightened but kept her hand firmly clasped in his. "I daresay every man here would cheerfully slit my throat for the opportunity to take my place."

She laughed. "And what of the women?"

"I suspect the women would cheerfully slit your throat."

She raised a brow. "To be with you?"

"Modesty forbids my agreeing with you but . . ." He grinned in a knowing manner that would indeed have any woman made of flesh and blood swooning with anticipation. "If I were to kiss you right here and now I would wager every woman in the theater would happily kill to be in your shoes."

"If you were to kiss me right here and now there would be a scandal of immense proportions."

"Indeed there would." He flashed that wicked grin again and her knees weakened. "But well worth it nonetheless."

She shook her head. "There will be enough for the gossips tomorrow simply because we have been seen together."

"I didn't think gossip bothered you. I thought you liked the reputation you have."

"I do and it doesn't," she said quickly, then sighed. "It does a little, I suppose. I have lived my life to suit myself, and there is a price for that. Society is not generally forgiving of those who do not adhere to its rules."

"Yet you have lived that life in a discreet manner and have had few ill effects from breaking those rules."

"No, I've been fortunate." She had indeed been lucky. She had not been ostracized from society for a number of reasons. Discretion of course was at the top of the list. She was a widow, which allowed her certain freedoms. She'd never been knowingly involved with a man who was either married or betrothed. And she had a great deal of money. Any number of things in this world were forgivable if one had a great deal of money.

"And clever."

She smiled. "Definitely clever."

"I have always found the only thing I like as much as a beautiful woman is one who is as clever as she is lovely."

"I don't believe you for a moment." She laughed. "You're the kind of man who doesn't want his opinions or anything else challenged by a mere female."

He winced. "That's rather unkind of you." He grinned. "True but unkind." He paused for a moment. "I will admit I never saw the appeal of an intelligent, independent woman until I met you."

"You are entirely too charming, my lord." She

drew a deep breath. "It is a rather unsettling surprise, this continuing discovery that you are not at all as I thought you were."

He gasped. "You did not think I was charming?"

"A blind woman long dead could see your charm," she said wryly.

"You thought me arrogant though." He heaved a forlorn sigh. "I was quite distressed by the charge."

"You were not," she scoffed. "You admitted it."

"I did, didn't I. You can attest then to my honesty." He leaned a shade closer. "What else do you think I am?"

She drew her brows together. "Flaws, you mean?"

"Good God, no. I am all too aware of my flaws. Tell me how I am different than you expected." His gaze searched hers as if he were looking for something quite, quite naughty. Or something special.

Without warning, the moment changed. The very air between them seemed alive with promise, with anticipation and desire. She could feel the beat of her heart in her chest.

"I thought you were cold."

"I am exceptionally warm." His voice was low and seductive.

She swallowed hard. "I thought you were aloof. Reserved."

He leaned even closer. "I am as friendly as a new pup."

"You are not." She laughed. "But you are most

amusing. I did not expect that. I did not expect you to make me laugh."

"I very much like making you laugh." In spite of his words, the look in his eyes had little to do with laughter. He leaned closer. There was scarcely more than a few inches between his lips and hers. "And making you sigh with delight." She could, indeed, she should move back and put a respectable distance between them. But his gaze held her mesmerized and she had no desire to move in any direction but his. "And gasp with pleasure. And I especially like making you make that funny little noise you make when—"

A sharp rap sounded at the door of the box. Heat washed up her face and she jerked away from him. He smiled in an overly satisfied manner, as if he knew exactly the effect his words had on her, and straightened. The door swung open. A matronly woman of indeterminate age and indomitable attitude swept into the box like an avenging angel.

"Gideon, my dear boy, I had no idea you would be at the theater tonight."

Gideon rose to his feet in an easy manner. "Of course you did, Aunt Louisa. I mentioned it to you only this afternoon."

"It must have slipped my mind. My memory isn't what it used to be." The lady heaved a dramatic sigh. "I'm getting quite old, you know."

Gideon shook his head. "You've scarcely passed your fiftieth year, your memory is excellent, and nothing slips your mind."

"Nonsense. My mind and my body are failing even as we speak." She angled her cheek toward him. "Now do greet me properly as if you are pleased to see me and I am not simply an unwelcome intrusion."

"Even if you are?" He dutifully brushed a kiss across her cheek.

"Especially if I am."

"You know Lady Chester, I believe?" Gideon said.

"No, Gideon. I have seen her on occasion but I don't think we have actually met." The older lady favored Judith with a cordial smile. In spite of her agreeable manner, Judith had the distinct feeling Gideon's aunt's appearance was not merely a social pleasantry.

"Aunt Louisa, may I present Lady Chester. Lady Chester, this is my aunt, Lady Radbury."

"It is a pleasure to meet you," Judith said, her manner as cordial as the older woman's smile and every bit as feigned. "Lord Warton speaks of you fondly."

Lady Radbury snorted. "I can't imagine Gideon speaks of me at all, let alone fondly."

"When I do speak of you, Aunt Louisa," Gideon said with a coolness that belied the amusement in his eyes, "it is with great fondness."

"Only because I have a great deal of money."

"I have a great deal of money." Gideon's voice was firm, and Judith had the distinct impression this discussion was not new. "I do not need yours."

"More's the pity." Lady Radbury shook her head. "It's a dreadful thing when a woman in my position can't threaten her relatives with impoverishment to get what she wants." She cast Gideon an annoyed glare. "You could at least let me have that simple joy, Gideon."

"No doubt I should squander my fortune in an attempt to make you happy," Gideon said dryly.

"That would be lovely and much appreciated." She settled into Gideon's vacated seat, her gaze fixed firmly on Judith. "Now then, be a good nephew and fetch us some refreshment. I should like a private word with Lady Chester."

Gideon glanced from his aunt to Judith and back. "No."

"No?" Lady Radbury raised a brow. "What do you mean, no?"

"I mean absolutely not," Gideon said smoothly. "I don't think that's particularly wise."

"Don't be ridiculous, my boy. I do not intend to eat her alive and I daresay Lady Chester can take care of herself."

"Indeed I can although I doubt I shall need to." Judith's gaze met Gideon's. "I think a chat with your aunt will be most delightful. Besides, I find I too am somewhat parched."

Gideon shook his head in a warning manner. "This is not a good idea."

Lady Radbury huffed. "I don't know what you think I'm going to do." She nodded at Judith. "I am generally quite well mannered. Indeed, I can be extremely charming when I wish to be."

"See that you are." There was a distinct threat in Gideon's voice. He looked at Judith. "Are you certain?" A hint of concern showed in his eyes. The loveliest feeling of warmth washed through her.

"I am." Judith cast him a brilliant smile.

"Very well then." He glanced at his aunt. "Behave yourself." He nodded at Judith. "I shall not be long."

"Do close the door behind you." Lady Radbury waved him away.

Gideon cast a last glance at Judith and then took his leave.

"Are you enjoying the play thus far?" Lady Radbury asked.

"Indeed I am. It's quite well done," Judith said with a smile. Idle chatter was not what she expected from Lady Radbury. This was no doubt a preliminary. "I always enjoy Shakespeare. *As You Like It* is one of my favorites."

"Really?" Lady Radbury's brow furrowed. "I find it a bit silly. All that 'who ever loved that loved not at first sight' nonsense."

"You think it nonsense?"

"Most certainly." She pinned Judith with a firm stare. "Don't you?"

"Not at all. I find it . . ." Judith thought for a moment. "Hopeful, I think. Promising. Very much an ideal."

"Perhaps." Lady Radbury nodded in a thoughtful manner. "You're looking lovely this evening, my dear, but then you always do."

"How very kind of you to say so," Judith said, wondering when the older woman would dispense with pleasantries and get to the true purpose of this chat. Unless she planned on discussing the weather next.

"Although we have never met, I am well aware of you."

Apparently the weather would be dispensed with. Judith braced herself. "Is that good or bad?"

"Both." Lady Radbury studied her for a moment. "Before I continue, I should tell you that while I have been a widow for these past twenty years, I have not spent the last two decades entirely without male companionship."

"Really," Judith said faintly. This was not at all what she had expected.

"We have a great deal in common, you and I. We both have the means, financially, to live our lives exactly as we see fit. And to do so without the undue interference of men. We are extraordinarily lucky."

Judith nodded slowly but remained silent. Better to hear exactly what Gideon's aunt had to say.

"So you see, my dear, I understand you far better than you think. However." She caught Judith's gaze and leaned forward slightly. "I think you are entirely wrong for my nephew."

"Do you?" Judith said slowly.

"Yes I do." Lady Radbury settled back in her chair. "First of all, you are far too intelligent for him as well as too independent. He needs a woman who will, without question, live her life for him and him alone. And be eternally grateful in the process."

"Lady Radbury, I—"

"Beyond that, you're really too old for him."

"Too old?"

"Yes." Lady Radbury's assessing gaze swept

over Judith. "You can't be more than a year or two younger than he is."

"I'm thirty," Judith said faintly. "Barely."

"Exactly. Lord knows, I have tried to introduce him to proper young women through the years but thus far he has not been especially interested. In truth I have not seen him taken with a woman, any woman, until you."

"We have scarcely—"

"He brought up your name more than a month ago." Lady Radbury met Judith's gaze directly. "Oh, he was very casual about it, as if it was of no significance whatsoever, but he is not as clever as he thinks and I am far more clever than he suspects. Tonight is the first time I can recall his being seen in public with a woman in a very long time." She paused as if debating the wisdom of her next words. "What do you know of Gideon's past?"

"Very little."

"Do you know about his marriage?"

"I know he was married briefly."

"It was a dreadful time for him and she was a horrid, beastly creature." Lady Radbury pressed her lips together. "Gideon, of course, was something of an idiot, but then men who fancy themselves in love generally are."

"I can't imagine ever describing Lord Warton as an idiot," Judith murmured.

"He was not the same man then that he is now. Dear girl, this all happened, oh, nine years or so ago." The older woman drew her brows together. "It was all kept very quiet but inevitably there were rumors floating about. You didn't hear about it at the time?"

"Not that I recall." Nine years ago, Judith was still mourning her own loss and wasn't the least bit concerned with gossip or anything else outside the confines of her own sorrow.

"That's something, I suppose," Lady Radbury muttered. "At any rate, Gideon fancied himself in love with a young woman and believed she loved him back. He further thought he was saving her from an unwanted marriage. She was already betrothed at the time." Gideon's aunt heaved a heartfelt sigh. "They eloped, and were discovered immediately by her father and her fiancé. The marriage was annulled. Gideon was devastated."

"I don't understand." Judith drew her brows together. "If they were in love—"

"And therein lay the problem. He was in love with her but she was simply using him for her own purposes. To make her fiancé jealous." Lady Radbury's eyes narrowed in a menacing manner. "She was a vile, vile creature."

Judith stared. "She married him to make someone else jealous?"

"I don't think she intended it to go that far. I don't know this for a certainty but I suspect she planned for them to be caught before the wedding actually took place. When poor Gideon realized how ill used he'd been . . ." Lady Radbury shuddered. "His heart was broken. It took him well over a year to recover."

"I did hear that," Judith said quietly. Gideon must have been in great pain to have reacted in the manner in which he did. Her heart twisted for him.

"I came to live with him shortly afterward. My husband's heirs decided it was past time to fully assert their claims to all my husband's property even though they had no need for it." Lady Radbury huffed in disdain. "I was left without a home and Gideon offered me one. I certainly could have purchased a house of my own but Gideon has a lovely large house here in town and a charming estate in the country. Besides, we are all that's left of our family and he's much more sentimental than he lets on. Oh, we have some distant, assorted cousins. Annoying people really." Her gaze locked with Judith's. "I am exceptionally fond of my nephew. He is my only brother's only child. Indeed, I think of him as the son I never had. Do you understand?"

Judith chose her words with care. "I understand you wish him to be happy."

"Don't be absurd." Lady Radbury rolled her gaze heavenward. "Happiness is incidental."

"I should think nothing in life is as important as one's happiness."

"Nonsense. Living up to one's responsibilities in life is more important. I want Gideon well wed to an appropriate wife who will give him the heirs he needs."

"I fear I don't see what this has to do with me."

"Then you are not as smart as I thought you were," Lady Radbury snapped. "My apologies." Her tone softened. "This is not at all personal, Lady Chester—may I call you Judith?"

"I'd prefer—"

"Excellent. Judith it is then." Lady Radbury leaned closer and laid her hand on Judith's. "Judith, you should understand that I know far more about you than you can imagine."

"Do you?" Judith arched a brow and pulled her hand away. "Is that both good and bad as well?"

"Yes." Lady Radbury smiled in reluctant admiration. "I know, for example, that your reputation, while not extreme, might yet be somewhat exaggerated. I know as well you have never lifted a finger to correct that impression. Of course, I have always thought a particular type of reputation served to scare off certain men."

"A particular type of reputation?" Judith said curiously. "What exactly is a particular type of reputation?"

"Oh, I don't know . . ." Lady Radbury met Judith's gaze firmly. "One that makes it apparent a woman is not a usual sort. Most men want a woman who is nothing out of the ordinary. Oh, certainly they will seek out great beauty but when it comes to any characteristic they claim for their own— talent, intelligence, competence—they do not want a female who is in any way extraordinary. You manage your own affairs, Judith, and I mean that in every sense of the word. You are in charge of your world. That terrifies most men."

"It doesn't seem to have terrified Lord Warton." Still, hadn't he called her terrifying on the terrace at Susanna's?

"No." Gideon's aunt sighed. "I fear he is intrigued

by it. He has never met a woman quite like you. I daresay you have a lot in common with that creature he married too."

"I can't imagine—"

"Oh, you might not be as devious but she knew precisely what she was about. What she wanted, that sort of thing."

"I would never hurt him."

"No, I don't think you would. Not deliberately. I think you're a decent enough person, at least I have never heard otherwise." She studied Judith for a moment. "Gideon needs to marry. You are not the type of woman he should marry. There's really little more to say."

"You're right, there isn't." Judith's voice was firm. "I have not set my cap for Lord Warton. I have no intention of marrying anyone. Ever."

"Your intentions are not enough," Lady Radbury said mildly.

"Of course they are."

Lady Radbury shook her head. "If Gideon is obsessed with you, he will ignore his responsibilities."

"We have barely begun to see one another." Judith laughed. "I would hardly term it an obsession." Certainly she could not get him out of her head but she would not call it an obsession. As for Gideon, one wouldn't think a man with an obsession would allow a full two days to pass without seeing the object of said obsession. "The very thought is absurd."

"Perhaps." Lady Radbury shrugged. "But I know my nephew and I know him far better than he thinks I do. I have never doubted that he would do what was expected of him when the time came. The one thing I did not expect was you."

"Me?"

"You." Lady Radbury shook her head. "For as much as I know about you, I do not know you at all. You are the unknown ingredient. However, if you follow your usual habits, then admittedly I have nothing to be concerned about at all."

"My usual habits?" Judith could scarcely choke out the words.

"Your affairs never last more than a few weeks, perhaps a month or so. Then you and the gentleman in question part company in a manner far more cordial than I ever have. To this day, you and those gentlemen, a fairly small number I might add, share a friendship." Lady Radbury smiled pleasantly.

Judith stared in disbelief. "How on earth—"

"Come now, Judith. London is the greatest city on earth and the smallest village in the world. There are no secrets here. Not really. You cannot imagine your actions have not been observed and considered. Even, on occasion"—she bit back a grin—"wagered upon."

"I would be dreadfully disappointed if my actions were not the subject of wagers. I have managed to win tidy sums myself in the past. Completely unfair, of course, since I have always known what I would or would not do." Judith brushed aside a growing sense of annoyance and favored Gideon's aunt with a bright smile. "Are they wagering now?"

"Not yet but I'm certain they will be." Lady Radbury's smile was as brilliant as Judith's. "Unless, of course, you desist seeing my nephew."

"Then I would suggest we each decide exactly how much we can afford to wager." Judith leaned forward and lowered her voice. "Louisa, may I call you Louisa? Excellent. Louisa, first of all, Lord Warton is not obsessed with me. As the alleged object of his obsession I am confident I would be the first to notice such a thing. Secondly, regardless of gossip or wagers or even your own concerns in the best interests of your nephew, what transpires between Lord Warton and myself is both personal and private. And Louisa." Judith straightened and beamed at the older woman. "That is all I intend to say on the matter."

"And well said too. I am impressed. Which does not change my opinion. This, whatever it is between you, can only lead to disaster for him. I shall not stand idly by and see him destroyed by a woman again. He would be better served—no—I think you would both be better served if you sever your relationship before it proceeds any further." A sympathetic light shone in Louisa's eye. "It is something of a pity that you and he didn't meet years ago. I rather think—"

The door snapped open and Gideon stepped into the box carrying two glasses.

"Refreshments," he announced. "Or what passes for them. Lemonade, I think." His gaze slid from Judith to Louisa and back. "How are the two of you faring?"

"Quite well, Gideon." Louisa rose to her feet. "I

don't know why you were concerned. We have
had a lovely chat."

"And what have you chatted about?" he said
cautiously.

"Nothing of significance," Louisa said blithely.

"Nothing at all important." Judith smiled at
him. "You for the most part."

He met her gaze and for a moment the look in
his eye swept all thought of his aunt from her
mind. "And I am not important?"

"You are . . ." *Very important to me.* Judith forced
a teasing note to her voice. "You are arrogant and
very important to yourself."

"But charming nonetheless." He grinned.

"Charming nonetheless." She smiled up at him.

"Dear Lord," Louisa said under her breath, then
sighed. "I must be off. I have left my friends unat-
tended and they will no doubt find all sorts of
ways to get into trouble if I do not return to them
soon."

Gideon offered her a glass. "Your lemonade."

Louisa shuddered. "My dear boy, I despise lemonade." She turned to go, then looked back. "I
should like to have a long chat with you at home
later, nephew."

"What a startling coincidence, Aunt." Gideon's
gaze met Louisa's firmly. "I should like to have a
long chat with you as well."

"I shall look forward to it." Louisa glanced at
Judith. "Do enjoy the rest of the performance, Ju-
dith. In spite of the absurdity of it, I know I shall.
Good evening."

"Good evening, Louisa," Judith said without so

much as a hint of relief at the older woman's departure.

With that Louisa took her leave, closing the door in her wake. Gideon handed Judith a glass and took his seat.

"You called her Louisa?" His tone was mild.

"We shall be very good friends," she said in an offhand manner.

"I doubt that. Furthermore, I suspect your discussion was not insignificant."

Judith sipped at the overly sweet drink.

Gideon raised a brow. "You're not going to tell me what the two of you talked about, are you?"

"Pleasantries. The performance. The sorts of things one talks about during the intermission of a play."

He stared at her. "I don't believe you."

"You've found me out." She heaved an overly dramatic sigh. "We were discussing the state of the world. Whether there will be war with Russia. Whether skirts will be fuller next year."

He snorted. "Hardly possible."

"It was nothing of significance." She turned her gaze toward the stage. "Now, the play is beginning."

It was indeed the truth. Louisa's concerns weren't at all valid and therefore had no significance. Judith had no intention of marrying Gideon. Certainly her relationship with him thus far had not followed her usual *habit*, but then Gideon made her feel as no man had since her husband. *Or as no man ever had?* She brushed the thought away. That was as absurd as Louisa's charges.

Still, even at the beginning of her other adventures she had always contemplated the end of them. The thought of ending this with Gideon, of never seeing him again, caught at something inside her. *Her heart?* That too was nonsense. It was nothing more than the intensity of their passion coupled with the romance of the play.

He leaned closer and spoke softly into her ear. "I do not believe you for a moment."

"Hush."

"I shall find out exactly what passed between you and my aunt." He paused. "Later."

Anticipation shivered through her. *Later.*

"And I shall use whatever means at my disposal to get that information." He straightened and turned toward the stage but she could hear the smile in his voice. "Later."

It was impossible to sit next to the man and not want to throw herself into his arms.

She sighed softly in surrender. "I shall look forward to it."

Chapter 6

What was it about this woman?

Gideon lay on his side with his head propped in his hand and studied Judith's profile in the faint light that drifted in through the tall windows of her violently feminine bedroom. He scarcely knew her at all, yet he felt as if he had known her forever. As if being with her was somehow inevitable. Silly romantic nonsense of course. Probably put into his head by the play they'd seen.

He wondered if she was asleep and resisted the urge to find out. A faint stuttering snore sounded from the far side of the room. Obviously someone was asleep. For a small dog, Arthur was exceedingly noisy. And stubborn as well. Gideon had made certain to slip the beast a biscuit upon their return from the theater. The blasted creature had taken the biscuit and had come dangerously close to taking Gideon's fingers with it.

"You're staring at me, aren't you?"

Gideon chuckled. "I thought you were asleep."

"No," she said softly, "I was just thinking."

"Oh?" He found her hand and brought it to his lips, kissing her fingers one by one. "About me I hope."

"Is it inconceivable to you that I would be thinking of something else?" A smile sounded in her voice.

"Something else? When I am lying here beside you? Naked?" He scoffed, "It is indeed inconceivable."

She laughed, rolled onto her side, and mirrored his position. "Do you wish to know what I've been thinking about?"

"Thought, at a time like this, seems"—he reached out and traced a finger along the edge of the sheet that barely covered her breasts—"unnecessary."

"Very well then."

Indeed, *thought* was the last thing on his mind. He ran his hand lightly over the sheet concealing her breast and felt her nipple beneath the linen tighten at his touch.

"Your aunt thinks I am entirely wrong for you," she said in an offhand manner.

"Oh, you are. Utterly, unquestionably wrong." He trailed his fingers along the underside of her breast. There was something remarkably exciting about the feel of a woman's warmth covered only by fresh linens.

"She believes I will ruin your life." Judith paused. "She didn't use those precise words but her meaning was clear nonetheless."

"And what a lovely ruination it will be." He leaned forward and kissed her shoulder. "I can scarcely wait."

"She thinks you are obsessed with me."

How could one woman taste so delicious? He murmured against the sweetness of her flesh, "I am. Completely obsessed."

"She fears that I will break your heart."

He stilled, his lips lingering on her shoulders. *Talk* was close behind *thought* on the list of what he had no desire to do at the moment. Still, Judith had evaded any discussion of what had transpired with Aunt Louisa, had indeed distracted him in an altogether thorough and exciting manner, until now. Reluctantly, he returned to his previous position. "My heart is substantially harder than it once was."

"Your aunt thinks otherwise."

He blew a resigned breath. "My aunt is an annoying woman who thrives on interference and refuses to accept that I am no longer ten years of age and am well capable of handling my own affairs. Particularly those of a personal nature." He considered his next question for a moment, then shrugged to himself. "What else did she say?"

She laughed. "Now you're interested?"

"You have piqued my curiosity. Obviously your conversation with my aunt has stayed in your mind, so yes, I am interested."

"I know so little about you," she murmured.

"There is not a great deal to know." Apparently, if he were to hear more of Judith's conversation with Aunt Louisa there was a price to be paid. "My aunt is the only sister of my father. My father died shortly after my twenty-first birthday. My mother died when I was very young, I scarcely remember her. Aside from Aunt Louisa, I have a handful of distant cousins, several of whom keep a close eye on my health and my marital state in hopes that I will die without an heir. Preferably before they are too old to enjoy my title and my fortune." He chuckled. "I should love to see the jostling for position that will ensue when I have breathed my last."

She laughed.

"You may laugh all you wish but I suspect it will be quite a ferocious fight."

"They should know that you have no intention of dying without an heir," she said lightly.

"No, I do not." He drew a deep breath. "She told you about my ill-fated marriage, didn't she? Although something that lasts less than a day can scarce be called a marriage."

"She mentioned it."

"I should like to have heard her version of the story. We have never talked about it." He considered his words carefully. "I have never spoken of it to anyone."

"You needn't do so now," she said quietly. "If you wish to—"

"No, it's past time to speak of it." Even as he said the words he realized they were true. He rolled onto his back, folded his arms under his head, and stared upward into the dark. "I was young and foolish enough to believe in love and silly stories about damsels in distress."

"And the gallant knights who provide their rescue?"

He chuckled. "Precisely. I was the gallant knight rescuing the fair damsel from a fate worse than death—an unwanted marriage. Except that I wasn't gallant so much as I was stupid, misled by a pretty face and a flirtatious manner. I thought she was the most wonderful creature I had ever met. An angel come to earth."

"I daresay I have never met an actual angel."

"As it turned out, neither had I," he said wryly. "Although she certainly looked like an angel. Her eyes were an amazing shade of violet and matched her name."

"That is angelic," she murmured.

"One would think so." He glanced at her shadowed figure. "Did you know her? Violet Smithfield? The daughter of the Earl of Traverston?"

"Not that I recall."

"Pity. I would be curious as to what your impression was of her. At any rate, my fair damsel, this angel, wanted the man she was to marry to express his feelings in a more . . ." He thought for a moment. "Passionate manner, I suppose. Her fiancé was known for his reserved nature. For whatever reason, convenience more than anything, I suspect, she turned her attentions toward me with an eye toward making the poor man jealous."

"Probably because she knew the moment she

met you that you were dashing and gallant and courageous enough to come to her rescue," Judith said firmly. "Women recognize such things, you know."

"They also recognize a fool when they meet one, and that's precisely what I was when it came to her." He shook his head. "I can only attribute it to the stupidity and passion of youth. Suffice it to say one thing led to another. Well before dawn one day we slipped out of the city and were married, a scant quarter of an hour before her outraged father and equally outraged fiancé made their appearance." He snorted with amusement. "I can tell you the man was no longer the least bit reserved about his feelings."

"You can laugh about it now?"

"I suppose I can." Surprise coursed through him. He hadn't imagined he would ever see humor in the incident. "It had all the makings of a theatrical farce: outraged father, indignant fiancé, lovely but devious ingénue, and hapless, hopeless swain."

"It would be most amusing onstage or in hindsight but not at all funny at the time."

"True enough. When one risks everything for the woman he loves and then learns not only did the woman in question not return his feelings but was, in truth, using him to incite another man's emotions, well, it can be most upsetting."

"Upsetting?"

"Upsetting," he said firmly. He was not about to use words like *devastated* or *crushed* or *heartbroken*.

He had been all that and more but now it seemed both long ago and surprisingly insignificant. Without conscious thought through the years he had indeed put his marriage behind him and gone on with his life. It was a startling, and satisfying, revelation. "The marriage was annulled without delay, she married the man she had intended to marry all along, and I lived in a hell of my own making for a time."

"I see." She fell silent for a long moment. "That's more or less what your aunt said."

"Probably more accurate and less sensational."

"Not really."

"Now, turnabout is fair play, you know."

"What?"

"It's your turn to tell me about your past, your marriage."

"There's very little to tell. I was rather sheltered as a child and probably spoiled as well. I was barely seventeen and had just begun my first season when I met Lucian, Lord Chester. He was but a few years older than I. Dashing, handsome, and terribly romantic, he quite swept me off my feet. We married within two weeks of meeting. My parents died the following year, my husband two years later. He had a sister but I have no other family." She shrugged. "There's little more to say than that."

Her recitation struck him as matter-of-fact and unemotional. How very odd. Judith was not an unemotional woman. "Come now, Judith, surely there's more to say than that."

"Not really." She sat up and slid out of bed.

"Where are you going?"

"Nowhere." He watched her shadowy figure find the frilly concoction she called a dressing gown and wrap it around herself. "But you are." She lit a lamp and cast him a pleasant smile, as if they had just returned from a stroll in the park instead of a night of exquisite passion. "It's very late or rather very early, and you should probably be on your way."

He sat up and stared at her. "You're making me go because you don't want to talk about your past?"

"Don't be absurd." She waved away his comment. "I'm making you leave because it's nearly dawn. It would be best for all concerned if no one noted your comings and goings."

"I daresay your servants are used to gentlemen coming and going at all hours." The words were out of his mouth before he could catch himself.

"Indeed they are," she said coolly. "I was thinking of your servants as well as your aunt. I wouldn't be at all surprised if she hasn't been watching for your return."

"Judith." He scrambled out of bed, grabbing his trousers, and yanking them on. "I didn't mean—"

"I know exactly what you meant, my lord." She shrugged. "It's not the least bit important at the moment."

"I am sorry. I wasn't think—"

"If the situation were reversed . . ." She crossed her arms over her chest. "If I were the one making reference to your . . . *adventures*, as it were, you wouldn't be offended. Why should I?"

"Well, you shouldn't, of course. There's no reason why you should." He pulled his shirt on over his head. "Although you are a woman."

"I thought you had noticed. But what might have escaped your notice is that I have nearly as much property as you do and my fortune might even be a tiny bit larger. In addition, neither of us has extensive family, we are close in age, and I would immodestly suggest that both of us are considered excellent specimens, in term of appearance, of our respective genders. What I am saying is that our lives and circumstances are remarkably similar and we should be considered in a similar manner. Why then is it perfectly acceptable for you, a man, to share a woman's bed without benefit of marriage but it is considered scandalous when I, a woman, does the same?"

He stared in disbelief. "Because"—he emphasized each word slowly—"you are a woman."

"And you are an idiot," she snapped. "And it scarcely hinders you at all."

"An idiot?" He sputtered with indignation. "An idiot?"

"Yes. I-d-i-o-t. Do you need the word defined as well as spelled?"

"Bloody hell, Judith." He tried to pull on his socks and hop toward her at the same time. "You're being irrational."

"Well, what can one expect? I'm a woman, aren't I? And therefore prone to being irrational."

"I didn't say that." And was grateful he had ignored the impulse to say exactly that. He was in enough trouble with her already for speaking without thinking. "I am sorry. I am truly, truly sorry. I was a cad to make such a comment."

"I told you, it doesn't matter. Now." She nodded at the door. "Get out."

A low growl sounded from the other side of the room. He ignored it. "If it doesn't matter and it's not important and you aren't angry with me—"

"Not in the least," she said loftily. "At least not for your comment."

"But it does serve as a convenient excuse to make me leave."

She snorted. "Apparently not with any sense of urgency."

He stared at her, the answer at once apparent to him. He should have seen it before. "Do you ever speak about your marriage?"

She glared at him. "Do you?"

"I did to you."

"I have told you everything there is to tell." She rolled her eyes toward the ceiling in exasperation. "I was young. He was a poet, very romantic, intense, and quite irresistible. And when he died . . . How did you put it?" She narrowed her eyes. "Oh yes. I lived in a hell of my own making for a long time. Is that enough?"

"No!"

"Well it shall have to do."

"Damnation, Judith!" He sat down hard on a chair that appeared far too delicate to handle anyone sitting hard, and continued putting on his socks and shoes. "This is not at all like you."

"How do you know what is and isn't like me? For all you know I could be irrational most of the time. We have spent two evenings together, scarcely long enough for you to become an expert on my nature. You don't know me at all!"

"This conversation is over." He got to his feet, grabbed his coat, and tugged it on. "But only for the moment."

"Then you shall be conversing with yourself as I have no intention of continuing it!"

"We shall see." He started toward the door. "Tonight, you and I made our association known to the rest of the world. There shall be a certain amount of gossip. No doubt a wager or two as to how long we will be together. I warn you right now, I intend for that to be a very long time."

"We shall see," she mimicked.

He again headed toward the door, then pulled up short. Damn it all, he was not going to leave this way. He turned, strode to her, and yanked her into his arms. At once Arthur launched himself across the room, yapping and nipping at his heels. Gideon ignored him and stared into Judith's eyes, raising his voice to be heard above the din of the dog. "You claim to be a book all of London has read. But I think you allow the world to see only what you wish it to see. I have never known a woman like you and I want to know everything about you. How you think, what you feel, and yes, I want to know about your past." He kissed her hard. "And I intend to find out."

She glared up at him but did not pull away. "You are even more arrogant than I thought!"

"Yes, I am." He kissed her again. "I shall call on you tomorrow."

She huffed. "I shall look forward to it."

He kissed her once more, softer, slower, and he felt her body relax against him. At last he released her. "Tomorrow then." He nudged the still yapping dog away, stepped to the door, pulled it open, and glanced back at her. "But you're wrong, Judith. I may not know the assorted details of your life, but I have known you from the moment I first looked into your eyes."

She stared at him with anger and annoyance and what he thought, what he hoped, might well be the tiniest hint of longing.

He nodded and started through the door. At that moment he heard a growl and realized he had made a serious mistake in turning his back on the fur ball of a dog. Gideon felt a sharp tug at the back of his trousers just below the right buttocks and heard a ripping sound. He glanced behind him to see Arthur sitting proudly with a piece of Gideon's trousers in his mouth. He could have sworn the nasty beast was grinning. He raised a brow and glanced at Judith. "Even he will not dissuade me. Good morning." He shut the door behind him.

Gideon was in his carriage and well on his way home before he realized he had indeed meant everything he'd said to her. And realized as well the hole in his trousers was larger than he'd thought.

"Bad dog," Judith murmured, still staring at the closed door.

Arthur trotted over to her, laid the swatch of fabric from Gideon's trousers at her feet, and gazed up adoringly. She bent down and scratched him behind the ears. "You shouldn't have done that, Arthur. It was quite naughty of you."

Arthur thumped his tail on the floor in an unrepentant manner.

"Yes, of course, I wanted to do exactly the same thing." She smiled wryly. "Well, perhaps not exactly the same thing, although I daresay biting him in his rear end would have been . . ." Without warning a wave of desire passed over her. "Never mind." She nodded at his basket. "Back to bed now." Arthur obediently ran to her bed, jumped on it, and settled himself firmly at the foot. She frowned at him. "Is every male in my life these days determined to ignore my wishes?"

Arthur cocked his head and wagged his tail.

"It's most annoying, you know." Judith crossed her arms over her chest and paced the room. "I don't want to talk about Lucian. Not to Gideon, not to anyone." Not even Susanna knew the details of her brief, tempestuous marriage.

Susanna had asked on occasion but had never pressed for answers. Admirable of her, really, since Judith knew virtually everything there was to know about Susanna's marriage with Charles. Charles had been the love of Susanna's life, and she reveled in her memories. Judith found her own memories had not withstood the test of time particularly well.

Oh, she had no doubt that she had loved Lucian with all the fervor of a seventeen-year-old girl who believed she had found her soul mate. And she had no doubt he had loved her as well, in his fashion. She had spent so many years not thinking about their time together, it was difficult now to think of it at all. But it had been ten years and was past time to do so.

The beginning had been glorious. Even now she did not doubt that. Lucian was full of life and passion and more exciting than she had ever dreamed. They had thrown wild, extravagant parties for his equally wild, extravagant friends. They were all of an artistic nature—poets and writers and artists. Many with more money than talent. Her world had been confined to her husband and his friends, and she had never for a moment questioned that they did not move in the more refined circles of her parents or the other girls she'd known. Indeed, what few friendships she'd had before she married faded with each passing day, and his world had become hers. When her parents had died, she'd had no one at all save him.

He had shown his temper on occasion in the beginning but it had been nothing of significance. He was a poet, after all, a genius, and one overlooked the imperfections of men of his creative temperament. It was in the last few months of his life that the incidents of anger had grown more frequent, more violent.

Without thinking, she glanced at her hand and the little finger bent so slightly, even she scarcely noticed it. The smallest thing would send Lucian into a rage. The stupidity of critics or mistakes made by servants or the presence of his sister. Or the wrong word from her. He would accuse her of being unfaithful, of infidelity with his friends. It was the furthest thing from the truth, of course. He was her life. Afterward he would be filled with remorse and apologize profusely and take her in his arms, and all would be well again. For a while. But the periods of harmony grew shorter. Even so, he had never hurt her, she had never imagined he would, and she had never feared him. A day before his death, something so insignificant she never could recall it had triggered his fury. He had called her a whore. Had again charged that she had been with other men. She denied it but he'd refused to listen. He'd thrown in her face what she had begun to suspect: hers was not the only bed he frequented. Her own anger erupted.

And therein lay her mistake. She had never spoken back to him before, never raised her voice. And her anger only served to increase his. He had forced her to her knees, gripping her hands so tightly, he had broken her little finger. She had fought against him, and he had struck her hard across the face. He had taken her then, brutally and with a violence that had torn her heart to shreds much as he tore her body. Had taken her in a manner that had nothing to do with love or passion and was in fact a cruel and awful punishment.

Later, he had wept with remorse outside the locked door to her rooms. He had promised never to hurt her again, had begged her forgiveness. She refused to open the door and swore she would never forgive him. She told him she was leaving. Perhaps she would have relented when the soreness had left her body and her finger had healed and the bruise had faded from her face. But the next morning his body had been found at the bottom of the terrace. He and his friends had been fond of drinking on the flat rooftop of the house. From the empty bottles on the roof and the position of the body, it was agreed Lucian had been in a drunken state and had fallen to his death. Regardless of the official cause of death, Judith had known better.

"It was my fault," she said quietly. Arthur rested his head on his paws and watched her pace. "I should have forgiven him at once." But she hadn't, and no amount of regret could change that.

And if she could change it, would she? Of course, she had loved Lucian. She would never have wanted him dead. A huge part of her had died when he'd died. Still, he had been growing more and more violent and less and less rational. Even now, she refused to consider exactly what his behavior had signified. Refused to so much as think the words *mad* or *insane*. Still, she couldn't help but wonder: if he hadn't died, would she have lived the rest of her life in fear? Indeed, would she be alive today?

"Is it any wonder that I prefer not to discuss my marriage?" she said to the dog. Arthur raised his head. "It was wonderful in the beginning; he was wonderful. The end of it should not negate that."

But she knew it would if she spoke of it aloud. If she dwelled on it in her own mind. The tragedy would become so much more important than the joy.

She had mourned for two full years, then had

firmly and deliberately put it all behind her and had gone on with her life. Not until now, not until Gideon, had she spent more than an occasional few moments considering her marriage.

What was it about that man?

She huffed and continued to pace. This wasn't supposed to be at all serious. Why, at this point with Jonathon or Harold or Samuel—Lovett certainly never got to this point—she'd be casually considering the end rather than still feeling they had just begun.

That was another thing. Or rather three things; Jonathon, Harold, and Samuel—Lovett still didn't count—but especially Jonathon. She was not the least bit ashamed of her past. She was a wealthy widow and she could well behave as she wished. And dear Lord, in spite of Susanna and the other friends she had made, she'd been so desperately lonely and so very alone through the years. It was a reason more than an excuse. She certainly didn't need an excuse. Still, it seemed she was somewhat more thin-skinned about her *adventures* than she had thought.

She glanced at Arthur. "As much as I denied it, I was annoyed by his comment."

Arthur yawned.

"Still and all, it doesn't seem to me that three lovers in ten years is an exorbitant amount. And without an occasional adventure, life would be unbearable." She blew a long breath. "It's exceedingly difficult to live entirely by oneself, you know."

Arthur barked once and wagged his tail.

"My apologies, I do have you." She stepped to the bed and sat down beside the dog. At once he put his head in her lap and she scratched behind his ears. "I must confess, it's difficult to consider your life and wonder if every decision you've made regarding marriage or adventures or, well, *men* has been a mistake. I don't think it has. Not all of it anyway. I have no apologies to make to anyone and no real regrets."

The dog sighed with contentment.

"So why should I be bothered if he cares about my past? Why, he probably doesn't care at all. It was an offhand comment. The sort of thing one says without due consideration." She grimaced. "The sort of thing one says because it has been on one's mind.

"Nonetheless, it scarcely matters. It's not as if either of us are in love or considering marriage. I certainly am not. This will end with him the same way it ended with Jonathon and Harold and Samuel."

Beneath her fingers, she could feel Arthur's warm body breathe evenly and knew the dog had fallen asleep. She suspected sleep would be somewhat more difficult for her. Too many thoughts and questions filled her mind for rest. None of which had answers.

"I just don't understand why I have said things to him I have never said to anyone," she said softly. "Or why when he said he wished to be with me for a long time, I didn't object. I was glad.

Unreasonably glad. And I don't understand at all"—she heaved a frustrated sigh—"why I cannot wait to see him again."

Gideon nodded to the young footman who silently opened the door to the grand house that had been the London residence of Pearsalls for generations. On the console table in the front entry a glass of brandy waited, thanks to the efficiency of his butler. Wells had been with him since shortly after Gideon's father had died. Good man, Wells. Gideon picked up the glass and drew a long swallow, savoring the taste of the liquor. There was nothing like a brandy before bed, especially if one wanted to sleep as opposed to allowing one's mind to dwell on an annoying, perplexing enigma of a woman.

"She cannot have children, you know," Aunt Louisa said from the shadows of the stairway.

"Who cannot have children?" Gideon asked, even though he knew exactly who she meant.

"Lady Chester." Aunt Louisa came down the stairs into view like the goddess of interference descending Mount Meddling.

"And how, my dear aunt, would you know that?"

Aunt Louisa paused. "Admittedly it's an assumption but not without merit," she added quickly. "She has been married and she has not been entirely celibate in her widowhood, therefore it's logical to assume she cannot have children."

"It's not the least bit logical," Gideon said coolly.

"It's a conclusion based on nothing more than speculation. Besides, it scarcely matters. I am not interested in children with Lady Chester."

"She's too old for you," Aunt Louisa said firmly.

He laughed. "She's two years younger than I am."

"It's not enough." Aunt Louisa shook her head. "You need someone much, much younger. Someone pliable, who will obey you without question—"

"I believe I have servants for that."

She ignored him. "Someone with an impeccable reputation. Someone, well"—she drew out the word slowly for emphasis—"*untouched*, as it were."

"A virgin for sacrifice on the high altar of continuance of the family name, Aunt Louisa?"

"Nonsense." She sniffed. "Marriage to you wouldn't be a sacrifice for anyone, virginal or otherwise."

"That is a matter of some debate, I suspect." The last thing he wished to do at the moment was have yet another discussion with his aunt about his need to marry. She would point out that he was not getting younger. He would counter with numerous examples of men far older than himself fathering children. She would propose he casually peruse a list of young women she had carefully selected, said list changing from year to year with Aunt Louisa's whims and the eligibility of the young ladies in her sights. He would thank her for her concern and strongly suggest she return to playing cards with her friends and working for charitable causes and leave his personal life, especially when it came to the selection of a wife, bloody well alone.

He had no desire to deal with this particular topic tonight but it appeared he had no choice. Aunt Louisa was like a terrier with a bone when she wished to be. "May I retire to my rooms and enjoy the oblivion of slumber, or are you determined to discuss this now?"

"*Determined* is such a hard word. Let us simply say I *wish* to discuss it."

"Ah yes, *wish* does make it more palatable." He tossed back the rest of his drink and started toward the library. "Very well then. But if I am going to be forced to discuss something I have no desire to speak of at the moment, I wish to at least wash down the proceedings with another brandy."

She trailed behind him. "You drink entirely too much."

"You criticize entirely too much."

A lamp was lit on the desk in the middle of the small library, a decanter and another glass were conveniently placed beside the lamp. No doubt Wells had left the lamp burning and the brandy ready when he realized Aunt Louisa's intention to ambush Gideon upon his return home. The butler was probably even now lurking about should Gideon feel the need for rescue, although Aunt Louisa would much prefer there be no witnesses. Gideon refilled his glass and glanced at his aunt. "Well? Go on."

Aunt Louisa squared her shoulders and clasped her hands in front of her. "Gideon, I think it would be best if you cease your attentions toward Lady Chester."

"Imagine my surprise. Do tell me, aside from the fact that you think she is too old, too child-less, and too *touched*, as it were, why?" He took a sip of his brandy. "Have you considered that she is also too lovely, too charming, and entirely too clever?"

"Actually I have." She stepped to the decanter, poured a glass of her own, and took a long sip. Aunt Louisa had a capacity for alcohol that ri-valed that of most men of his acquaintance. "That—all of that—is also why I think you should stop seeing her."

He raised a brow. "If you want me to seriously consider your opinion in this matter you shall have to try harder to make sense."

"I am making perfect sense," she snapped. "Lady Chester is indeed charming, quite pretty, as well as intelligent. But she is not the right woman for you."

"You're right as always. Why on earth would I want a woman who is charming, pretty, and intel-ligent?"

She narrowed her eyes. "I do hate it when you act as if you have no idea what I am talking about."

"It's the best weapon at my disposal." He blew a long breath. "My dear aunt, I appreciate your con-cern. I know you think I should be actively hunt-ing a wife, although the thought alone conjures visions of tracking wild beasts through the dark-est reaches of Africa. Frankly, I see no particular hurry—"

"Unless, of course, you die unexpectedly and your cousins get all that should rightfully go to your sons."

"I assure you I shall do everything in my power to avoid unexpected demise to preserve the inheritance of those as yet nonexistent sons."

"That does indeed ease my mind," she said sharply and drained her brandy.

"It should." He plucked her glass from her hand, refilled it, and handed it back to her. "You have my word I shall not die before I have provided for the continuation of the family name."

She snorted.

"However, until that time comes I intend to see whomever I choose, including and especially Lady Chester."

She shook her head. "She is a dreadful mistake, Gideon."

"Not at all, Aunt Louisa. I find her . . ." Exciting. Vulnerable. Fascinating. "Quite refreshing."

She cast him a sharp glance. "You're falling in love with her."

He laughed. "I most certainly am not. I am not the least bit interested in love, nor is she. If anything we have fallen"—he cast his aunt a wicked glance—"in lust."

"Do not look at me like that. As if I should faint dead away by the so much as a mere mention of the word *lust*. If you think you can shock me you are sadly mistaken. I am made of far sterner stuff than that. Besides, I am not completely unfamiliar with lust myself."

"That admission is more than I prefer to know.

However"—he eyed her thoughtfully—"as you are familiar with lust, then you of all people should be able to recognize it."

"I do. I recognize something else as well." She studied him for a long moment. "Gideon, do understand I like Lady Chester a great deal. I agree with everything you have said about her. She is bright and amusing and lovely. If the stakes were not as great, I would accept your feelings for her—"

"I have no feelings," he said quickly.

"I might even encourage you. As it is, I am certain"—her gaze met his—"this will end badly."

"Nonsense."

"I should hate to see your heart broken again," she said quietly.

"As would I. But my heart is not involved."

"You protest entirely too much, my boy." She sighed in resignation. "You have the look of a man about to fling himself off a very high cliff without concern as to the rocks waiting below."

"That's remarkably poetic, but I will tell you yet again, I am not flinging myself off a cliff. I am not falling in love, and my heart is not at risk. Lady Chester and I have not as yet spent a great deal of time together, but do understand, my dear aunt, I intend to remedy that. As I said, I appreciate your concern, misguided though it may be." He thought for a moment. "You should understand as well that I am not the same man I was nine years ago. I am older and, God willing, wiser. Regardless of what might happen, my heart will not be broken. I will not permit it."

"You are an arrogant man, Gideon Pearsall. As your father was before you and our father before him." She shook her head. "Your arrogance will be your downfall exactly as it was theirs."

Gideon laughed. "My grandfather died in his bed at a rather impressive age and my father was felled by influenza. Neither of which could be blamed on arrogance.

She sniffed in a haughty manner. "It was only a matter of time."

"I was under the impression you thought a woman would be my downfall," he said mildly

"One and the same, Gideon, one and the same."

It was pointless to argue with the woman. The only side of an argument she ever acknowledged that had any merit whatsoever was her own. Past time to end it, at least for tonight. Gideon was under no illusions that the topic was put to rest. Not with Aunt Louisa.

"This is getting tiresome, Aunt." Gideon finished the last of his brandy and set the glass on the desk. "It's long past the time we should both be in our beds."

"I daresay you have already—"

"Yes?" A warning sounded in his voice.

"—been up entirely too long." Aunt Louisa smiled innocently. It was a dangerous smile and the one thing guaranteed to make Gideon's fingers itch to wrap themselves around her neck. That too innocent smile was a weapon he had no defense against and as such was most infuriating. Aside from that, arguing with her was almost fun. "Do sleep well, Gideon."

"Aunt Louisa." He nodded, turned, and strode out of the library.

"Did you know you have a hole in your trousers?" she called after him. "You should do something about that. It's not the least bit . . ."

He started up the stairs, firmly ignoring the chastisement that trailed after him. Of course he knew he had a hole in his blasted pants. He could tell by the air that wafted down the back of his leg. It was worth it, though. A pair of trousers was a small enough price to pay for what had truly been a splendid evening. Oh, certainly there had been a few difficult moments when Judith had refused any discussion of the past. He had never known a woman who was so determined not to talk about her life, especially one who to all appearances had little to hide. Judith wasn't quite the well-read book she had claimed but she was not anonymous either. Perhaps Helmsley was right. Perhaps there had been something wrong regarding her husband and her marriage.

He absently opened the door to his rooms and stepped inside, grateful, as always when he arrived home at this hour, that he had long ago reached an understanding with his valet. Unless the man was awakened by Gideon's riotous arrival home, which typically meant His Lordship had had entirely too much to drink and therefore lacked the skills to undress himself, he was not to attend him. Gideon was grateful as well that his aunt's rooms were in the opposite wing of the house.

The wisest course, the easiest thing to do, would be to abide by Judith's wishes and leave the past in the past. Besides, he'd never been especially interested in a woman's background before. Why was he so interested now? He had no idea nor did he care. He simply wanted to know everything about her. It was probably idle curiosity. After all, didn't one always want to uncover a secret? It was no more important than that.

He doubted anyone else would agree. His aunt's tirade was tiresome, but so too was the insistence of everyone around him that his heart would surely be broken by Judith or that hers would be broken by him. Blast it all, he was certainly not interested in love. Nor was she. They'd said as much to each other right from the start. Hadn't they? Not in so many words perhaps but the meaning was clear. He shrugged off his coat and dropped it on a chair. Still, it would do no harm to find out exactly what her thoughts were on the subject of something beyond friendly affection between them.

Abruptly a thought struck him. It would be wise to determine exactly what his thoughts were as well. In spite of what he'd said to his aunt or Helmsley, at this particular moment he wasn't at all sure he knew the answer.

Chapter 7

"This has gone far enough, Gideon." Judith sat across from Gideon in his carriage on their way to who knew where. She tried to sound commanding but suspected she sounded far more delighted than demanding. Which, in fact, she was. "I insist you tell me where we're going at once."

"I am kidnapping you and spiriting you away to the south of Spain where we shall live the remainder of our days frolicking on sun-drenched beaches and wearing very few clothes," he said in a casual manner as if he were suggesting nothing more unusual than a drive in the country.

"Oh." She paused thoughtfully. "That could be something of a problem."

"Do you think so?" It was too dark to see the expression on his face but she could hear the smile in his voice.

"Well, I haven't a thing with me that would be suitable for the sun-drenched beaches of Spain or frolicking for that matter."

"Hence the need for very few clothes." He chuckled. "I suspect you'll adapt."

"Oh, I would think so." At once the image of white sand beaches and palm trees and exotic plants flashed into her mind. A brilliant sun blazed in blue skies, reflected in even bluer waters. It was a vision of exceptional warmth touched with hedonistic decadence and much more than a little bit wicked. Particularly since, there in the blue water, without benefit of any clothing whatsoever, Gideon grinned at her. His skin was darkly tanned and his hair ruffled by the wind. He looked like anything but an English gentleman and his laugh wrapped around her very soul. In spite of herself, a slight wistful note sounded in her voice. "Are we really going to Spain?"

He laughed and her stomach tightened. "Not tonight. Tonight is a surprise."

"Spain would be a surprise," she murmured, firmly thrusting aside the look in the eyes of a completely uncivilized Gideon.

"Indeed it would but tonight's surprise is not quite as exotic." He thought for a moment. "Somewhat exotic I should think, at least in subject, but not up to the standards of sunny Spanish beaches."

"Pity." She paused. "Exotic, did you say?"

"You are like a child at Christmas."

"Indeed I am. I like surprises, good ones that is. Don't you?"

"I suppose," he said slowly. "Although I daresay I've never given it much thought."

"One doesn't think about surprises. One simply enjoys them."

He chuckled. "I shall have to surprise you more often."

"See that you do," she said in a prim manner that belied the excitement simmering inside her. Not just for whatever this surprise of his was, but simply because he did that to her. Blasted man.

It had been nearly three weeks since their altercation and rather remarkable weeks at that. There had been no actual apologies on either side; she certainly had nothing to apologize for and apparently he felt neither did he. There was something of an unspoken truce between them on subjects she did not wish to speak of, although they certainly did not hesitate to discuss anything and everything else. Politics, art, literature, gossip. They found themselves in accord on a number of things. Both were intrigued by photography and concerned about the inevitability of war with Russia. Anything they disagreed on, they disagreed on with fervor. Which was every bit as much fun as agreement.

She had spent nearly every night locked in his arms, swept away by passion and fire or bewitched by tenderness and affection. He had accompanied her again to the theater. She had gone riding with him in the park. They had wandered together through several museums perusing artifacts and art. There too, they were not always in agreement, but debate proved to be as enjoyable as everything else. He had escorted her to yet another endless evening of entertainment at Susanna's where their hostess had seemed slightly ill at ease, which wasn't the least bit like Susanna, but then Susanna had not been approving of their relationship in the first place. When he was not with her in the flesh he was always firmly present in the back of her mind. And on those rare nights when he was not in her bed, he was in her dreams, and she woke each day with a smile on her lips. All in all, Judith's life had never been so full. Or so passionate.

The carriage rolled to a stop. Gideon climbed out of the vehicle, then turned to assist her.

"Here we are," he said, with a definite note of satisfaction in his voice. He stepped aside, and she found herself looking up very familiar steps.

"Oh dear." Judith winced.

"It's the Horticultural Society," Gideon said proudly. "There's a lecture tonight about the discovering of new varieties of South American orchids by the very man who led the expedition."

"Is there indeed?" She forced an enthusiastic note to her voice. "How very interesting."

"I thought you would . . ." He narrowed his gaze. "Did you already know about this?"

"I am sorry, Gideon, of course I knew. I can't believe I completely forgot about it."

"You're probably a member of the society, aren't you?" His voice had the tone of someone who already knew the answer to his question.

"I have been for years," she said apologetically.

He blew a resigned breath, took her elbow, and started up the stairs. "Blast it all, you are an incredibly difficult woman to surprise."

"Spain would have been a surprise," she murmured.

"I thought this would be perfect."

"Well, I am surprised as I had forgotten all about it." She favored him with her brightest smile.

"You could have pretended, you know," he muttered.

"We agreed to honesty between us."

He snorted. "Only a certain amount. I remember that distinctly. You said too much would take all the fun out of it." He smiled in a grudging manner. "I suppose if I would try to avoid places you had already intended to go or resist giving you plants you already own, a surprise might be easier to achieve."

Judith bit back a grin and adopted a solemn tone. "I was very surprised by the orchid."

"I'm certain you were." He chuckled. "I shall try to do better the next time."

"Surprise or not, the thought was lovely and is most appreciated. I am delighted that you would even think of accompanying me tonight. I know your passion for exotic plants is not as great as mine."

"I have no passion for exotic plants."

"Exactly." She studied him for a moment. "These lectures can be dry at the best of times. For someone with no interest in the subject at all, it might well be deadly dull."

"I don't expect to be the least bit bored," he said coolly. "I shall be with you."

A delightful warmth washed through her at his words. "You are a charming devil, my lord."

"I know."

"There is a reception afterward," she said in as enticing as manner as she could.

"I dearly love warm lemonade and stale biscuits." He leveled her a firm glance. "Which I will gladly endure for you."

"No doubt the price you pay for being a charming devil."

"No doubt," he said under his breath.

The doors were opened at their approach by invisible hands. She glanced at Gideon and marveled that he would be willing to spend the evening doing something he had absolutely no interest in doing just to make her happy. It was at once hard to believe and quite, quite wonderful. What was even harder to believe was that, for the first time in longer than she could remember, she felt, well, happy. Not that she had been particularly unhappy, but this was different. This was . . . bliss. The thought struck her that she should not become accustomed to it, simply enjoy it while it lasted.

"Just affix a charming smile to your face"—she grinned in a wicked manner—"and think of Spain."

By God, Gideon would have wagered nothing could surpass the tedium of listening to Lady Dinsmore's relentlessly untalented relations spout bad poetry or sing in a decidedly off-key manner. He would have lost.

He stood by himself at the moment, dutifully sipping at the glass of what passed for punch, and watched Judith move gracefully around the surprisingly full reception room. He had no idea there was this much interest in plants in the entire world, let alone in London. There were even a few people here that he knew. Secret botanists apparently.

If there were a true element of surprise to the evening it was Judith herself. He had known she had a passion for her conservatory and her orchids, but he had not realized the extent of her expertise. Here, he'd watched her speak as an intellectual equal with gentlemen who were obviously experts and, even more astonishing, had watched them respond, not to her feminine charms, but to her mind. Gideon had known she was clever, but observing her now, he realized he hadn't had the faintest idea just how knowledgeable she was. She hid it well, but the woman was a bloody expert. He couldn't help but wonder what else she might be hiding.

"It's rather dull for the uninitiated," an older gentleman at Gideon's side observed.

"The punch more than makes up for it." Gideon smiled at the other man. "Lord Thornecroft, isn't it?"

"Very good, Warton. It's been a long time." The Earl of Thornecroft chuckled. "Not since that actress—"

"Indeed it has," Gideon said quickly. Thornecroft was an amicable sort with a penchant for ladies of the theater. They had indeed crossed paths in the past, the exact details of which were probably better left in the past. "I had no idea you were interested in orchids."

"Oh, I am fascinated by all manner of exotic plant life. I am especially interested in ancient Egyptian and tropical flora. My interest, however, is not common knowledge, and I prefer it that way." The older gentleman grinned. "Wouldn't do to be known as a stuffy old scholar. It would spoil my reputation."

Gideon laughed.

"Nothing could spoil that reputation." Judith stepped up beside them, favored Thronecroft with an affectionate smile, and held her hand out to him. "I understand it is well earned."

"It would be better earned." Thornecroft kissed her hand and cast her a wicked smile. "If I had had the opportunity."

Judith laughed and addressed Gideon. "He does indeed hide it but His Lordship is considered an expert on the flora of ancient Egypt."

Thornecroft shrugged in a modest manner. "Nothing more than a hobby really."

"No one except you would call it a hobby. Lord Thornecroft helped me a great deal when I first began gathering specimens for my conservatory." Judith smiled with genuine warmth at the older man. Something suspiciously like jealousy stabbed Gideon. He ignored it.

"She has become quite the expert herself." Affection and pride shone in the older man's eyes. "Her collection, as well as her knowledge, is most impressive."

"So I've noticed," Gideon murmured. It was absurd to be the least bit jealous of the earl. Why, he was old enough to be her father. Not that age had ever dissuaded Thornecroft, from what Gideon had heard. Indeed, it could be said that Judith was too old for him. Still, it seemed these two shared a mutual passion and a friendship forged from that passion that had nothing whatsoever to do with the usual relationships between men and women. And that, Gideon realized abruptly, was precisely what he envied.

Judith drew her brows together suspiciously. "I thought you were supposed to be braving the waters of the Amazon in search of rare species of lily?"

"I was forced to change my plans. My nephew and only living relative decided to at last return to London. He's been gone for years." He shook his head. "Exploring the wilds of South America can wait."

"I'm not entirely sure how much longer I can wait." Judith sighed. "I should like to see the orchids of Colombia for myself."

"I hear there is an expedition forming in Paris." Thornecroft studied Judith in a speculative manner. "Or perhaps we could sponsor our own?" Excitement sounded in his voice. "I know it sounds far-fetched but I should have thought of it long ago. Between the two of us, we have the funds to attract—"

"I wanted to explore jungles when I was a child," Gideon said without thinking, then cringed to himself. *I wanted to explore jungles?* Where on earth had that come from?

Judith and Lord Thornecroft stared at him.

Gideon smiled weakly. "Somehow, it just slipped my mind over the years."

"Pity." Judith tried and failed to hide a smile.

"Perhaps you may yet, my boy. Should we indeed decide to pool our resources and fund an expedition of our own, why, you could join us."

"Excellent," Gideon said firmly. An expedition to look for flowers in the jungle? Not bloody likely. Still, he was not about to let Judith go off into the wilds of South America with anyone, let alone Thornecroft.

The earl considered Gideon as if he knew exactly what the younger man was thinking. "As much as I may seem like an aging, incorrigible rake, and admittedly in many ways I am, I have a fondness for Judith that has nothing to do with my disreputable reputation regarding women. I feel affection for her that is no less than that which I would feel for a member of my own family."

Gideon raised a brow. "Like a daughter?"

"Good Lord, no." Thornecroft shuddered. "I have watched the fathers of daughters and I have no wish to experience that hell." He nodded thoughtfully. "More like a niece."

"I am honored, Frederick." Judith reached up

and brushed a kiss across his cheek. "And you are my favorite uncle."

"I thought you would be here tonight." A tall, blond woman stepped up behind Judith.

Judith stiffened almost imperceptibly but Gideon noticed. She forced a smile to her face and turned to greet the newcomer. "Good evening, Alexandra. I had no idea you were interested in orchids."

The blond smiled in a pleasant manner that nonetheless struck Gideon as anything but pleasant. "Whatever interests you, sister dear, interests me."

Sister?

"Good evening, Miss Chester," Lord Thornecroft said in a manner too polite to be considered curt.

Miss Chester?

"If you will excuse me, I see someone I have been meaning to speak with." The earl cast Judith an encouraging smile, then glanced at Gideon. "I leave Lady Chester in your capable hands." His gaze met Gideon's and there was a distinct warning there. Gideon wasn't entirely sure if it was in reference to Miss Chester or to Judith. Probably both. After all, the man did think of Judith as a niece.

"Lecherous old goat," Miss Chester muttered.

"Not at all," Judith said staunchly. "He is a very kind man."

Miss Chester sniffed in disdain and turned to Gideon. "And you are?"

"My lord, may I present my sister-in-law," Judith

said. "Miss Alexandra Chester. Alexandra, this is Viscount Warton."

"A very great pleasure to meet you, Miss Chester." Gideon took her offered hand. He wasn't at all sure why, but he didn't like this woman. She was pretty enough, a few years older than Judith, her hair a paler blond, taller and much more slender, but there was something in her manner and in her eye that made Gideon distinctly uneasy. He brushed a kiss across the back of her hand and released it. She, however, did not release his.

"You're Judith's *friend*, aren't you?" She studied him curiously.

"I consider myself a friend, yes," Gideon said coolly.

"Are you with friends this evening, Alexandra?" Judith said quickly.

"Lucian wouldn't have liked him, Judith." Miss Chester's gaze slipped over Gideon in an assessing manner.

Gideon raised a brow. "Oh?"

"He is entirely too handsome." Miss Chester shook her head. "Lucian wouldn't have liked him at all."

"Alexandra," Judith said sharply.

Miss Chester released his hand and trailed her fingers over his shoulder. He resisted the urge to shrug her away. "His shoulders are quite impressive. Lucian would have been envious." Her gaze met his. "Is that a trick of your tailor or are your shoulders really that broad?"

"That's quite enough," Judith snapped.

"One can never have too good a tailor," Gideon said smoothly.

"Alexandra." A warning sounded in Judith's voice.

"I'm having fun, Judith. His Lordship understands perfectly well that I am teasing. Do not begrudge me that much." Miss Chester smiled suggestively at Gideon, then turned to Judith. "You have not been to see me since Christmas Eve."

"I have been remiss. My apologies." Judith's voice was cool and unemotional.

"Will you come soon?" It was a command more than a request. "Tomorrow?"

"I'm not sure." Judith studied the other woman. "Is there a problem?"

Miss Chester glanced at Gideon. "She pays me, you know."

"I provide Alexandra with an allowance which is adequate for her needs," Judith said.

"In truth, it's exorbitant and far more than I deserve. And yet"—Miss Chester shrugged—"I have no idea where it goes."

Judith smiled in a remote manner. "Are you alone or did you accompany friends here tonight?"

"You've already asked that. I wouldn't have come here on my own even to see you. I am with friends. I have a great number of friends, Judith," her sister-in-law said sharply. "I do not sit in that house by myself all day, you know."

"Of course not, Miss Chester. I am certain Lady Chester did not mean to imply that you did." Gideon favored her with his most charming smile. "However, your friends might well be missing you by now."

"Probably." She huffed, then smiled in a wicked manner. "I'm quite mad, you know."

"You are not," Judith snapped. "Simply maddening."

"Well, if I can't be mad, maddening shall have to do." She eyed Gideon. "Don't you agree, my lord?"

"You seem neither mad nor maddening to me," Gideon said gallantly even though Miss Chester did indeed appear both.

"Really? I shall have to try harder then." Miss Chester glanced at her sister-in-law. "I shall see you soon, Judith."

"I shall look forward to it," Judith murmured.

Gideon watched Miss Chester make her way through the crowd. "She doesn't seem to like you," he said in a low voice. "And you don't seem overly fond of her."

"She hasn't liked me from the moment I first met her brother. It would have been lovely to have had a sister. I tried very hard to become her friend." Judith shrugged. "Afterward it scarcely mattered." She slanted him a wry glance. "One gets used to being disliked, you know."

"Yet you support her," he said slowly.

"Her brother made no provision for her in the case of his death. She had no inheritance, no prospects for marriage, and no money of her own."

Judith's gaze returned to her sister-in-law's retreating figure. "I would have supported her regardless."

"Regardless?"

Judith hesitated. "Of her dislike for me."

"The way she speaks of her brother ..." He knew full well Judith did not want to speak of her husband or marriage, yet this was an opportunity to learn something that he did not wish to pass up. "She seems very protective." Or possessive. "Was she older than he?"

"Worse." Judith's gaze met his. "She was his twin."

"That certainly explains a great deal."

"More than you know," Judith muttered. She drew a deep breath and smiled up at him. A twinkle shone in her eye, and he knew at once the topic was closed. "An explorer?"

"I was very young. You mustn't hold it against me."

"I don't hold it against you at all. I think it's quite enlightening." She leaned toward him and lowered her voice. "With any luck at all we can rediscover the explorer you wished to be as a child."

"That would be an adventure." He grinned. "And at least I have managed to provide you with one surprise tonight."

A slow smile spread across her face. "Perhaps, later this evening, I can provide you with a surprise of my own."

"I've never been one for surprises but"—he

chuckled—"I am willing to keep an open mind."

In spite of her lighthearted manner, and whatever delights she had in mind for later tonight, Judith was suspiciously quiet on the drive to her house. Gideon decided it was best to leave her to her own thoughts. Besides, she had probably already said more than she had intended. And there were any number of things he wished to consider himself.

It had been an evening of surprises thus far although not at all what he had intended. Indeed, most of the surprises had been for him. He had known Judith had a sister-in-law, but Alexandra Chester was not at all what he would have expected. He wasn't sure he had ever seen hate before but it was surely hate that glimmered in Miss Chester's eyes when she looked at Judith. The woman was clearly dangerous, and Gideon vowed to himself he would do whatever was in his power to protect Judith.

Miss Chester was definitely a surprise but no more so than the revelation of Judith's horticultural expertise. Simply by virtue of the extent of her conservatory he had known she was no dilettante dabbling in growing pretty flowers. But the extent of her knowledge and, more, the respect shown that knowledge by others tonight, was not merely surprising but something of a shock. He had sadly underestimated her. There was far more to Judith Chester than he had ever imagined. A lesser man, perhaps a less arrogant man, would have been intimidated by Judith's intellect and her position in the rarefied community he had observed tonight. Gideon was not the least bit intimidated. Rather, he was proud. Proud to be seen with her, proud to have her on his arm for however long that might be. It struck him as well that he hoped that would be for a very long time.

And that was the biggest surprise of all.

Chapter 8

"I told you I would come to see you." Judith folded her hands on top of her desk and stifled the urge to scream that Alexandra usually provoked in her. "It was not necessary for you to come here."

"Oh, but I like calling on you, sister dear." Alexandra wandered aimlessly around Judith's library, examining a book here, studying a painting there. "This house is a pleasant change from mine. It makes one feel so very proper. I can see why you prefer it here. Besides, I was doing you a favor." Alexandra glanced at Judith. "You don't like coming to Chester House."

Judith hesitated, then sighed. "No, I don't."

"Even your obligatory day-before-Christmas visit is difficult for you."

"Not at all," Judith said lightly. "It's your birthday and I don't mind coming in the least."

"It's *his* birthday as well and you hate it." Alexandra turned back to the books and perused the shelves. "It's to be expected, I suppose. The house has dreadful memories for you."

"It has some wonderful memories," Judith said firmly. "But this is my home and this is where I choose to live."

Judith had moved back to the house her parents had left her after Lucian's death. She had wanted to deed Chester House to Alexandra when Lucian died, but his family's solicitors had been adamant about her not doing so. It seemed the only way to save Alexandra's legacy was not to let her have it. It had something to do with obscure, unbreakable clauses in Lucian's father's will. Apparently he did not think highly of his daughter's ability to manage her own affairs, and his complicated legal maneuvers made certain she never would. The old man had left everything to Lucian with the understanding that Lucian would provide a suitable dowry for his sister when necessary. Unfortunately, he had overrated his son's sense of financial responsibility. The elder Baron Chester had died when the twins were barely nineteen. His solicitors had forced Lucian to make a will on the occasion of his marriage, but he'd had no interest in such details and had instructed them to leave everything to his new wife. He would deal with his sister's future at a later date. He never had. Lucian had not expected to die at the age of four-and-twenty.

Judith maintained Chester House with the fortune left to her by her husband. Her own trusted solicitors, who had served her parents well, handled the details of servants' salaries and upkeep of the building and a continuous succession of companions for Alexandra. In addition, Alexandra received a monthly allowance, far too generous, Judith's advisers thought. But Judith felt strongly that the Chester fortune should be used in support of the last remaining member of the Chester family. She certainly didn't need the money; her parents had left her exceptionally well off. At least once a year, she was urged to place the house and the fortune in a trust and wash her hands of it entirely. She'd always refused. In many ways, her continued involvement was a sort of penance, and she saw it as the least she could do.

"I am thinking of moving away from Chester House," Alexandra said idly.

"Oh?" Judith ignored the relief that washed through her at Alexandra's comment.

"I am considering marrying Nigel Howard, and of course I shall live with him."

Judith shook her head. "I don't know Mr. Howard."

"He's a poet. Quite good really. His brilliance has yet to be recognized but it will be soon." Alexandra paused. "Although I daresay he would rather live with me. We could be quite happy at Chester House."

"Can Mr. Howard support a wife?"

"I wouldn't think so but I can support him." Alexandra shrugged. "Or you can. It scarcely matters, I suppose."

"It matters a great deal if you are to be married," Judith said coolly.

"Then I won't marry him," Alexandra snapped. "I shall simply keep him in my bed until I tire of him and then toss him away liked a well-read newspaper. Or I shall lock him out of my rooms and refuse to have anything further to do with him. Isn't that what you do with men you no longer want?"

Judith clenched her jaw. "What do you want, Alexandra? Why are you here?"

Alexandra arched a brow. "Now, now, Judith. Mustn't be rude to your only living relative. All we have is one another."

"Indeed we do." Judith drew a deep breath. "How may I be of assistance to you?"

"That's much better." Alexandra sailed across the room and settled in the chair closest to the desk in the fluid, graceful manner that only tall women can master but that always reminded Judith of a cat nonetheless. "I should like to resume my travels. Live for a time in Paris perhaps. I have been in London far too long and I am finding it deadly dull."

Alexandra had spent more of the past ten years traveling Europe than she had living in England, for which Judith was eternally grateful. It lessened the potential for unexpected meetings like last night's. One never knew what Alexandra might do or say at any given moment. It lessened as well the possibility that her sister-in-law would involve herself in public scandal, although, to give the other woman her due, she confined her more out-rageous activities to that same artistic community that had been her brother's world.

"What about Mr. Howard?"

"Nigel is a dear, dear man but I must admit he's a little too dear." Alexandra wrinkled her nose. "A little too nice, too earnest as it were. He would make an excellent husband, aside from his severe lack of funds, that is, but you and I both know I would make a horrible wife." She traced random patterns with her fingers over the arm of the chair. "It would do Nigel a great disservice to allow him to think he was getting a wife worthy of him when in fact"—she glanced up at Judith—"he wasn't. It might lead a man to do something horrible."

"Then it's best for all concerned that you not marry him."

Alexandra studied her for a moment. "Have you ever considered that he might not be worthy of me?"

Judith chose her words carefully. She had fallen into Alexandra's traps far too often to let her guard down now. It was always the same. Alexandra would say something that would trigger Judith's sympathy and make Judith wonder, if only for a moment, if she'd been too harsh. If perhaps this might at last be the opportunity to become, if not sisters, cautious friends. "I think that's possible."

Alexandra flashed a smug grin. "You'd be wrong. He is entirely too good for me."

Judith sighed. "I've been wrong before."

"It's a pity really." She narrowed her gaze in a

thoughtful manner. "He's very handsome, isn't he?"

Judith frowned in confusion. "I told you, I've never met Mr. Howard."

"No, I meant your Lord Warton, although Nigel is as well."

"He is not my Lord Warton."

She snorted. "He certainly is if he accompanied you to that endless, tortuous lecture." She considered Judith curiously. "Are you in love with him?"

"No," Judith said quickly but apparently not quickly enough.

"I see." Alexandra's tone was thoughtful. "He'll never marry you if he knows—"

"I have no intention of marrying him."

"Perhaps he—"

"Nor does he have any intention of marrying me."

"It's been ten years since Lucian died." Alexandra stared at her. "Isn't that long enough?"

More than long enough. "Long enough for what, Alexandra?"

"I don't know." She blew a long breath. "But it seems a very long time."

It struck Judith that it had been a very long time for Alexandra as well. Judith had moved on with her life but Alexandra had wandered through hers, without purpose or bearings.

Judith drew a deep breath. "I have no desire to marry again."

"It appears to me a man like Warton would be more than sufficient to ignite such desire."

"What do you want me to say, Alexandra?" Abruptly, Judith had had enough. "Yes, Lord Warton is indeed sufficient to ignite desire of any sort. Yes, he is handsome, and yes, he likes me well enough to accompany me to a lecture. These are all among the reasons why I like him."

Alexandra eyed her coolly. "Ah, but will he still like you if he learns your secret?"

"There is no secret. Now." Judith grabbed a piece of writing paper and picked up a pen. "I will send instructions to my solicitor directing him to deposit funds into your account." She dipped her pen in the inkwell. "I will make certain you have enough for . . . six months?"

"A year would be better."

"A year it is then." Not that that meant Alexandra would actually be away for a year. She would be back when her money was gone, probably long before the end of a year.

Judith penned the note quickly, by habit really. Lord knew she had written enough of them. She glanced up at her sister-in-law. "By the way, you should probably stop telling people you've just meet that you are mad."

"You're absolutely right." Alexandra nodded solemnly. "I should wait until I know them better to tell them."

Judith sighed in exasperation. "That's not what I meant."

"I know what you meant but I don't see why. I rather like being considered mad. It's a wonderful excuse for bad behavior."

"Nonetheless." Judith's gaze met hers. "Someday someone will lock you up and then it will be up to me to come to your rescue."

"Splendid." Alexandra eyes narrowed. "I do live to make your life difficult, you know. It is my greatest joy."

Alexandra hated her, and who could blame her. To Alexandra, Judith was the woman who had stolen her brother's love, her home, her fortune, and any independence she might have claimed for herself. Judith might well have hated Alexandra if the situation had been reversed.

"At some point, Alexandra, you may wish to reenter the circles of polite society," Judith said with a sharpness she couldn't quite hide. "Madness might not be quite the asset you think it is."

"I always thought the very best families had madness in them," Alexandra murmured. "I should fit in nicely."

"Do as you wish." Judith shrugged. "Regardless of what I say or the wisdom of your actions, you will do exactly as you please anyway."

"My *will*, Judith"—Alexandra's eyes glittered in the late-afternoon light—"is the only thing in my life that remains under my control."

Judith stared at her for a long moment. Not for the first time, she wondered if Alexandra wasn't the most tragic figure in all of this. Certainly, Judith had lost a husband, but the strength of self that was as great a legacy from her parents as anything of a monetary nature meant she would survive. Alexandra had lost her father's affection, if she'd ever had it, years before his death and had then lost her brother, her twin. The only person in the world whose affection she could ever truly count on. Even though in the end, he had failed her too.

"I am sorry," Judith said and realized how very insignificant her apology was.

"Sorry? For what?" Alexandra shook her head. "Even I can see that you have had very little hand in shaping the circumstances I find myself in. The blame for that lies squarely with my father and my brother, may they both rest in peace. Perhaps not my father, but then I daresay where he is, peace is not possible." She got to her feet and smiled pleasantly. "Nonetheless, I cannot find it in my heart to think of you with anything but hatred." She nodded at the note Judith had written. "Shall I deliver that for you?"

"No, but I do appreciate the offer." Judith's smile matched Alexandra's and was just as feigned. She rose. "If I allow you to take the note, when presented to my solicitor it will no doubt be for two years' funding instead of one."

Alexandra winced. "Now, now, sister, it's not at all kind of you to think I would do such a thing."

Judith raised a brow.

"Perceptive but not kind."

"When do you plan on leaving?"

"Soon I think. Nigel is . . ." The oddest look passed over Alexandra's face. If one didn't know better, one would think she was concerned for someone other than herself. She shook her head as if to clear it. "Soon. I detest England at this time of year. And Chester House is especially grim in the winter."

"You will let me know of your plans."

"Most certainly. " Alexandra's gaze met hers, and the women stared at each other awkwardly, as if each had something to say but neither quite knew what it was. It was in those rare moments like this that Judith always wondered if Alexandra regretted their relationship as much as Judith did. It was a pity really. They were both so alone in the world. She and Alexandra could have supported one another through the years. Life might be remarkably different for both of them if they had.

"Explain to me again why you think trudging through the park on a day like today is a good idea," Norcroft said in a mild manner.

"I find myself increasingly restless these days. That, coupled with a desire to share a cordial conversation with one of my oldest friends, is why I asked you meet me in the park," Gideon said. It was entirely true, as far as it went. "Besides, it's a beautiful spring day."

"In hell perhaps." Norcroft huffed. "It's cold, it's damp, the sky is an ugly shade of gray, and as it's only the beginning of March, the very word *spring* bespeaks of an optimism I didn't know you had."

"Nonetheless, I find it invigorating."

"Since we are forced to walk at a brisk pace simply to keep from freezing, I can certainly agree with *invigorating*." Norcroft paused for a moment. "Although *distracting* might be a better word."

"I have no need for distractions."

"I've never seen a man who looked like he needed a distraction more." Norcroft chuckled.

"I'm not sure if seeing you in this state is horrifying or carries a great deal of satisfaction."

"Don't be ridiculous." Gideon stared straight ahead, his step didn't falter. "And I'm not in any state."

Norcroft snorted.

"I simply don't know . . . That is to say I'm not sure . . ." Gideon glared at his friend. "I don't know anything. There you have it. Are you happy?"

Norcroft stifled a grin. "Blissful."

Gideon raised a brow. "Not horrified?"

"Oh, that too."

"Why?" Gideon narrowed his gaze. "I can understand *satisfied*—"

"Because it means you are as human as the rest of us?"

"All too human apparently," he muttered. "Why horrified?"

"Horrified is the natural reaction one has when one realizes the world as we know it has surely come to an end." Norcroft shook his head. "Gideon Pearsall, Viscount Warton, felled by a woman."

"I have not been felled," Gideon snapped, although in truth he felt rather felled. "I'm simply confused, that's all."

Norcroft chuckled. "Generally, I'd say that's enough."

Gideon and Norcroft tipped their hats to two other intrepid souls hurrying in the opposite direction.

"Have you ever been in love, Norcroft?"

"Love?" Norcroft stopped in his tracks and stared. "You're in love?"

"I didn't say I was in love." Gideon glanced back at Norcroft over his shoulder. "I asked if you'd ever been in love."

Norcroft hurried to catch up. "Once or twice, I suppose. Nothing serious."

"Then you have never been in love. Love is extraordinarily serious."

"So," Norcroft said idly as if neither question nor answer mattered. "Have you ever been in love?"

"Once." Gideon shook his head. "It was a disaster."

"Ah yes." Norcroft nodded. "Violet Smithfield."

Gideon stopped and looked at his friend. "You do know about Violet Smithfield then?"

"Of course." Norcroft met the other man's gaze directly. "As do Helmsley and Cavendish. Oh, the incident of your marriage was kept exceptionally quiet, but between my mother and Helmsley and Cavendish's large number of female relations, all of whom delight in a juicy morsel of gossip, we heard something about it."

Gideon stared. "You, none of you, ever said a word."

"*You*, my friend, never said a word." Norcroft shrugged. "And because we are your friends, we realized you had no desire to do so, so we never have."

Gideon studied Norcroft for a long moment. Norcroft, Helmsley, and Cavendish were indeed his closest friends. If truth were told, they were his only friends. They had shared a great deal through the years but they had never shared this.

That they had never mentioned his ill-fated marriage, even while under the influence of excessive alcohol, said a great deal about that friendship. Gideon smiled in a wry manner. "It must have been difficult for Cavendish to hold his tongue."

Norcroft grinned. "It's always difficult for Cavendish to hold his tongue. Now"—he rubbed his gloved hands together briskly—"why don't we finish this discussion in front of a warm fire with a brandy in hand?"

"I'd prefer to walk, it helps me to think." Gideon grinned. "If you can bear the elements, that is."

"I shall attempt to bravely carry on." Norcroft sighed in a dramatic manner and they started off.

They walked for several minutes in silence. Gideon had no idea exactly what he had to say but he was tired of talking to himself. He had nothing but questions. While he doubted Norcroft had any answers, it was good to have a friend to listen to his troubles. A friend. He had known he and the others were friends but it hadn't seemed quite as significant as it did now. It had been little more than a word. Now that he needed, well, *friends*, when apparently he had not needed them up to now, it became much more.

"The problem with falling in love with a woman who is not in love with you," Gideon said at last, "is that the sense of betrayal is as great as the heartbreak. Particularly if you *believed* she loved you as well. It's a violation of your trust and shatters your belief in things you've always held true."

"Love." Norcroft nodded in a sage manner.

"Actually, I was referring to honor. Frankly, until then I had never given undue consideration to love. Oh, I had certain romantic notions fueled by literature and poetry but they centered more around gallantry and chivalry than love. But I had always believed in honesty and the sanctity of one's word. That someone I could have intense feelings for did not share that belief was as devastating as everything else." Gideon glanced at Norcroft. "More than you wished to know?"

"Not at all," Norcroft said staunchly. "I am willing to listen for as long as you wish to talk. It's most enlightening." He paused for a moment. "However, I am a bit confused."

Gideon snorted. "Aren't we all?"

"Are we discussing Violet Smithfield or Lady Chester?"

"Both I think." Gideon blew a long breath. "My past with Violet affects my present with Judith. I understand that. It makes perfect sense. It might explain as well why I wish to know everything about her."

"Wouldn't do to have an unexpected fiancé turn up again."

"Oh, I knew about Violet's fiancé." Gideon shook his head. "What I didn't know was that he was the man she wanted. She kept that secret from me quite well. I never even suspected the truth. Judith has all kinds of secrets and things she does not wish to talk about and I want to know everything about her."

"To eliminate surprises?"

"Perhaps, but it's more than that." Gideon paused

beneath a tree and snapped off a twig. "I'm not sure why or how but it's more. It's not so much a matter of trust as a matter of . . . thirst. Or hunger. To know how she thinks, what she feels, and why she is the woman she is today. Everything about her. Does that make sense?"

"Not at all. Go on."

"Judith and I agreed at the beginning to be honest with one another and I'm confident she has been honest in everything she has said to me. It's what she hasn't revealed that concerns me."

"So it's not your past that you fear but hers?"

"Possibly."

"The past always shapes the future. It's the nature of man." Norcroft studied Gideon for a thoughtful moment. "Forgive me for being obtuse but I don't understand why this is a concern at all. I was under the impression that what was between you and Lady Chester was of a temporary nature. Enjoyable interlude, I believe you called it. Nothing at all serious."

"It was," Gideon said simply. "Or at least it was intended to be."

"And now?"

"Now?" Gideon blew a long breath. "I don't know. I don't know what she wants. I don't know what I want."

"I see."

"Do you?"

"Not really." Norcroft shrugged. "I might understand all this better if I were warm."

"Nonsense. The cold makes one's blood move

which surely assists in thinking." Gideon started off down the path.

"I know what I'm thinking," Norcroft muttered and fell into step beside him.

"My aunt is right, though," Gideon said more to himself than to his friend. "Judith is not the type of wife I should be seeking."

"So marriage has raised its ugly head now, has it?"

"It all seems to lead to that, doesn't it?" Gideon slanted a glance at the other man. "My aunt feels Judith might not be able to bear children. If she is right, marriage to Judith would mean the end of my line. Certainly I have cousins who would inherit my title, but the Pearsalls would be at an end. I have always considered it my sole responsibility in life to make certain that does not happen. But now . . ."

"Now you are torn between doing what you should do and what you want to do." Norcroft chose his words with care. "It seems to me that you would not be discussing marriage if love was not a consideration as well."

"That's a distinct possibility." As soon as he said the words he knew Norcroft was right. Love was indeed a consideration.

"If it is love you wish to talk about, I fear you have come to the wrong man. Helmsley is—"

"I have no desire to talk to Helmsley about this," Gideon said firmly.

"About her you mean."

"Yes. Blast it all, Norcroft, I realize it's irrational.

The relationship between Helmsley and Judith is long over. I understand that. She and I are both adults with histories of our own that have nothing to do with one another. But . . ." He snapped the twig in his hand. "I don't like it. I don't like that she's been with Helmsley and I don't like that they remain friends. I don't like that she's been with other men at all." His voice hardened. "And I'm not at all pleased that she's been married before."

Norcroft's eyes widened. "I see."

"Don't look at me like that. I am not a raving lunatic." Gideon tossed away the pieces of twig and brushed off his hands. "I am simply—"

"Jealous?" Norcroft said in a helpful manner.

"Not at all." Gideon met the other man's gaze. "Or insanely so." It was true even if he hadn't acknowledged it to himself yet. "I find I don't want her to have lived before that moment when our eyes met at the Twelfth Night Ball. I want her life to have started with me. Only me."

"Then, as I see it, you have two choices." Norcroft studied his friend. "You can go on with your life precisely as you have planned. Do exactly what's expected of you. Find a suitable wife. Possibly continue as you are with Lady Chester—"

Gideon shook his head. "She would not be willing to do so if I were married. Nor, I think, would I ask her to."

"Very well then. You live your life as expected and you do it without Lady Chester. Or . . ." Norcroft paused.

"Or?"

"Or you can abandon all the expectations you've lived with your entire life until now and follow your heart."

Gideon grimaced. "My heart is as confused as my head."

"It seems to me that you can live your life the way others think you should and be unhappy," Norcroft said slowly, "or you can live your life in a manner that will make you happy. Life is entirely too short to waste on regrets. Of course, I am a selfish sort." Norcroft's gaze locked with his. "I want to meet those expectations as well as be happy. But then I have not yet met a woman who would make such a choice necessary."

"What would you do?"

"Oh no." Norcroft shook his head. "This is not my dilemma. However, I do think the first thing you need to do is determine your feelings. And hers."

Gideon blew a long breath. "I have as little idea how she feels as I do how I feel." He thought for a moment. "But there is a kinship between us, Norcroft. A bond of sorts. It was immediate and has not faded even a bit. At first, I thought it was simply desire."

"And now?"

"Now . . ." Gideon shook his head.

"Now we have come full circle. Back to love."

"It's a wicked circle, I think." Gideon sighed. "Love, that is."

Norcroft chuckled. "So I've heard."

"She and I have not discussed love," Gideon murmured. He had intended to bring up the topic, casually, as if it were of no importance. But it had never seemed the right time. He wondered now if he hadn't failed to introduce the subject of love because he feared what she might say. Or what he might confess. Or admit. "Indeed, I was under the distinct impression love was not to enter into our arrangement at all. Not that we ever said as much. I think—"

"Bloody hell, Warton." Norcroft stopped and glared at his friend. "You are the last person in the world I would ever have described as indecisive. You've asked for my advice—"

Gideon stared. "I don't recall asking for your advice."

"You asked what I would do."

"That was hypothetical and about—"

"I have no idea what I would do and it scarcely matters. But here's what I think you should do." Norcroft ticked the points off on his finger. "First, I would determine if Lady Chester feels any affection for you whatsoever. Secondly, you need to recognize or accept or simply understand your own feelings. Are you in love or aren't you?"

"I—"

"If you're going to say you don't know, I would prefer not to hear it," Norcroft snapped. "If you don't know your own feelings, or claim you don't, that alone is an indication that you are in a position you have never been in before. For good or ill."

Gideon raised a brow. "That was advice?"

Norcroft shrugged. "It's the best I can do."

"Still, I think you might have something," Gideon said thoughtfully. "I can't make any decisions about anything until I know how she feels. Until I understand how I feel. If indecision alone is an indication"—he chuckled—"perhaps I am in love."

"Or mad," Norcroft muttered.

"One and the same, I would think. Now, old man." Gideon clapped his friend on the back. "I think a warm fire and a brandy is long overdue." He grinned. "It's damnably cold out here."

Chapter 9

"Surely there is somewhere else we need to be this evening?" Gideon murmured into Judith's ear while keeping a polite smile on his face. "Perhaps, I don't know, trapped in a burning building?"

Judith's gaze skimmed Susanna's crowded ballroom and she resisted the urge to laugh. "Come now, Gideon, it's not that bad."

"We were just here a fortnight ago." Gideon nodded to an acquaintance who smiled knowingly at Gideon and Judith. "I wouldn't hazard to think what entertainment by her less-than-talented nieces and nephews Lady Dinsmore might have in store for a gathering this size. Good Lord." A look of sheer horror passed over Gideon's face. "You don't think she'd make them all perform together, do you? Like some sort of grand, off-key chorus?"

"Don't be absurd." Judith bit back a grin. "It's a ball, not one of Susanna's typical entertainments. There is music and dancing, and I would wager not one of her relations will be pressed into service for the torture of her guests."

"Thank God," he murmured and gazed down at her. "Still, I was rather hoping for a quiet evening together. I have a great deal I wish to talk to you about."

"Do you?" She raised a brow. "Anything of a serious nature?"

"Intensely serious." His tone was light but there was indeed a somber gleam in his eye. He heaved a resigned sigh. "It can wait, I suppose."

"I'm not sure I like it when you're serious."

"Then for you, and for you alone, I shall endeavor to be nothing but lighthearted and gay for the remainder of the evening." He cast her a hopeful look. "A short evening perhaps?"

"Perhaps. But . . ." There was nothing she would like better than to spend the evening talking with Gideon. Talking with Gideon was almost as much fun as being in his arms. It was the oddest thing. The more she was with him, the more she wanted to be with him. Still, they had plenty of time to be together and later tonight they would be. She shrugged in a helpless manner. "Susanna has been planning this ball for months. It's in celebration of her grandmother's birthday, you know."

Gideon nodded at an elderly woman seated at the far end of the ballroom surrounded by various other guests, all, no doubt, relations. "The antique at the end of the room?"

Judith choked back a laugh. "If you're referring to the distinguished elderly lady, then yes, that is the dowager marchioness, the matriarch of Susanna's family."

Gideon considered the older woman. "She looks like she's eaten something that has disagreed with her."

"At her age I suspect everything disagrees with her." Judith studied the lady thoughtfully. "Still, it must be quite wonderful to reach advanced age and find yourself surrounded by your children and their children. Family, people who care for you, who will miss you when you're gone from this world." A familiar pang of longing stabbed Judith and she thrust it aside. Silly, really, to envy what you could never have.

He glanced down at her. "You will be missed."

"Not like that." An annoying wistful note sounded in her voice.

"Why not?"

She shook her head. "One accepts the realities of one's life, Gideon. What can be and what will be and what can never be. One's destiny, as it were. And that, dear man, is far too somber a topic for tonight." She firmly ignored the sense of regret that washed through her and cast him a brilliant smile. "And as much as I would love to spend the evening alone with you engaged in conversation or anything else, we are indeed trapped here. It would not do to leave too early, especially since Susanna says the queen is expected to make an appearance."

"I doubt in this crowd our absence would be noted by the queen or anyone else."

"Susanna would notice and I would not offend her for the world. She is my dearest friend."

"Your dearest female friend," he said under his breath.

She stared at him. "What an odd thing to say."

"It is odd and uncalled for and you have my apologies." He smiled. "I have a great deal on my mind."

She studied him. "If one didn't know better, one might think there was a touch of jealousy in your comment."

"Just a touch?" He cast her a genuine smile.

Judith had no desire to experience a man's jealousy ever again. But this was Gideon, who was not the least bit like Lucian, and in spite of herself it was hard not to be a little pleased. If he was jealous, perhaps he cared. Not that it mattered. They would not be together for long. Still, it was nice.

"Just a touch," she said firmly.

"Judith!" Susanna swept up to them in a flurry of rustling skirts and a cloud of determination. Her mass of dark curls was, as always, the tiniest bit disheveled, as if her hair had a mind entirely its own. She brushed a kiss across Judith's cheek. "I am so glad to see you."

"You saw me when we came in." Judith grinned. "Or was it another Lady Dinsmore who greeted us upon our arrival?"

"No, no, it was me. I am thankfully the only Lady Dinsmore left." She glanced at Gideon. "My mother-in-law was an overbearing woman who thought she knew everything about everything. Rather like your aunt, I should think." Her eyes widened and she stared at Gideon. "Dear Lord, I can't believe I said that."

"I can't believe you said it either." Gideon chuckled. "Although it was most insightful of you."

"Nonetheless you have my apologies, my lord." Susanna smiled weakly. "I am a bit overwhelmed tonight"—she waved at the gathering—"with all this. Having a large family is usually quite wonderful but at the moment I have one sister criticizing everything from the quality of the champagne to what the orchestra is wearing. Another helpfully trying to solve problems that don't actually exist. Two sisters-in-law who have decided this is the perfect time to stop speaking to each other. Brothers who have vanished altogether. Several nieces flirting outrageously with the obvious intention of provoking scandal or at the very least gossip, and cousins too numerous to mention all doing their very best to drive me mad."

Gideon stared in disbelief or perhaps terror. Not that anyone would blame him. Susanna's extensive relations were enough to strike fear into the hearts of the uninitiated.

"So all is progressing exactly as expected?" Judith grinned at her friend.

"Unfortunately yes." Susanna laughed and turned to Gideon. "Would you mind terribly if I were to steal Judith for a few moments? I saw your aunt earlier. You might wish to find her or . . ." She gestured aimlessly. "Well, something. I desperately need to speak to Judith on a matter of some importance."

Judith raised a brow. "Another family crisis?"

"Not yet." The slightest look of unease washed across Susanna's face.

Judith glanced at Gideon.

"I find I am exceptionally parched," Gideon said at once. "May I fetch the two of you some refreshment?"

"That would be lovely. And most appreciated." Susanna nodded gratefully, hooked her arm through Judith's, and briskly steered her away.

Judith glanced over her shoulder at Gideon, who shrugged and grinned with obvious amusement. She glanced at her friend. "Whatever is the matter?"

"Nothing really." Susanna stopped a passing waiter, grabbed a glass of champagne for herself, handed one to Judith, then led her out a side door and into the corridor that served both the ballroom and the music room and could lead one to Susanna's terrace. "This will do."

Judith studied her friend curiously. "This will do for what?"

"For the moment." Susanna downed her champagne, then looked at her empty glass with disgust and dropped it into a potted palm. "It wouldn't do to have anything but champagne for tonight, you know. Frankly, I thought if the entire family was to be on hand we should have something much stronger than champagne available. A nice punch with brandy and rum might be up to the task." She shook her head. "No one would dare to miss

Grandmother's birthday. They all live in fear that when she passes on she will leave all her money to orphaned cats or some other charitable organization."

Judith tried not to laugh. "Orphaned cats?"

Susanna grinned. "Something of that nature. It's just the sort of thing Grandmother would do to thwart the more mercenary members of the family. At any rate." Susanna sobered. "I gather your *adventure* with Lord Warton continues."

Judith sipped her wine. "Indeed it does."

"You've been together for more than a month now."

"Indeed we have."

Susanna's brow furrowed. "That's longer than your adventures have ever lasted."

Judith grinned. "Indeed it is."

"Is it serious?"

Judith paused for no more than a fraction of a second. "No, of course not."

"It is, it is." Susanna groaned. "I can see it in your face. You look, well, *happy*. You positively glow with happiness."

"My apologies," Judith murmured.

"Don't be absurd, I'm glad to see you happy. I just—"

"You just think Warton is a mistake," Judith said slowly.

"Yes. No. Well, not for the same reasons I did initially." Susanna wrung her hands. "I have not been a very good friend, Judith. *Cousin*."

Cousin? Judith winced. "Oh dear."

"I should have told you when you first became

involved with Warton. In truth I didn't think it was necessary. I never imagined . . . And frankly, I was torn." Susanna's gaze flitted around the corridor as if she were afraid to look Judith in the eye. "Divided loyalties and all that. There you, my dearest friend in world, are on one hand, and on the other is a member of my family." Susanna wrinkled her nose. "Although, to be perfectly honest, I've never liked her and I don't think she's ever especially liked me either."

"Who has never liked you?" Judith stared in confusion. "What are you talking about?"

Susanna drew a deep breath. "I'm talking about Lady Braxton. She's my cousin. Not like you and I are cousins, she's actually my cousin by blood. Well, marriage really. She was married to my second cousin on my mother's side."

"How nice for you all." Judith shook her head. "But I still have no idea what you're talking about."

"When I told you about Warton's marriage the reason I knew everything that I knew was because the woman in question was my cousin." Susanna met Judith's gaze reluctantly. "Violet Smithfield. Now Lady Braxton."

"You said you couldn't remember her name," Judith said slowly.

"Yes, well, one hates to admit that someone who could do something that vile to a man is a relation. One particularly hates to admit it to one's dearest friend. It's really quite embarrassing, you know."

Judith raised a brow. "You were embarrassed?"

"Mortified. And I was also afraid that you would think I disapproved of you and Warton because of what had happened with Violet and I didn't want that to make you ignore my concerns." She paused. "Which are still valid, you know, except for that happiness of yours." She shook her head. "I did not expect that. It puts everything in an entirely different light."

"Does it?"

Susanna nodded. "It certainly does."

Judith thought for a moment. The fact that the woman who had broken Gideon's heart was related to Susanna was of interest but not overly significant. Still, Susanna's failure to disclose it had obviously weighed heavily on her friend's mind. "I don't see that it really matters. It's over and done with and in the past."

"Oh, without question," Susanna said in a too-bright manner.

Judith studied her friend. "There's more, isn't there?"

"Only that Violet is a widow now. Her husband died two years ago."

Judith raised a brow. "And?"

"And while she spent much of her married life in the country or on the continent, she is no longer in mourning." Susanna winced. "And has decided to live in London."

At once Judith realized what Susanna was so loath to say. The oddest feeling settled in the pit of her stomach. She met the other woman's gaze. "And she's here tonight, isn't she?"

Susanna nodded reluctantly.

"Gideon should know at once." Judith drained the rest of her champagne. "It would be dreadful for him to come upon her unawares." She started for the door.

"Judith." Susanna caught her arm. "I suspect . . . that is to say . . ."

"Out with it, Susanna," Judith said sharply. "What?"

"She asked if he would be here tonight. I think . . ." Susanna cringed. "I think she wants your Lord Warton back."

"He's not my Lord Warton. But you are right about one thing." Judith thrust her empty glass at her and turned to go. "We could have used the rum."

"It's been a very long time, my lord."

The lilting, feminine voice sounded behind him and Gideon groaned to himself. Not again. He had scarcely been able to make his way around the ballroom without seeing one acquaintance or another. Many of whom had casually asked after Judith. No doubt gossip was running rampant about the two of them. Not that he particularly cared. He affixed a polite smile on his face and turned.

Shock smacked him hard in the stomach and stole his breath.

"Good evening, Gideon." Violet Smithfield—no, Lady Braxton—smiled at him in a pleasant manner. As if they were mere acquaintances passing on the street. She nodded at the glasses of champagne he held, one in each hand. "Is one of those for me?"

"No," he said, handing her one without thinking. And at once found himself at a similar ball nine years ago. He shook his head to clear the image.

She raised a brow. "Gideon?"

It was not at all surprising that her presence now would sweep him back to another time. She looked very much the same as she had then. Her hair just as sleek and dark, her lips just as scandalously red, her eyes . . . violet.

"Gideon?" she said again.

What in the name of all that was holy was he doing? He gathered his wits about him and nodded curtly. "My apologies, Lady Braxton, I fear you have me at a disadvantage. I had no idea you would be here tonight."

"Are you pleased?"

"I am . . . surprised."

"Yes, I can see that." She studied him for a moment and he returned her perusal. At first he had thought she looked unchanged but he was wrong. Her face was slightly leaner, more mature. But then it would be, wouldn't it? He had certainly changed since they were last together. "Would you have stayed away if you had known?"

"No," he said without hesitation. "In truth I must admit, I expected us to encounter one another long before now. In many ways, London is a very small town."

"I have scarcely spent any time in London at all since my marriage." Violet shrugged. "When we were not traveling the continent, William preferred living in the country to residing in London."

"And yet, here you are." Gideon smiled politely

and was grateful he could do so. He wasn't at all sure how he felt about Violet's abrupt reappearance in his life. Not that she was in his life. She was simply . . . here.

"Indeed, here I am." She sipped the champagne thoughtfully. "How are you, Gideon?"

"My health is excellent. My investments are sound. My friends are loyal." He noted the arrogant, cool tone in his voice and was inordinately pleased. He was face to face with Violet, and aside from the first few moments, was completely under control. "And you?"

She laughed lightly. "I'm very well."

"And Lord Braxton"

She stared at him. "You don't know?"

"Know what?"

"My husband died two years ago."

"My sympathies." He shook his head. "I had no idea."

Astonishment shone in her eyes. "I don't believe you."

He chose his words carefully. "I am sorry for your loss, Lady Braxton, but I assure you I would not have asked after him if I had known. I do not play those kinds of games."

"No, of course you don't." The smile returned to her face, and her gaze met his. He had forgotten how tall she was, barely a few inches shorter than he. "Do you realize everyone in this room is watching to see what will happen between you and me?"

"I doubt that." He took a sip of his wine. "It's a very large room."

"And a fair proportion of the people here are relations of mine." She paused. "Which means they probably remember our . . . circumstances."

"Nonsense." He shrugged. "It was a long time ago. Far juicier scandals have occupied people's attentions since then. I daresay most have forgotten ours altogether."

"Have you?"

"One tends to put unpleasantries aside and go on with one's life. So, no, I have not forgotten, just as I have not forgotten being stung by a bee when I was eleven or a nasty spill from a horse when I was fifteen." *Or having my heart broken at the age of three-and-twenty.*

"I remember the two of us quite clearly."

"The two of us?" Gideon smiled pleasantly. "If I recall, there never really was an *us*, was there? There was a *me*. There was definitely a *you*. And I seem to remember a *he* but never truly an *us*."

She laughed. "You are exceptionally droll, Gideon. I don't remember you being quite so . . ."

He raised a brow, "Charming?"

"No, I remember your charm." She studied him curiously. "*Cynical* was the word I was going to use. And arrogant, I think."

"Time, my lady, marches inexorably on and takes with it the innocence and trust of youth."

"Oh my." She winced. "That was cynical."

"As well as accurate." He nodded. "Now then, Lady Braxton—"

"Violet. You always called me Violet."

"Yes, well, now you are Lady Braxton. The rules of behavior between us have changed."

She stared at him. "I did not expect you to be so cold."

What did you expect? "Once again, my apologies. My intention was not to be cold. I was simply trying to be polite."

"Is it difficult? To be polite to me?"

"Not at all. I am unfailingly polite to people I scarcely know."

"I see." Her gaze searched his. "You're not glad to see me then?"

"I am neither glad to see you nor dismayed. My reaction can best be described, as we noted earlier, as surprised. Even *shocked* would be reasonably accurate." He chuckled. "One does not expect to be confronted with the mistakes of one's youth at a gathering in honor of an elderly lady."

Her eyes narrowed. "And I was a mistake?"

"Perhaps my greatest. But I was young and foolish, and mistakes are often made by the young and the foolish." He leaned closer to her and lowered his voice. "I should advise you to keep a smile on your face. You wouldn't want those watching to think this encounter was anything but pleasant."

At once a smiled curved her lips. "You're right of course. You should know, you are not the only one who made mistakes."

He raised his glass to her. "Oh, I was well aware of that."

"You might not be aware, however, that I have realized my errors and I regret each one." She paused for a moment. "It's not too late to correct them."

"I am not certain exactly what you are saying, Lady Braxton." Gideon chose his words carefully. "But I have found some mistakes can never be corrected and are best left in the past. Especially those of youth and stupidity."

She shook her head. "We have a great deal to talk about, you and I."

"Again I'm afraid I disagree." He looked firmly into her violet eyes. "We have nothing to talk about. Oh, perhaps if we meet on the street, the topic of the weather would be of interest to us both. Or if we again come face to face at a party like this one, the quality of champagne or the stuffiness of the room might be something we can exchange a word or two about. Beyond that, I see nothing whatsoever that you and I have to talk about. Now, if you will excuse me."

"Of course." The look in her eyes belied the sweetness of her smile. "But this discussion is not yet over, Gideon."

"On the contrary, Lady Braxton. Any discussion between us ended nine years ago." He nodded politely, turned, and made his way through the crowd.

There were indeed any number of eyes focused on him. And her. He hadn't the slightest doubt anyone watching would have seen nothing whatsoever to remark upon. But Violet was right. Their meeting would have been fodder for gossip had either of them reacted with anything other than feigned politeness. Damn, he needed to get out of here. At the very least, he needed fresh air and a few minutes to compose himself.

To say he was surprised by his unexpected encounter with Violet was an understatement. Why, he'd been stunned into insensibility. Had become a blithering idiot. Or nearly so. It had, he supposed, all things considered, gone as well as could be expected, given he hadn't the faintest idea she would be here. Not that he hadn't rehearsed this meeting over and over again through the years, although admittedly it had been a long time since he had done so. Seeing her again was a shock, of course, and at the moment, he wasn't at all sure how he felt about it. Or rather, about her. Her appearance brought up all kinds of emotions he'd thought were long since put to rest. No, not emotions exactly, but definitely confusion. The question now was why. Surely he had no lingering feeling for her. Indeed, at this point in his life he shouldn't feel anything whatsoever about her, let alone confusion.

He skirted the edge of the ballroom, found a door, stepped into the corridor, and came face to face with Judith.

"Gideon." Her eyes widened with surprise. "I was just—"

Without thinking he grabbed her shoulders, pulled her to him, and kissed her long and hard. It was an impulse and not an especially smart one at that, particularly for a man who had just escaped one situation fraught with the potential for gossip. Still, it—Judith—was exactly what he needed.

"Dear Lord." A groan sounded behind Judith.

At once he released her and stepped back. Judith stared up at him.

"Are you insane? Have you no sense at all?" Lady Dinsmore glared at him. "You cannot go about kissing people willy-nilly in corridors. Especially if you have no idea if you are alone or who might be watching. Why, there might have been a . . . a *flock* of people standing behind Judith instead of just me. Fortunately, I am extremely discreet."

"You're right." Gideon nodded. "I don't know what came over me. You have my sincere apologies for my inappropriate behavior, my gratitude for your discretion, and my deepest regret if I have caused you any embarrassment whatsoever."

"I rather liked it," Judith murmured.

"Well, admittedly, it did not look unpleasant," Lady Dinsmore said grudgingly. "Even so, Judith has gone to great pains through the years to be circumspect in regard to her . . . *adventures*."

Judith's eyes widened. "Susanna."

Lady Dinsmore ignored her. "Not that this is at all like any of her other three adventures. You have already lasted well beyond any of them and spent far more time in her b—"

"Susanna!" Judith snapped. "That's quite enough!"

Lady Dinsmore gasped and clapped her hand over her mouth. "Lord help me. I cannot believe I just said that. Judith—"

"Perhaps it's best if we end this discussion with apologies all around," Gideon said quickly, "and forget everything any of us has seen or heard."

Lady Dinsmore's brows drew together. "Would you really do that? Forget what I just said?"

"Will *you* forget what you just saw?" Gideon stepped closer, took her hand, and raised it to his lips. He kept his gaze trained on hers. "If you can find it in your heart to do so, I shall be eternally in your debt."

The hint of a smile curved the lady's lips. "You are a charming devil, my lord. I can certainly see why Judith—"

"Susanna," Judith said through clenched teeth, "I think you've said more than enough, particularly if you wish to continue to be considered discreet. Although"—her eyes narrowed—"I believe that ship has left the port."

"Yes of course," Lady Dinsmore said weakly and wrinkled her nose. "I do tend to do that on occasion."

"Do what?" Gideon adopted an innocent air. "I can't recall a thing you might have said or done here that is the least bit objectionable. It seems to me we were discussing nothing more than the success of the party." He leaned toward her. "A rousing success, I might add."

Lady Dinsmore brightened. "Do you really think so?"

"I do indeed." Gideon nodded solemnly.

"Although the queen has not yet arrived." Lady Dinsmore sighed.

"And when she does," Gideon said firmly, "your grandmother's birthday party will be an even greater success than expected." He paused in a knowing way. "Think of what your sisters will say."

Judith snorted.

Lady Dinsmore grinned. "That's exactly what I was thinking." She studied him for a moment. "I further think I might have been wrong about you."

He smiled slowly, the kind of slightly wicked smile he had long ago learned could be an effective weapon. "I do hope so, my lady."

Lady Dinsmore stared. "Yes, well . . ." She cleared her throat. "I should return . . ." She waved vaguely at the door to the ballroom.

"Absolutely. I cannot imagine that you have not already been missed. I say." He leaned toward her in a conspiratorial manner. "Do you think it would be a mistake if I were to spend a few private moments with Lady Chester? On the terrace perhaps?"

"It would most certainly be a mistake. But then what between the two of you is not a mistake?" Her eyes twinkled. "As it is rather a brisk night, I shouldn't be too long if I were you."

"Thank you, Lady Dinsmore." He opened the door for her.

Lady Dinsmore's gaze slipped to Judith and then back to him. "About that slip of the tongue that I—"

"Now, now." Gideon wagged his finger at her. "You said nothing and I heard nothing."

"Yes, of course." Lady Dinsmore looked at Judith and smiled weakly. Gideon could have sworn some unspoken message passed between them in that language women have that men cannot decipher. She glanced at him once more, then disappeared back into the ballroom.

"What exactly do you think you were doing with Susanna?"

"I believe I was charming her." He took Judith's hand and started toward the terrace. "I was good, wasn't I?"

Judith laughed. "As always. But why—"

"Because she is your dearest friend and I wish for her to like me."

"I think it worked," Judith said under her breath. "Why are we going to the terrace?"

"I wish to speak to you about something." Judith should know Violet was here. It would be most awkward for Judith to come face to face with his former, well, *wife*, regardless of the brevity of that marriage.

"There is something I must speak to you about as well," she said.

He opened the door, and she stepped out onto the terrace. He followed and closed the door behind them. The air was cold but the night was still, and he found the change in temperature refreshing.

"There's a hint of spring in the air." She glanced at him. "Do you feel it?"

He chuckled. "You are overly optimistic. I feel nothing but the cold. However." He shook his head. "I should not have dragged you out here. You will catch your death of cold. Your shoulders are bare and that gown is most revealing."

She laughed. "Too revealing?"

"Well, I like it and it is the fashion so I shall have to bear with the annoyance of knowing other men like it as well. Here." He opened his arms, and she stepped into his embrace. "Does that help? Are you warmer?"

"Delightfully so," she murmured against him. "What did you wish to talk to me about?"

"I . . ." No, there were better things to talk about than Violet Smithfield. "Have you given any consideration to . . . us?"

She drew back. "Us?"

He wished he could see into her eyes, but the light from the door provided far too little illumination. "Yes, you and I."

"I'm aware of what *us* entails," she said slowly. "But I fear I don't understand what you're asking."

"When we began this . . . *adventure*, you set certain boundaries."

"Yes?"

"They were quite explicit in regard to"—he searched for the right word—"expectations."

"Go on."

"We agreed to be honest with one another, and I wish to be honest with you now. It's simply difficult to find the words."

"I see." She blew a long breath and took a step back. "Perhaps I should save you the effort, then."

He drew his brows together in confusion. "The effort?"

"It's been a great deal of fun, Gideon. No." She shook her head. "It's been really quite remarkable, and in that, completely unexpected. But we did agree—"

"Did we?" *Agree to what?*

"Indeed we did and I do understand." Her voice was cool, remote. "I would have preferred that you had chosen a more private setting, although I daresay no one else would come out of doors on a night like this."

"A private setting for what?" he asked cautiously. What was she talking about?

"For this. For what you have to say although there's really no need to say it aloud. It's always rather awkward, isn't it?" She laughed in an odd sort of self-conscious manner. "It would be best, therefore, if we both save ourselves any further embarrassment. Now, if you will excuse me, I think I shall take my leave. I feel a headache coming on. Good evening, my lord," She nodded and started toward the door.

"Judith." He grabbed her arm. "What are you talking about? Where are you going?"

"I'm going home if you would be so good as to release me." Her voice was calm but there was the slightest hint of a tremor underneath. "And I'm talking about our agreement."

"I'm not about to release you." He shook his head. "What agreement?"

"You know perfectly well what agreement," she said sharply. "We agreed that when either of us decided that we wished to discontinue our relationship, we could do so with no recrimination. Although I must admit"—she drew a deep breath— "I have never been on this side of it, and regardless of how civilized or cordial, it's really not at all pleasant. Especially as I thought . . . that is to say . . ."

"What?" He pulled her closer.

"I thought everything between us was, well,

quite, quite wonderful. Obviously I was wrong." She twisted free. "And I hate being wrong."

At once he realized what she was saying and laughed with the absurdity of it all.

"It's not the least bit funny," she snapped. "You don't like being wrong either."

"No, I don't." He grabbed her again and firmly pulled her into his arms. "And I rarely am. But you, dear Judith, are entirely wrong." He kissed her for a long moment until he felt the tension ease from her. "Do you want to know what you are wrong about?"

"Not especially," she said in a lofty manner. "Now let me go."

"I don't think so."

She tried to push out of his arms but he held her fast. "Do release me, my lord. It's for the best. I can certainly see that. If we part now, before, well, *before*, it would save us both—"

"I have no intention of parting now. I intend for us to be together for a very long time."

"But someday, when you marry—"

"Someday perhaps, but not now." He shook his head. "It was not my intention to end our relationship."

"It certainly sounded like—"

"Well, it wasn't." He kissed her again quickly. "In setting your boundaries, we had never discussed affection between us. Or the possibility of love. And that is what I wished to talk about."

"Oh." She paused. "That's entirely different then." She thought for a moment. "I misunderstood."

"No, you didn't. One misunderstands when a statement has been made and interpreted incorrectly. You never let me get the words out of my mouth. You, dear Judith"—he brushed his lips across hers—"jumped to unfounded conclusions.

"I suppose. Possibly—"

"There is no *possibly* about it." He chuckled. "You were wrong and I insist you admit it."

"I'd prefer not to." He could hear the smile in her voice. "It sets a nasty precedent." She paused. "Is there . . . affection between us?"

"I think so." *I hope so.*

"Or . . . love?"

"I don't know." He nuzzled the side of her neck. "But I should very much like to find out. Will you give me the opportunity to do so?"

"It seems only fair." Her voice had a slight breathless quality. "Although I'm not sure it wouldn't be a huge mistake. On both our parts."

"At the moment, I don't especially care."

"And when the moment passes and you come to your senses?"

"I shall never come to my senses," he murmured. And was it, in truth, inevitable that he do so? He was as unsure about that as anything else regarding this woman. The future wasn't even remotely clear. But he hadn't a doubt about tonight. "I would wager neither the queen nor anyone else would note our absence if we were to—"

"I know all the private corridors and passageways in Susanna's house." She reached up and kissed him softly, a promise as much as a kiss, and he wondered if she would always have this effect on him. "We can take our leave without drawing any attention whatsoever."

"Excellent." He kissed her once more, then released her, stepped to the door and pulled it open, then paused. "Oh, wasn't there something you wished to speak to me about as well?"

"There was but . . ." She smiled up at him. "It can wait." It was no doubt the light from the doorway reflecting in her eyes, but there was a warmth and a glow there that caught at his breath. Or his heart. "Let us be off."

Chapter 10

*A*unt Louisa burst into Gideon's library,
slammed the door closed behind her, and
flattened herself against it as if to hold back ma-
rauding armies determined to loot and plunder.

"I have always thought there was a useful purpose to having a library on a ground floor instead
of an upper level and I can see now I was right,"
Aunt Louisa said with the fervor of a temperance
worker.

Damnation. The last thing he needed at the moment was an overly dramatic scene with his aunt.
A letter he'd just received from his estate manager
indicated necessary repairs were proving more
complicated and more costly than initially assumed. Gideon was going to have to leave at once
for a quick trip to the country to assess the problems for himself. It couldn't be helped, he supposed.

He glanced up at his aunt. "I shall probably regret asking this, but what is the useful purpose to having a library on a ground floor?"

"Escape." She waved at the tall windows that marched along the back wall of the room. "It's scarcely any drop at all to the ground from here, while you could well break your neck climbing out of one of the upper-story windows."

"Indeed you could." As he well knew from his much younger days. "But I am at a loss as to why I should wish to escape by climbing out a window on any floor."

"Because"—she paused dramatically—"*she's* here."

Gideon drew his brows together. "Good Lord, Aunt, I know you do not think Lady Chester is—"

"Oh, not Lady Chester." Aunt Louisa scoffed. "Judith Chester is a virginal saint in comparison. I am speaking of"—she narrowed her eyes—"Lady Braxton"

"Lady Braxton is here? Now?"

"Indeed she is." She nodded at the window. "Quickly now, Gideon, go. Out the window with you. Before it's too late. You can spend the afternoon at your club. I shall send word when it's safe for you to return and I shall be happy to make your excuses to Lady Braxton. Indeed, I shall relish it."

"I have no intention of climbing out the window of my own home like a thief in the night." So Violet had come to see him? How very interesting. "I'm not going anywhere."

Aunt Louisa's eyes widened and she abandoned her position by the door and moved closer to his desk. "Are you insane?"

"I don't think so, although it is possible, I suppose."

"You're going to see her?"

"I have already seen her. Last night."

"Yes, I saw her as well although I didn't speak to her. Not that I had any desire to do so." She sniffed in disdain. "Apparently, now that she is a widow, she has taken up residence in London." She studied her nephew as if to gauge his reaction. "She has two children, you know, and gossip has it she is looking for a new husband."

"Gossip is not always as accurate as you might think."

She snorted. "Don't be absurd. I would trust the veracity of gossip long before I would believe anything I read in the papers." She eyed him carefully. "I do hope you are not considering having anything whatsoever to do with her."

"I do wish you would stop telling me who I may and may not see."

"This is entirely different, Gideon." She waved off his comment. "Lady Braxton is dangerous. She is a vile, vile creature who cannot be trusted. Lady Chester is quite charming and I think she has a good heart. She is simply . . . wrong."

"Nonetheless, I shall do as I think best."

"You don't think best when it comes to women. Honestly, Gideon, you're involved with one who has not been, shall we say *alone*, through widowhood—"

A mere three *adventures*, Lady Dinsmore had said last night. It was not at all what he would have thought—what he had thought—given Judith's reputation. Three lovers in ten years. To condemn her for that was certainly the pot calling the kettle black.

"And there is another on your doorstep who deceived you and has probably returned to do it again!"

"I sincerely doubt that." Still, it was curious that Violet had come to call. He rose to his feet. "It would be rude not to find out precisely what she does want."

"It wouldn't be the least bit rude," Aunt Louisa snapped. "It would be wise."

"I appreciate your concern, Aunt, misplaced though it may be."

"It's not misplaced and I—"

"However," he said firmly, "I am not the foolish young man I once was."

"You are still a man and men are always foolish when it comes to women."

"Probably." He chuckled. "Even so, I daresay I can hold my own. If you would be so good as to show Lady Braxton in, we shall see."

"We shall indeed." Her tone softened. "Don't say I didn't warn you."

"Oh, I would never say that."

"Do be careful, Gideon." Genuine concern shone in her eyes. In spite of her commanding manner and true belief that she and she alone knew what was best, her fears on his behalf were somewhat endearing. "I shall be in the parlor if you have need of me."

He grinned. "If I find myself in dire straits I shall surely call for rescue."

"You are not the least bit amusing, Gideon." She huffed, turned, and swept from the room.

Gideon blew a long breath. He wasn't at all sure he wished to have the confrontation Violet surely had in mind. She was very much in the past as far as he was concerned. Over and done with. Even so, it nagged at him that he hadn't mentioned her presence last night to Judith. It had seemed rather pointless, really. They were leaving the ball and there was no possibility Judith and Violet would encounter each other. And later, well, he had been preoccupied with much more delightful pursuits to consider anything the least bit unpleasant. He fully intended to mention Violet to Judith, probably when next he saw her. Still, he felt the oddest bit guilty about his failure to say anything. Silly, of course. It's not as if he were hiding something.

"Good day, Gideon." Violet sailed into the room as if she belonged there. "Who is that dragon who wanted to send me on my way? It was all I could do to get a servant to take my hat and cloak between her glaring and unconcealed disdain. She was obviously too well bred to say anything truly nasty but I did expect to see flames shoot out of her nostrils at any minute to roast me where I stood."

He stepped out from behind the desk. "That

dragon is my aunt. Did she fail to introduce herself?"

"Apparently she felt no introductions were necessary, although I didn't know you had an aunt. Let alone one who resided with you."

"I suspect there are a great many things about me you didn't know."

"Fewer than you might think." She smiled and held out her hand. He took it, barely brushed his lips across it, then tried to release her, but she held on to his hand. Violet stepped closer, scandalously closer, and gazed into his eyes. "How are you really, Gideon?"

"I told you last night. I am quite well. Really." He firmly disentangled himself from her and stepped back. "Why are you here?"

"That's extraordinarily blunt." She shook her head. "I'd rather hoped we could chat for a bit. I know you won't throw me out. You're far too civilized for that."

"I wouldn't wager on it if I were you." He studied her for a moment. "So you've come for a chat?"

"I thought it was past time for you and me to talk and this appears to be an excellent place for it." She glanced around the library. "I do so adore libraries. They simply reek of wisdom and men. And I have always loved this room."

He laughed shortly. "You have never been in this room."

"I shall love it from this day forward then." She cast him a brilliant smile. Charming and all too familiar.

A knock sounded at the door, and almost at once Wells appeared with a tea tray. As much as Aunt Louisa did not approve of Violet's presence, she would still feel obliged to offer refreshment.

"Excellent." Violet waved Wells to a side table. "Do set it there. I shall pour, so you may take your leave."

"As you wish, my lady." Wells followed Violet's instructions but cast a discreet questioning glance at Gideon. Gideon nodded slightly. It was pointless to counteract Violet's orders even if she had no business issuing them in his house. The butler set the tray on the table and then quietly left the room. Gideon had no doubt Wells would remain nearby, just as he was certain his aunt was doing exactly the same thing.

"Would you care for tea?" Violet stepped to the table and picked up the teapot.

"No, thank you." He propped his hip on a corner of the desk and folded his arms over his chest. "But please help yourself."

"Indeed I shall." She poured her tea and Gideon noted she played the part of mistress of the house very well. It was obvious that her face was not the only thing to have matured through the years. Violet moved to one of the two chairs positioned in front of his desk and sat down in a graceful manner without spilling so much as a drop. "You need more seating in here, Gideon. Perhaps a sofa or a settee or something along those lines."

"Are you quite through criticizing my library?"

"For the moment." She took a sip of her tea and

glanced up at him. "Are you going to stand there glowering at me?"

"Probably."

"It's most disconcerting, you know."

"I do know."

"I feel as if I were on trial," she murmured.

He raised a brow. "And are you prepared to tell the truth?"

"I have very little left to hide." She set her cup on the table between the two chairs and gazed up at him. "I owe you an apology, Gideon."

"An apology?" He stared in disbelief. "A mere apology?"

"Not the least bit *mere*. Admittedly a large apology." She rolled her gaze toward the ceiling. "I did you a dire disservice. Is that better?"

"I would scarcely call it a disservice." He forced the words out through clenched teeth. "You married me."

"That was not my intention." She shook her head. "I truly believed William and my father would find us before it went that far."

He could hardly believe his ears. The woman showed no remorse whatsoever. She acted as if the incident that had broken his heart was nothing more than a prank gone wrong. "When they didn't, you certainly could have stopped the ceremony. There was no need to go through with it."

"Again, in hindsight, that was a mistake. You said it yourself last night that young people make mistakes."

"Your actions could scarcely be called a mistake," he said coolly.

"I was mistaken in my judgment, which naturally led to my actions. However, at the time, I realized that you and I going off together had created a compromising situation that I would not have been able to survive, socially that is. Therefore I thought it would be best to marry you in case William and my father did not appear."

"You married me to save your reputation?" He tried and failed to keep his voice level.

"You needn't sound so shocked. Women marry to save their reputations and avoid scandal all the time. And it's not as if I didn't like you. I did, you know."

"You liked me." He could scarcely choke out the words.

"Of course, a great deal. I certainly could have chosen anyone else to, well . . ."

"Deceive? Betray? Mislead?"

"Assist me in my plans," she said in an almost prim manner. "However, from the beginning I did realize if something went awry—"

"If?" he sputtered. "If?"

"Yes, *if*. I certainly did not expect problems, however if they occurred, I could well end up married to the wrong man for the rest of my days. And I would not have minded being married to you at all. You were"—she smiled pleasantly—"my second choice. I daresay I could have been quite happy spending the rest of my days with you."

"Well, that makes all the difference then, doesn't it?"

"No, it doesn't. I realize now that I hurt you terribly. I heard you even became quite disreputable for a time." Her gaze slipped over him in an assessing manner. "I would have liked to have seen that."

He ignored the comment and the implication it carried. "Is this the apology then?"

"Yes, I think so." She thought for a moment, then nodded. "That's all I wish to say on that matter." She drew her brows together. "Is that good enough?"

"Hardly."

"Well, it sounded much better in the carriage on the way here," she murmured.

What did he expect? Violet was Violet after all, and Violet had always done what was best for Violet. At least that had been his experience. It struck him for the first time how little he really knew of her. Looking back on it, their *romance*—for lack of a better word—had been swift and had consumed him. Perhaps if he hadn't been so smitten with her, he would have kept his wits about him, but at the time he would have followed her to the moon. Now he couldn't quite remember why.

"So," she said brightly, "am I forgiven?"

He smiled in as pleasant a manner as he could muster and found it wasn't difficult to do so. "Absolutely not."

She huffed. "Do you plan on holding this against me for the rest of my life?"

"More than likely." He studied her for a moment. He would never truly get over what she'd done to him; in many ways it changed his life. But there was no longer pain associated with it. There was a residue of anger, and that might well always exist. But it had been years since he'd given her so much as a second thought. "However, you should know that I have put what happened between us in the past. I have put you in the past."

She lifted her chin. "I don't believe you."

"You should."

"I cannot imagine you did not know my husband had died or where I was in any given year." She met his gaze pointedly. "I knew where you were and what you were doing."

He said the first thing that came to mind. "In order to make your husband jealous?"

She shook her head. "That wasn't at all nice, Gideon."

She was right, the comment was beneath him. "My apologies. That was uncalled for."

She waved off his comment. "Yes it was. It was also most insightful of you. You have come in quite handy through the years."

"I'm glad I could be of service," he said wryly.

"Gideon." Her gaze met his. "I should like to be completely honest with you."

He snorted. "If that's possible."

"I have thought about you a great deal through the years. Not that my marriage was not a happy one," she added quickly. "I did not make a mistake in marrying William. However, the manner in which I forced him to face his feelings for me was cruel to you. I see that now. I should like to make it up to you."

"What?"

"I am free now, Gideon. And we are both far past the age of consent." She rose to her feet and stepped closer to him. Entirely too close for propriety. "I am a widow, and from what I hear you like widows—"

"I like one widow in particular." He resisted the urge to move away. She would surely see that as a sign of discomfort caused by desire for her. Not bloody likely. He held his ground. "Not widows in general."

"Pity." She considered him for a long moment, and at once he understood how a luncheon selection might feel. "I have decided to have a party, Gideon. Let us say a week from now. That should be enough time. Something to announce that my days of mourning are over and I am back in London. Small, intimate, nothing like last night's pretentious debacle."

"And yet your grandmother seemed to enjoy it."

"William's great aunt actually." She thought for a moment. "I will have to invite Susanna, I suppose, although she doesn't like me, she never has."

"Lady Dinsmore is an excellent judge of character."

She ignored him. "I shall have the invitations delivered tomorrow." Violet furrowed her brow in thought. "Possibly even today if I hurry."

"I'm afraid I must decline."

"I know what you're thinking, Gideon." She laughed. "You think I'm not inviting anyone else, don't you? That this is simply a plan to lure you into my evil grasp? Perhaps seduce you?"

"I admit the thought had occurred to me."

"Did you like it?" She gazed at him in an innocent manner he didn't believe for a second.

"No," he said simply.

"Pity it didn't occur to me, it's really quite brilliant. I should be happy to invite your widow if that's what I need to do to ensure your attendance."

"Even so—"

"Come now, Gideon." She sighed in annoyance. "I am trying to start my life anew here in London. I would prefer to do it without old gossip hovering about. If you do not attend my very first party, there will be talk as to why you didn't. The only way to show the world that we harbor no unpleasant feelings toward one another is for you to come."

"Perhaps."

"There is no *perhaps* about it. We can be polite, cordial, even friendly. That should quench any rumor about ill will between us."

He hadn't the slightest desire to attend a party given by Violet although it might be most entertaining. "I will consider it." He straightened. "Now then, if your apology, and I use the term loosely, is at an end, I must bid you good day. I have pressing matters of business I must attend to."

She hesitated. "Gideon."

He blew a long-suffering breath. "Yes?"

"I do wish to be honest with you."

"What an intriguing idea."

"Therefore I feel I should tell you I have found I do not like this business of being unmarried. I don't like having to manage my own affairs. I don't like not having a man about." She cast him a confident smile, and the hairs on the back of his neck rose. "I want a new husband, Gideon, and the one I want is you."

"Therein lies a problem," he said smoothly. "As I do not want you."

"Oh, but you will." She stepped closer to him. "I am quite willing to offer you now what I was not willing to give you before." She laid her hands lightly on his lapels and gazed into his eyes. "I am no longer an innocent virgin."

He firmly removed her hands from his coat. "You might well have been virginal but you were never innocent, my dear."

"It's my fault you're so cynical, isn't it? I did this to you. I do regret that. Well." She lifted a shoulder in an offhand shrug. "I shall have to do my best to make amends."

"Let us simply consider the matter over and done with."

"Oh, I couldn't possibly." A determined gleam shone in her violet eyes. "I don't like being alone, without a husband. I became used to marriage and I intend to be married again. And I warn you." She looked him straight in the eye. "I want you, Gideon, and I will have you."

"I should warn you as well, I am not the same youth who could be so easily fooled by a pretty face and a charming manner."

"I have no intention of fooling you." She leaned closer to him and lowered her voice in a seductive manner. "But I have every intention of making you again feel for me what you once did."

"And you shall fail." He smiled slowly. "Never again, Violet."

"We shall see." She turned and started for the door, then paused and looked back at him. "Do keep in mind, I wanted William and I let nothing, not even you, dear, dear Gideon, stand in the way of getting him. I am no less determined now." She smiled pleasantly. "Good day, Lord Warton." A moment later, she was gone.

"Good day, Lady Braxton," he murmured.

If he lived a hundred years, he never would have expected that particular conversation. Oh, certainly, in the beginning he had played their reunion scene in his mind where Violet had pleaded for his forgiveness, declared her undying love, and begged him to take her back. Naturally, he had then scorned her advances or he had graciously taken her back, depending upon his state of mind at the time.

Nine, eight, perhaps even seven years ago, her declaration that he was the one she wanted would have meant everything to him. Now it was no more than a matter of curiosity. Intriguing but not overly interesting. There were any number of feelings he had expected to have if this time ever came. He wasn't even sure if he was indeed still angry with her. Or if he cared at all. How very odd. There was a time when she was all he wanted in the world. Now all he wanted was Judith.

And what, precisely, did that mean?

He had no idea but it was past time to find out. He had told Judith he wanted to be with her for a very long time. What did that mean? Marriage? Marriage was never supposed to be part of this and yet . . .

A few days in the country would serve him well. He would have a chance to think clearly without his thoughts being clouded by her presence. When he returned he would know his own mind. And perhaps even his heart.

First, of course, they had to survive Violet's party. Judith and Violet in the same room did not seem especially wise. Still, Violet had a point. Ignoring her invitation would only fuel more gossip. His appearance at her soiree might well show the world there was nothing further between them. Especially with Judith on his arm.

Although the chances were just as good it could be a disaster of biblical proportions.

"So, even though you fully intended to tell him at the ball that Violet was back in London, you didn't?" Susanna perched on a stool in Judith's conservatory and watched her friend in a manner Judith thought was entirely too observant.

"It didn't seem necessary at the time." Judith glanced up from the plant she was repotting. "I am sorry we missed the queen though. It must have made the evening a rousing success."

"It always does but you didn't miss a great deal. She didn't stay very long, which was a relief to all concerned." Susanna drew her brows together thoughtfully. "It always seems to me, when I see

Her Majesty at any social event, that she looks the tiniest bit as if she would prefer to be dancing across the ballroom floor rather than being . . . royal. Of course, Prince Albert always looks the tiniest bit disapproving."

Judith smiled absently.

"And you didn't tell him about Violet yesterday either?"

"I never had the opportunity. He sent me a note saying he had to leave for the country on some sort of emergency involving his estate. It's awkward to tell the man you're involved with that the woman who broke his heart has returned." Judith shrugged. "Although by now I daresay he already knows."

"I think we all know. And I believe they spoke at the ball."

"I see." Judith kept her expression carefully composed. It was to be expected that Gideon might have spoken to Lady Braxton. And not especially odd that he would not have mentioned it. After all, she did not mention Lady Braxton's presence to him.

"Did you receive an invitation to her party?"

"It arrived this morning." Judith carefully dislodged the roots of the small fern. "I thought it surprising given that I've never met her."

"I don't think it's the least bit surprising. I think it's quite diabolical. Obviously she wants Lord Warton to come and is clever enough to realize he won't if you don't." Susanna sniffed in disdain. "Rather short notice for a party, I think, and highly suspicious as well. I would wager she's up to something." She studied her friend. "Did you know you have taken that same plant from one pot to another three times now?"

"Don't be absurd." Judith scoffed and looked down at the fern. "It's four times I think." She blew a long breath. "I don't know what's gotten into me. I can't seem to concentrate on the task at hand."

"Obviously your mind is elsewhere."

"Perhaps." Indeed her thoughts were squarely on Gideon's abrupt departure. His note had been brief and to the point. Almost curt, although she was probably reading more into it than he had intended. They had parted amicably enough the morning after Susanna's ball. Indeed the morning, as well as the night before, had been quite wonderful. But then it always was with Gideon. More and more she disliked every time they said goodbye, regardless of how long they would be apart. More and more she wanted . . . more and more. It was a ridiculous thought. There could never be more. She shook her to clear it. "I have sadly neglected the conservatory recently."

"For, oh, say, the last month or so?"

"For precisely the last month or so." Judith glanced around the glass room. "I had this built shortly after I returned here to live after Lucian's death. I have poured a great deal of my heart into it, and it in turn has sustained my soul through the years. There is a comfort I find here that I find nowhere else. In the way life flourishes. In the scents of earth and growth. And in the sound of water splashing in the fountain. Admittedly, the fountain is an affectation for a serious conservatory but I think the earth is not complete without water."

"How very philosophical of you."

"Not at all. I simply like fountains." Judith smiled and shook her head. "Beyond that, I consider it practical in many ways. It keeps the air moist. Water is as necessary as earth for life to flourish."

"And what of passion?"

Judith raised a brow. "Passion?"

"You have always had a great passion for this conservatory and these plants. Even love." Susanna chose her words with obvious care. "If they are neglected now, is it perhaps because that love is directed elsewhere?"

"They are not neglected, I misspoke," Judith said quickly. "I have highly skilled gardeners whose duties include tending to everything inside the conservatory in addition to the garden. What I do is little more than play."

"You did not answer my question."

"I'm not sure it needs an answer, although I will admit my attention of late has not been on the conservatory." How could it be? Every waking moment had been filled with thoughts of him. What had the man done to her? This was not supposed to happen. She was not supposed to feel as if her life was not complete without him. She was not supposed to feel anything at all about him save lust and perhaps friendship. She forced a casual note to her voice. "I am thinking about breaking it off with him."

Susanna stared. "Why?"

"I misunderstood what he was saying the other night. That, coupled with the knowledge of Lady Braxton's presence, led me to believe he was ending our relationship."

"You never jump to conclusions." Susanna narrowed her eyes thoughtfully. "Indeed, you have always been one of the most rational people I know."

"Past tense apparently." Judith shook her head. "And when I thought he was ending things, well, I did not like the feeling at all."

"No, I can't imagine you would." Susanna chuckled. "You have always been the one to decide when an adventure was over." She sobered. "Why end it with him now?"

"I've let it go on far too long as it is." Judith couldn't quite believe the casual note in her voice. As if discontinuing her relationship with Gideon didn't matter. When it mattered terribly. "It seems best for all concerned."

"I see." Susanna thought for a moment. "No, I don't."

"I would simply prefer to end it before anyone gets hurt." Judith didn't want to break it off with Gideon and perhaps if he hadn't left London, if he were here, she wouldn't have the time to think about it at all. His very presence would be reassuring. But when she'd misunderstood his intentions at the ball, she had felt something very much like the beginning of heartbreak. She would prefer to avoid that and end it with him before she reached a point where the pain would be unbearable. If indeed it wasn't already too late.

"Who?"

"I don't know who." Judith huffed. "Someone, anyone."

"Who?"

"Honestly, Susanna, you sound like an owl."

"Who?" Susanna said again firmly.

"Me," Judith snapped. "That's who."

"Why?"

"This is quite enough of—"

Susanna pressed. "Why?"

"Because I'm in love with him!" Judith glared. "There! Are you happy?"

"Not especially."

"It's what you wanted to hear, isn't it? It's what you've been trying to make me say."

"It's not at all what I wanted to hear," Susanna said quietly.

"That's right, you don't like him. You thought our being together was a mistake."

"If you recall, I thought your being together was a mistake because I feared you would be hurt," Susanna said slowly. "I have changed my mind."

"About my being hurt?"

"No, about Warton himself."

"Of course you have." Judith brushed dirt off the apron she wore over her dress. "He's charming. How could you not like him?"

"Not about that although I do agree, he's really very nice. Surprisingly so. But that's not what I meant." Susanna met her friend's gaze. "I have changed my mind about you and him being together. He makes you happy, Judith. I'm not sure I have ever seen you truly happy before."

"Nonsense." Judith waved away the comment. "I am usually happy. Indeed, I am an extraordinarily happy person all in all."

"No," Susanna said carefully, "you are a very private person."

"One can be private and happy. One does not preclude the other."

"Possibly, I suppose." Susanna slid off the stool, clasped her hands behind her back, and wandered idly toward several glossy-leaved jasmine trees. "Do you realize . . ." She leaned forward to sniff a pristine white blossom, her tone suspiciously offhand. "In the long years you and I have been friends you have rarely mentioned your husband or your marriage."

"Haven't I?" Judith absently removed the fern from its present pot and replaced it where it had been before. "Well, we were very young. We married. Three years later he died."

Susanna straightened and glanced at her. "It sounds like a recitation, Judith. An exercise in memorization."

"There's little more to say."

"I have talked about my husband a great deal since his death."

"Yes, you do tend to go on," Judith said in a manner sharper than she intended and immediately regretted her words. "I am sorry, Susanna. I wouldn't offend you for the world."

"I am not offended at all." Susanna smiled wryly. "I do speak of Charles and our life together more frequently than I should. Silly, I know, but it keeps him alive for me." She shook her head.

"With each passing year, the things that I wish to remember fade. The sound of his laughter, the touch of his hand, the feel of his kiss. I live in terror that one day I will not remember anything at all, and the void that he left in my life will consume me."

Judith's heart caught. "Dear Lord, Susanna, I had no idea."

"Nor should you. It is . . ." She smiled. "Private." Susanna drew a deep breath. "But we are speaking of you now."

"Must we?" Judith said with a weak smile.

Susanna studied her for a moment. "I've watched you through all three of your adventures, Judith. You carry on a long flirtation, then you allow the gentleman of the moment to share your bed a time or two, then you discard him."

Judith waved away the observation. "It was never serious with any of them."

"They could have become serious. Every man you've been involved with has cared for you. Indeed, two of the three are as yet unmarried. They could have loved you given time and encouragement but you would not permit it."

"Nonsense. I—"

"You've always ended it before it had the opportunity to become something special. Something permanent." Susanna's gaze met Judith's. "You run away, Judith."

"Don't be absurd. Why, I scarcely travel at all."

"That's not what I mean and you know it." Susanna shook her head. "You flee from anything that might smack of serious emotion."

Judith stared. "Susanna, I scarcely think—"

"You run away," Susanna said firmly, "by refusing to let any *adventure* become more than superficial. I admit, I do it as well. I suspect I run away by indulging in spirits entirely more than I should. You fill your empty life with all this." She waved in a wide gesture at the plants surrounding them. "I fill mine with my family and nieces and nephews. In spite of that, I am the loneliest woman I know." Her gaze locked with Judith's. "Except for you."

"I'm not the least bit lonely." The moment she said the words, Judith knew they were a lie. There was an aching, empty lonely hole inside her that had been filled recently by the man she could never have. "Why, I have lots of friends."

"You have acquaintances. People to share an evening with, to converse with at social gatherings, or to discuss the various aspects of orchids or exotic plants. To fill your house in the country at those extravagant parties you host. You have people who amuse you and occupy your time and your mind but never, never your heart."

"I have you."

"And I have you." Susanna heaved a heartfelt sigh. "And we are not enough."

"Have you ever considered that there might be people who are destined to spend their lives alone?" Judith chose her words carefully. "I have no real family. My parents are gone. My husband is dead. The only true relation I have is a sister-in-law who cannot abide my very presence. Perhaps I'm . . . cursed."

Susanna raised a skeptical brow.

"Not cursed then but perhaps some of us are fated to be alone in this world."

Susanna stared in disbelief. "If I believed that, Judith, if I thought for so much as a moment that I was destined to live the rest of my life alone, I would fling myself under a carriage this very day and end it all. The only thing that keeps me sane is the thought that someday I shall find a man who will love me, a man I can love as I did my husband." She shook her head. "You and I are very much alike in our circumstances but I am not willing to give up hope. And you shouldn't be either."

"Hope?"

"Hope." Susanna blew a long breath. "I will tell you this, cousin, if I ever meet a man who could make me feel the way Lord Warton makes you feel I shall not let him out of my sight."

Judith stared at the other woman. "What would you have me do, Susanna? There is no future for us. We agreed at the beginning that marriage was not a consideration."

"Agreements can be broken." Susanna snorted. "And why isn't marriage a consideration?"

"I'm not the kind of wife he needs, nor am I what he wants in a wife. He can't marry me."

"We're back to that, are we?"

"You said it yourself. He needs the kind of wife I could never be."

"Well, I'm an idiot. I don't know anything. Anyone will tell you that. Judith." Susanna leaned toward her. "The man is a handsome, wealthy viscount. He can do whatever he bloody well pleases."

Judith widened her eyes at the obscenity. "Susanna!"

"Oh for goodness' sakes, Judith, you needn't look at me like that." Susanna rolled her gaze heavenward. "I just find this all so annoying. He makes you happy. You love him. There's no reason why you can't be together."

"You have forgotten a few minor points." Judith ticked them off on her fingers. "He hasn't said it but I think my past bothers him more than he lets on."

"And he's been saving himself for marriage? Hardly." Susanna huffed. "You are a widow. You have been most discreet. There's never been a real scandal associated with you. Whereas he ran off, wed, and the marriage was annulled. Now that was a scandal."

"It was kept very quiet," Judith murmured.

"It wasn't kept that quiet. Add to that the fact that he spent the next year or so in highly disreputable behavior—why, you should be the one bothered by his past."

"He's reformed."

"And, as of the moment you met him, you reformed."

"I have a certain reputation."

"It makes you interesting, besides, you've reformed remember? So." Susanna crossed her arms over her chest. "What else?"

"Gideon has never spoken of marriage. As for love . . ." Judith raised a shoulder in a helpless shrug. "I don't know what his feelings are. I'm not sure that he knows."

"Admittedly that is a hurdle to overcome. Obviously, you do need to find out if your feelings are returned."

"Obviously." How did Gideon feel? He'd said there was affection between them but he was uncertain about love. He'd also said he wished to be with her for a very long time. What did that really mean? Susanna was right. It would be foolish not to find out before she did anything irreparable.

"Promise me you will not do anything rash, you will not break it off with him without finding out how he truly feels." Susanna took Judith's hands and gazed into her eyes. "Promise me you will at least think about the possibility of spending the rest of your life with him."

"Dear Susanna." Judith cast her a weak smile. "I'm afraid I've thought of little else."

Chapter 11

"$\mathcal{I}$ would scarcely call this a small, intimate gathering." Gideon's gaze skimmed the crowded ballroom.

"There are at least sixty people here." Judith's gaze followed his. "Why did you think it would be small?"

"That's what Violet—Lady Braxton—said when she told me about this."

"Really." Judith paused. "When did you see Lady Braxton?"

"The day I left London. A week ago."

"You never mentioned it," she said in a casual manner. Entirely too casual.

"As I have been in the country and only returned today, I have not yet had the opportunity to say scarcely anything to you." He grinned down at her. "One might think you were jealous if one didn't know better."

"Then it is fortunate that one knows better," she said in a lofty manner.

Gideon chuckled. His apprehension about tonight was probably unfounded. They had gone through the receiving line upon their arrival without mishap. Much to his relief, Judith and Violet had met without the slightest hint of anything other than polite demeanor on either side. Of course, regardless of what either woman was thinking, there wouldn't be anything but the height of cordiality between them. Still, it was bloody awkward introducing your current lover to your former, well, *wife*. Particularly when said former wife wished to renew your previous relationship.

As for any decision about his relationship with Judith, he had come to the brilliant realization that no decision was necessary. There was no pressing need to decide anything at the moment. Why couldn't they go along as they had been? He felt a deep affection for her that might or might not be love. Indeed, the days away from her had seemed a lifetime. She had lingered in the back of his mind every waking moment and had been with him in his dreams at night. But he had felt what he'd thought was love before. Only recently had he realized it might not have been love at all. It might have been his pride as much as his heart that was shattered. Odd, until he'd seen Violet again, he'd never questioned whether what he'd felt for her was love. It was disquieting to realize he might not recognize love even when he found it. Yet another reason to continue with Judith exactly as they had been. The acknowledgment of love, if indeed this was love, could wait.

"What an unusual combination of people," Judith said more to herself than to him.

"Do you think so?" The gathering didn't seem the least bit unusual to him and not particularly interesting either. There were a number of people here that he knew and probably even more that Judith knew. "I see Lord and Lady Helmsley are here." He nodded at the couple on the far side of the room and said the first thing that came into his mind. "Is it odd, to see him with her?"

"Odd?" She glanced up at him.

"Well, you and he were—"

She laughed. "It's not the least bit odd."

He winced. "I shouldn't have said that."

"No, you shouldn't have but you are forgiven." She shrugged. "I suppose it's only natural for you to wonder about my feelings." She drew a deep breath. "It might be of interest to you to know that Jonathon and I were always better friends than we were anything else."

"So I've heard," he said more to himself than to her.

"Certainly there was an amusing flirtation between us that continued through the years but it was never . . ." She shook her head. "Important, I would say, serious, that is, in any way aside from friendship. I quite value his friendship and Lady Helmsley's as well. In truth, I encouraged him to pursue her. And I assisted her to pursue him in return." Her gaze returned to the newly wed couple. "They look extraordinarily happy, don't they?"

"I can't tell if you're smug or jealous," he said in a teasing manner.

"Oh, I am definitely proud of the role I played. As for jealous, perhaps I am. Or at the very least envious." There was a touch of longing in her voice so slight, Gideon thought he might have been mistaken. He resisted the urge to take her in his arms right here in front of Violet and everyone else and kiss her until the ache of longing became the demand of desire. "To be so in love with someone that happiness fairly glows from you like a beacon of light in the darkness. And to know that love will light your way for the rest of your days. That is indeed something to provoke envy."

"They are fortunate to have found one another," he murmured and realized he too was envious. And it struck him without warning that he needn't be. Perhaps he didn't need to make a decision about his relationship with Judith because he already had. Perhaps all he needed to do was to acknowledge it to himself. And, of course, to her.

Behind him, a throat cleared. "Lady Chester? Judith?"

Gideon turned to find a fair-haired man, slightly shorter than himself, grinning in a decidedly lopsided manner at Judith.

"Harry!" Judith favored the newcomer with an affectionate smile and held out her hands to him. "What a delightful surprise. The last I'd heard you were traveling the Orient."

"I was." *Harry* chuckled. "But I am home now for good."

"How wonderful. I know you have been missed. Do you know one another?" Judith said, pulling her hands from *Harry's*, who seemed annoyingly reluctant to let her go.

"Only by reputation." Harry nodded briefly at Gideon. "You're Lord Warton, aren't you?"

"I am." Gideon forced a polite smile. He wasn't sure why but he didn't like this man. He particularly didn't like the way he gazed at Judith as if she were a platter of rare roast beef and he was a meat-starved man. "And you are?"

"Lord Warton, allow me to introduce Lord Mountford," Judith said. "Lord Mountford is a very old friend."

"A very good friend," Mountford said firmly.

"I stand corrected. Old and good." Judith laughed. Gideon didn't like that either.

"Do you mind, old man, if I steal her away for a dance?" Mountford's words were directed at Gideon but his gaze was fixed on Judith. "We have a great deal of reminiscing to do."

Yes, I bloody well do!

Judith raised a brow. "Gideon?"

"No, of course not," Gideon said with a polite smile.

"Excellent." Mountford beamed and offered his arm to Judith.

Judith cast Gideon a curious look as if she knew exactly what he was thinking, then took Mountford's arm and allowed him to escort her to the dance floor. And *that* Gideon liked even less than anything else.

Damn it all, he was jealous. Jealous! Of this *old friend*. This *very good old friend*. That's what it was: pure and simple jealousy. He recalled jealousy back when he had fancied himself in love with Violet. At a ball very similar to this one he distinctly remembered this nasty, wrought-up feeling when she'd danced with her fiancé. Still, this was entirely different. He wasn't jealous that Judith was dancing with someone else, although he wasn't especially pleased by it, but that that someone else shared a history with her that Gideon did not.

"Oh dear, I see I'm too late." Lady Dinsmore stepped up beside him and stared at Judith on the dance floor.

"Too late for what?" Gideon said slowly.

"To warn Judith, of course."

"Warn Judith of what?"

"Well, Lord Mountford is here. She hasn't seen him in years, you know."

"Apparently," Warton said dryly. "They are very old friends."

"I suppose you could call him a friend." Lady Dinsmore thought for a moment. "Yes, *friend* would be appropriate, I think. Nor has she seen Viscount Nottingdon who is also apparently in attendance this evening."

Gideon raised a brow. "Yet another old friend?"

Lady Dinsmore nodded. "And then there's Lord Helmsley." Her brow furrowed. "Although she does see him on occasion. They are good friends after all."

"Yes, yes, I know. Good friends, old friends, the woman is surrounded by friends." He blew a long breath. "But as they are friends, I'm afraid I don't understand your concern."

"No, you wouldn't, would you?" Lady Dinsmore sighed. "It's quite lovely to run into old friends or old acquaintances or old what-have-you when you are expecting to see them, and something altogether different to come upon them unawares. For example, you weren't at all pleased to come face to face with Violet without warning, were you?" She smiled in an all-too-innocent manner.

Gideon stared. "How did you know about that?"

"You poor man." She shook her head in a pitying manner. "Everyone who was there knows about it."

"Does Judith know?"

"She didn't at the time but she certainly does now. It's not something you can keep a secret, you know. A meeting in the middle of a large crowd does not go unnoticed." Lady Dinsmore studied him for a moment. "You haven't mentioned it to her, have you?"

"I haven't had the opportunity," he said in a lofty manner and ignored the guilt that stabbed him. He had had the chance, he'd just preferred not to take it at the time.

"You should find the opportunity as soon as possible. Not revealing an encounter with someone from your past to someone who is very much sharing your present is a mistake fraught with the possibility of disaster. Especially when the someone from your present already knows about it."

He bit back a smile at the stern nature of her warning. Still, she was right. "I appreciate the advice, Lady Dinsmore."

"No you don't." Her gaze returned to the dancers. "I daresay this is no coincidence."

"What is not a coincidence?"

"These old friends of Judith's all being at the same gathering with you. A gathering hosted by a woman who is determined to get what she wants."

He stared at her curiously. "I can't say that I see the significance of friends of Judith's being here. Judith knows a great many . . ."

Not that this is at all like any of her other three adventures.

"Mountford, Nottingdon, and Helmsley?" He stared at Lady Dinsmore. "*Three* old friends? And you said she's had *three* adventures?"

"You promised to forget that," she said pointedly.

"I lied," he snapped.

"Imagine my surprise." Her gaze met his firmly. "Do you mind if I confess something to you?"

"I live for confessions from beautiful women," he said without thinking. *Three old friends?*

"If you're going to attempt to sway a woman with compliments you should try to sound more sincere."

"Probably," he muttered.

She studied him in a far too thorough manner. "I was looking for Judith to tell her of the unusual nature of the guests invited here tonight. I did see her leave your side to dance with Lord Mountford."

"So you deliberately told me that Judith's former friends were here?" he said slowly.

"Forewarned is forearmed, my lord."

"And you were warning me?" He did appreciate it, as odd as it seemed. He had a hard enough time coping with the fact of Judith's past relationship with Helmsley. Putting faces to the rest of Judith's adventures would be difficult indeed. "Why?"

"In many ways, Judith is just like any woman. A touch of jealousy in the man she cares for is relished." Lady Dinsmore paused. "However, more than that she considers . . . unpleasant. She has never said it, but I have always suspected it has something to do with her late husband. I suspect as well it is the surest way to lose her entirely."

"I shall struggle to keep my emotions under control," he said wryly.

"You have nothing to be jealous of save the past, and frankly, my lord, what's done cannot be undone."

"I shall try to avoid fisticuffs and I doubt that there is a dueling pistol lying about here anywhere."

"You may joke about this as much as you wish but do heed my warning." She stared at him. "Are you in love with her?"

"That's really none of your concern, is it?" he said mildly.

"On the contrary. Judith is my dearest friend. Her happiness is of great concern to me. Of late, she has been happier than I have ever seen her." She met his gaze firmly. "If you are not in love with her, I would hope that you would end things with her before it is too late. I have never seen Judith's heart broken. Indeed, she has guarded against that very thing through the years. I should hate to see it happen now."

"And if I am in love with her?"

"Then it seems to me you have a number of decisions to make. Not all of them particularly pleasant, I would think."

He studied her thoughtfully. "You care for her a great deal, don't you?"

She nodded. "She is as close to me as a sister. And, more often than not, I like her far better than I like my own sisters."

"Although I daresay she would not appreciate your telling me about the friends of hers here tonight."

"One does things for those one cares about that are not always to their liking, yet for their welfare all the same." She shrugged. "I have her best interests at heart."

He smiled. "She is lucky to have you."

"I hope I can say the same about you." Lady Dinsmore cast him a brilliant smile. "Now then, my lord, I should like nothing better than to dance."

"Then allow me the honor." He extended his arm and escorted her onto the floor.

He took Lady Dinsmore in his arms and, as they moved around the floor, he caught a glimpse of Judith with *Harry*. Gideon firmly ignored the annoyance that stabbed him at the sight of Judith laughing up at the not unattractive but definitely too short gentleman who held her entirely too close.

He did appreciate Lady Dinsmore's warning, it would not do to be caught unawares by Judith's past, but what was the woman thinking? He was not some callow youth who would fly into a jealous rage at the sight of Judith's former lovers. Certainly, his immediate impulse at the moment was to rip Judith from Mountford's arms and drag her away, but he could hold rein on his emotions. He was a civilized man after all. And yes, he had experienced some jealousy earlier in the evening and he did find the fact of her relationship with Helmsley somewhat bothersome, but he was certainly the master of his own feelings. Perhaps once he had allowed his emotions to rule his behavior but this was a different time, a different woman, and he was an entirely different man.

Besides, Judith was his now. Why, hadn't Lady Dinsmore just said Judith cared about him? He caught sight of her across the ballroom and tried to ignore the question that thundered in his head and perhaps in his heart, a question that had nothing whatsoever to do with jealousy.

Judith was his now, wasn't she?

"You are exactly as I remember you, Judith." Harry escorted Judith off the dance floor and managed to gaze into her eyes at the same time. But then Harry had always been talented if she remembered correctly. "You have not changed a bit."

"I do hope I have changed somewhat." She shook her head in a mock serious manner. "It wouldn't do to remain the same year after year after year. I think it would make a person frightfully dull."

"You're right, of course." Harry laughed, then sobered. "It's been a very long time."

"Not that long." Judith shrugged off the comment. "Five years or so I should think."

"Five years is a lifetime to be away from people you care for," he said in a firm manner.

"I would imagine so." There was something about him, something about the look in his eye that struck her as odd. No, not odd. Optimistic. Of course, she could be mistaken. Nonetheless, a tiny voice in the back of her head urged her to proceed carefully. "You have a rather extensive family if I recall. It must be difficult to spend so much time away from them."

"Yes, of course, but my family is not who I was referring to." He cast her a meaningful glance.

Judith laughed lightly as if he had just said something most amusing. Good Lord! Surely Harry couldn't be thinking there was a possibility of renewing their relationship? Shortly after she had ended their adventure, he had taken to traveling to India and the Orient and, from what she'd heard, had increased his family's fortune significantly. She had not seen him more than once or twice in passing since their days together, although she had not especially avoided him. However, avoiding his apparent intentions now seemed the wisest course. "Have you been back in England very long?"

"Nearly a year. Judith." He gazed at her with an earnestness that was disquieting. "We have a great deal to talk about."

She kept a pleasant smile on her face. "Do we?"

"Indeed we do."

"Harry." She chose her words carefully. Harry was a very nice man and she would not offend him for the world. However, there was an eager note in his voice, a fervent gleam in his eye that only a blind and deaf woman would fail to recognize. "I am fairly certain we said everything we needed to say to one another years ago."

"So was I." He grinned. "You can well imagine my surprise."

"Your surprise?" She arched a brow. "Why on earth would you be surprised?"

"You're right." He chuckled. "I shouldn't have been the least bit surprised. Fate and all that. Judith." He gazed deeply into her eyes. "I must talk to you alone. Surely there is a terrace or library or unused parlor or somewhere where we can speak privately."

"I have no idea." *And no intention of going anywhere with you alone.* "I believe this was Lady Braxton's parents' house and I have never been here before. However." She slanted a quick glance at the dance floor. Gideon was still dancing with Susanna and there would be no rescue from that quarter at the moment. "Why don't you . . . go.

Yes, that's good." She waved him away. "Go, see what you can find. Regarding a private location, that is. I shall wait for you here."

"Better yet, why don't you come with me?"

"I think it would be best if I were to remain here." She leaned toward him in a confidential manner. "Gossip, you know."

He scoffed, "If I recall, you were never overly concerned with gossip."

"There you have it." She beamed at him. "I have changed."

"Yes, well, I suppose." He eyed her longingly. It might have been most flattering under other circumstances. Or five years ago. But they had had their adventure, it was in the past, and she preferred to leave it there. "You will stay here, then?"

"Most certainly," she lied. "Riveted to this very spot."

"Excellent. I shall return shortly." He took a step toward her as if he were about to take her in his arms right there in front of the world.

She wagged her finger at him. "Gossip, remember?"

"Yes, of course." He sighed deeply, cast her one last yearning look, then turned and headed toward the main doorway.

"Do take your time," she said under her breath and stared after him. What on earth had gotten into Harry? And whatever was he surprised about? Whenever she had seen him through the years they had been pleasant enough to each other, even friendly, but he had never before looked at her with the eagerness of an unrepentant puppy.

"Champagne?" A waiter's voice sounded beside her.

"Yes, thank you," she said absently and accepted an offered glass. There was definitely something odd here and she wasn't at all sure if she wanted to find out what it was or flee. At the very least, she certainly wouldn't be waiting when Harry returned, although she couldn't let him believe there was the tiniest chance of a reunion between the two of them. What she needed was something to distract him. And what Harry needed was a nice woman who would make a nice wife. Not Judith, of course, but someone. Surely there was someone she could introduce him to. Preferably someone in this very room. It wouldn't do to let Harry go on thinking—

"I never really understood what you saw in him."

"He's very nice and quite amusing when you— what?" She jerked her head toward the waiter and groaned. "Dear Lord, not you."

Samuel, Viscount Nottingdon, grinned down at her. "Is that any way to greet an old friend?"

She stared at him for a moment, then favored him with a reluctant smile. "No, of course not. Your appearance simply caught me by surprise."

"Did it? I thought it might." He chuckled and sipped his wine.

Unlike Harry, her path and Samuel's had crossed on a regular basis during the three years since their adventure had ended. They were now and again at the same ball or party, usually those so large the crush of people prevented anything more between them than a smile or a nod or the brief exchange of pleasantries. For the most part, Samuel had always kept his distance. Judith was under no illusion that he did so because she had broken his heart or anything of that nature. They had parted long before anyone's heart could be at risk. But, as always, she had been the one to end it. She'd always thought it was more a matter of pride with him than anything else.

"It is good to see you see, Samuel."

"Is it?" He raised a brow. "Why?"

"It is always good to see an old friend," she said smoothly.

"You're lying and you were never very good at it." He sipped his wine and studied her.

"On the contrary, my lord." She grinned in spite of herself. "I've always been quite an accomplished liar."

"No, Judith, an accomplished liar would have made me feel as if I were the one ending it with her. You are annoyingly candid. Kind but honest." He heaved an overly dramatic sigh. "However, you did teach me never to fall in love with a kind but honest woman."

"Now you are talking nonsense," she scoffed. "You never fell in love with me."

"No, of course not," he said wryly. "I am not that foolish." He chuckled. "Nor were you foolish enough to fall in love with me."

"That would indeed be foolish." Relief swept through her and she took a long swallow of her champagne. At least Samuel, unlike Harry, had no illusions about what their relationship had been or could be now. Harry's behavior still made absolutely no sense.

"However, I do suspect someone thinks foolishness is in the air."

Judith drew her brows together in confusion. "What on earth do you mean by that?"

He considered her carefully. "You really had no idea I would be here tonight, did you?"

She shook her head. "Why would I?"

"There's something you should know," he said slowly. "However, I think it would be best for all concerned if we continued this discussion in private rather than here in the ballroom."

She narrowed her gaze and studied him. "You are not the first gentleman this evening to suggest a more private setting to speak with me."

"And I can't imagine I should be the last." He cast her a wicked grin.

"I'm not sure if I can trust you."

"You can't, of course, not for a moment." He met her gaze directly. "I wouldn't."

She smiled slowly. "Do you promise not to declare your undying love for me?"

He hesitated for so slight a time, she wasn't certain it had happened at all, then grinned. "Absolutely not."

She sighed in an exaggerated manner. "I suppose then it's a risk I shall have to take." She glanced around the ballroom and did not see either Gideon or Susanna. No matter, really. She would not be gone long. She drew a deep breath and looked at Samuel. "Well, where shall we go?"

He nodded at a different door from the exit

Harry had taken. "Out that door and down the corridor to the right, there is a billiards room. I shall meet you there."

She frowned. "Might not someone be playing billiards?"

"I would doubt it." He shook his head. "Lady Traverston, Lady Braxton's mother, never liked billiards, or rather never liked the way her husband and his companions gathered in the billiards room. The very existence of the room was apparently the subject of some dissension between herself and Lord Traverston. When he died, he left specific instructions that the table was not to be disturbed, and it wasn't." He grinned. "But Lady Traverston had the balls, the cues, and everything pertaining to the game removed."

She laughed. "How do you know that?"

"You'd be surprised at the things I know." He nodded toward the door. "We'll leave the ballroom separately to avoid undue gossip, and I shall join you in a moment."

"Very well." Judith discreetly made her way to the door and from there to the billiards room. She said a brief prayer of gratitude that the large room was empty save for a number of masculine-looking chairs, an intricately carved billiards table, and the faintest hint of long ago cigar smoke. The last thing she wanted was to come upon Harry while waiting to meet Samuel. And then there was Gideon to consider, although with any luck at all, she would be back in the ballroom before he noticed she was gone. Not that it really mattered. If she had seen him she would have invited him to join them.

Even so, she wasn't the least bit worried about meeting Samuel alone. There was something in his manner that indicated that his request to speak with her privately was sincere. Not that Harry wasn't sincere. She grimaced. She still couldn't imagine why Harry had decided there could be something between them again. She'd done nothing to encourage him. Why, she hadn't even seen him for longer than she could remember.

"My apologies for not being here sooner." Samuel stepped into the room and closed the door behind him. "I ran into Mountford in the corridor and pointed him in another direction."

"I am most grateful." She blew a relieved breath. "I have no idea what has gotten into him. Lord Mountford has always been so rational. But he seemed to think that he and I . . ." She shook her head. "Suffice it to say, he was under a misassumption. The question is why."

"I believe I have the answer to that." Samuel chose his words carefully. "As discreet as you've always been, it would not be at all difficult to identify those men who have been involved with you."

"Don't be absurd," she scoffed. "I've had flirtations with any number of men through the years."

"Yes, but those you have—what is the word you use?" He thought for a moment. "Ah yes, *adventures* with is substantially smaller. I had long ago determined I was the third of your adventures although I daresay Warton is number four."

She stared in disbelief. "How did you—no—why did you—"

"Nothing more than simple observation, Judith." His voice held a stern note. "Do not make more of it than that. We parted as friends and I should like to remain friends. I make a very loyal friend."

"There isn't a doubt in my mind." It was quite wonderful to realize that a man she'd been intimate with thought enough of her to remain her friend. She cast him a warm smile. "And I am most grateful for that friendship."

"As to the matter at hand." He leaned back against the billiards table and braced his hands on either side. "When I received the invitation to Lady Braxton's party I was surprised but not overly so. My mother and hers were great friends, and I've known Violet much of my life although I've never known her particularly well. Fortunately, my mother realized at an early age that her son and the daughter of one of her dearest friends would never suit so she did not push me in that direction." He shuddered. "Thank God. But that's how I knew the story of the billiards room." He glanced around the room and shook his head. "Pity."

"Go on."

"At the bottom of the invitation Lady Braxton had written that you would be here—"

Judith stared. "What?"

"—and that you were looking forward to renewing our acquaintance." He drew his brows together. "Or words to that effect. I would wager Mountford's invitation was similar although as Helmsley is now married, it probably suited Violet's purposes simply to have him present."

Judith stared, stunned. "I don't understand."

He snorted. "I understood the moment I saw you and Warton tonight."

"Then be so kind as to explain it to me."

"It's painfully obvious to anyone who sees the two of you together that you are in love with him."

"I'm not—"

"And furthermore, he is in love with you."

"Don't be . . ." She paused. "Do you really think so?"

"Indeed I do." He laughed in a dry manner. "As someone who thought, if only for a moment, that you might just be . . . well, it scarcely matters." He shook his head. "I was fairly certain you had no knowledge of what Lady Braxton had written on the invitation. It simply wasn't the way you do things." He met her gaze firmly. "If you had wished to renew our relationship you would not have gone through a third party. You would have come to me directly."

She raised a brow. "Is that a compliment?"

"Absolutely. A man likes to know where he stands with a woman, and one thing I will say about you, my dear." He chuckled. "From beginning to end, I always knew where I stood."

She winced. "I'm afraid I wasn't very straightforward with Lord Mountford this evening, but he caught me unawares. I cannot believe that Harry would think . . ." She shook her head, then glanced at Samuel. "You're much more perceptive than Harry."

"Perhaps." He shrugged. "Or simply more realistic."

Judith thought for a moment. "Why would she do something like that?"

"Do you know Lady Braxton at all?"

She shook her head. "We met for the first time tonight."

"But you do know about her and your Lord Warton?"

"He's not my Lord Warton," she murmured. But Lady Braxton might very well wish for Gideon to be her Lord Warton. And hadn't Susanna said Lady Braxton had set her sights on him?

"He gives an excellent impression of being your Lord Warton. Which is precisely why Violet would pull a stunt like this."

"Confronting me with the mistakes of my past?" He raised a brow.

"I didn't mean mistakes exactly," she said quickly.

He chuckled. "I know what you meant. But I don't think you were Violet's intended target. Judith." Samuel straightened and took her hands in his. "No man, no matter how intelligent or rational, likes the thought that the woman he loves has had a life of any sort whatsoever before him, let alone *adventures*. For the most part, that previous existence can be ignored. We men are foolish that way. We can easily pretend something has no substance if we cannot see it for ourselves. So, to have all of your fellow *adventurers* in the same room with you at the same time—"

"Would not only bring home to Lord Warton the reality of my past but would point out as well how very wrong for him I really am," she said slowly.

"Warton would come to his senses regarding you and—"

"Turn to her." Judith blew a long breath. "That's quite brilliant of her."

"I wouldn't call it brilliant."

"But it is. She didn't need to do much of anything save throw us all together and see what happens. Why, she scarcely needed to dirty her hands with this little plot. It is indeed brilliant." Judith gritted her teeth. "It is also, of course, diabolical, vicious, and more than a little mean."

He grinned. "And you'll make her pay for it, won't you?"

"I shall certainly try. If for no other reason than what she's done to Harry, poor dear man." She thought for a moment. "How, of course, is the question."

"You know what the French say?" His gaze caught hers. "About success being the best revenge?"

She smiled slowly. "That's good, Samuel, that's very good."

"Thank you," he said modestly. "Judith, I am not one to give advice on the matters between men and women. Lord knows, I have not been overly successful in that field myself. But I would advise you to take your Lord Warton—"

"He's not—"

"—and flee. Violet will not rest until she gets what she wants."

Judith laughed, "I'm not going anywhere. London is my home."

"Then marry him."

"I am not suited for marriage." She shook her head. "I tried marriage once, and once was quite enough."

"Perhaps you did not try it with the right man?"

"Nonsense. I loved my husband and my husband loved me," she said without thinking.

"And now you love someone else. It's not a sin, you know." Samuel's gaze searched hers. "If you had ever looked at me the way you look at him, I would never have let you go."

"Samuel." Judith widened her eyes. "What you and I shared was never intended to be serious."

"No, that was clear from the beginning. I did not expect more. However, I suspect what you now share with Warton was not intended to be serious and yet it has become so, hasn't it?"

She stared at him for a long moment and then smiled weakly. "I'm afraid so."

"Admittedly, you have lived your life in a somewhat unconventional manner. A little bit wicked perhaps but you have harmed no one. If he cannot accept that, if he does not love you enough . . ." He squeezed her hands. "Then it's not you who are not worthy of him but he who is not worthy of you."

Her breath caught at his words. "My lord, you are a wonderful man."

"Indeed I am." He grinned. "Pity you didn't realize that years ago. Well, your loss shall be some other lucky woman's gain."

"She will be lucky indeed," Judith said with a

laugh, impulsively leaned forward, and brushed a quick kiss across his lips.

"If I were a jealous man, I would be locating dueling pistols at this point," a familiar wry voice sounded from the doorway.

Chapter 12

$\mathcal{N}$ottingdon, or at least Gideon assumed it was Nottingdon, smiled down at Judith in a far too affectionate manner, released her hands, and stepped aside. "However, as you are also an intelligent man you can ascertain at once that this is not—"

"What it looks like?" Gideon said pleasantly although *pleasant* was the last thing he felt.

Judith studied him curiously. "And what does it look like?"

It looks like a test of some sort. Nonsense. He pushed the thought from his mind. Judith was not the sort of woman to pit one man against another. He chose his words carefully. "It looks like a moment of affection between friends. A brother and sister perhaps."

"Ouch." Nottingdon winced. "It looked like that, did it?"

"Indeed it did." Gideon nodded. "Pleasant enough but relatively passionless."

Judith bit back a grin.

"Are you sure you wouldn't rather just shoot me, Warton?" Nottingdon shook his head. "It would be much less painful."

"If you insist. The next time I shall be happy to shoot you." Gideon smiled. "Several times, if you wish, in extraordinarily painful places."

"I would be most appreciative." Nottingdon's gaze met Gideon's in a direct manner, and Gideon had the distinct feeling the man was assessing his character. It was most annoying as Gideon was not the one found in an unused room kissing another man's—what? *Friend?* If anyone's character was in question it was certainly not Gideon's. "At the moment, however, I must take my leave. I have a matter of some importance I should like to discuss with our hostess."

Gideon nodded toward the door. "I saw her a moment ago in the corridor. She directed me here."

"Of course," Nottingdon murmured, then turned his attention to Judith, took her hand, and raised it to his lips. "It was delightful to see you again, Lady Chester. Do feel free to call upon me if the need ever arises."

"Thank you, my lord." Judith smiled at Nottingdon with a genuine affection that made Gideon's stomach twist. He ignored it. "But the delight was mine."

Nottingdon glanced at Gideon. "Pleasure to see you again, Lord Warton."

Gideon nodded. "Lord Nottingdon."

Nottingdon cast a last smile at Judith, then took his leave, closing the door behind him.

Gideon looked at Judith. "You were remarkably quiet during all that."

She studied him in a cool manner. "I did not wish to interfere."

"You saw no need for defense? His or your own perhaps."

She shook her head. "Not at all. You and I are neither married nor are we engaged. I did nothing that warranted a defense."

He crossed his arms over his chest. "What if I had indeed decided to shoot him?"

She shrugged. "I might have said something then."

He narrowed his gaze. "You find this all most amusing, don't you?"

"I find it somewhat amusing. However." An admiring smile curved her lips. "You were most impressive, you know."

He chuckled. "I was good."

"Very good. Particularly that comment about kissing his sister. A lesser man might have seen something that wasn't there. Might have leaped to the wrong conclusions."

"You and I have agreed to honesty between us. We have also agreed that when either of us wishes to end our relationship we can do so without reproach." He gaze met hers. "I daresay if that happens, I shall not have to find it out by discovering you in the arms of another man."

She stared at him. "You trust me, then?"

"With my life," he said in an offhand manner. *With my heart.*

"I see." She drew a deep breath. "And there's nothing tonight, that, oh, I don't know, bothered you in any way?"

"You mean the fact that Mountford gazed at you like a lovesick cow?"

Judith choked back a laugh. "Well, that."

"By the way, I saw him in the corridor. I sent him in another direction."

She grinned. "That wasn't at all nice."

"No, it wasn't." He stepped to her and pulled her into his arms. "Or I could have been bothered by the fact that I found you kissing another man. As rational as I might have appeared, I did not like that in the slightest."

"And yet your behavior was impeccable." She wrapped her arms around his neck. "I was not merely impressed but proud."

"You should be." His lips met hers, and desire, familiar and demanding, rose within him. "Especially since I could have been extraordinarily bothered by all of your old *friends* being in the same room at the same time."

She drew back and looked at him. "You know?"

"I do."

"Susanna told you. I should have known she would have noticed although in that respect I must admit she was more astute than I." Her gaze searched his. "And you're not . . . jealous?"

"Not in the least," he said in a lofty manner.

"Not even a little?"

"How honest am I supposed to be?"

She smiled. "Reasonably honest."

He stared at her for a moment, then blew a resigned breath. "Blast it all, Judith, of course I'm jealous." He pulled her harder against him and gazed into her blue eyes. "I am jealous of everyone who came before me in your life: men, women, children. I am jealous of anyone who was ever important to you. I am especially jealous of anyone you ever loved."

She stared up at him. "Anyone I ever loved?"

"I hate the fact that you loved anyone before me." He drew a deep breath. "Is that reasonably honest enough for you?"

"Yes, I should think—"

"Now, Judith, now you may be quiet." His lips crushed hers and for a long moment he lost himself in the taste of her. Of champagne and delight and something . . . more. Her body molded against his and he could feel the heat of her through the layers of silk and satin. His body responded and he didn't care. At last he raised his head and stared down at her. "I have missed you more than I imagined I ever could."

Her voice was breathless. "I have missed you as well."

"I want you, Judith," he murmured and kissed the corners of her lips, then trailed his mouth along the line of her jaw. Her head dropped backward and he kissed her neck and tasted the hollow of her throat.

"Which works out nicely as I"—she gasped—"want you as well. We should probably . . . oh my . . . leave I should think . . . before . . ."

"Before . . ." He raised his head and grinned wickedly. "Before what?"

"Before . . ." Her eyes were glazed with desire. "Before . . ."

He pulled her tighter against him and wondered if she could feel his arousal. "How much do you want me?"

"Rather a lot at the moment." She twined her fingers in his hair and pulled his mouth back to hers. Her tongue met and mated with his, and need bonded them together.

He wrenched his mouth from hers. "It would be a shame to waste it, then."

"Yes . . . well . . ."

Without warning he released her, stalked to the nearest chair, grabbed it, and proceeded to wedge it under the door handle.

Her brows drew together. "Whatever are you doing?"

He tried the door and it held fast. "That shall ensure all the privacy we need."

"Privacy?"

He started toward her and nodded. "It wouldn't do for someone to walk in on us."

"It would be embarrassing of course but . . ." Her gaze dropped to the front of his trousers and the all too obvious evidence of his arousal. Her eyes widened and she met his gaze. "You can't be thinking—"

"I am indeed."

She stepped back. "You're not serious."

He chuckled. "I can't remember ever being more serious."

"We couldn't possibly." She moved back.

"We most certainly could." He stepped toward her.

"Well . . . well, I've never." Her voice was firm but there was a gleam of excitement in her eyes. "We shouldn't."

His hand slipped to the buttons of his trousers. "Why not?"

"There are dozens of people." She waved aimlessly, her voice weaker than a moment ago. "Right outside that very door."

"Hardly," he scoffed and continued toward her. "They're in an entirely different part of the house altogether."

"Still." She stepped back once more and bumped into the billiards table behind her. "Oh dear."

He raised a brow. "Trapped, are you?"

"I suppose I am." She stared into his eyes. "It appears I have no other choice."

"None whatsoever." He stood within a hand span of her now and knew her desire matched his own.

She licked her lips, and his stomach tightened. "I suppose the only thing to do is surrender gracefully."

"One always appreciates a graceful loser."

"Oh, I do not intend to lose." Her mouth curved upward in a wicked smile. She grabbed his jacket and pulled him closer. "No intention at all."

His lips met hers, and hunger gripped him. He

wanted her as much now as he had the first time, as much, he suspected, as he would tomorrow. He pushed her back harder against the table and attempted to slide her skirts up her legs. It was like trying to swim against a current. Damnation. "Judith, I cannot, well, get to you. Between your skirt and petticoats, blast it all, I'm drowning in fabric—"

"Honestly, Gideon, one would think you've never done this before." She choked back a laugh. "In a billiards room, during a ball."

"Astonishing, isn't it?"

"I would think if you remove my petticoats—"

"Excellent idea." He turned her around, leaned close, and kissed the back of her neck.

She sighed with pleasure, then bent forward and braced her elbows on the billiards table. "If you lift my skirt up, you can remove my petticoats."

"Gladly," he murmured. He pulled up her grown, arranged it over her shoulders, wondered in the back of his mind why he was being so tidy when what he really wanted to do was rip the clothes from her body, then quickly untied her petticoats and pushed them down to pile around her feet. Her nicely shaped derrière was covered by the sheer linen of her drawers.

She started to straighten and he firmly pushed her back down.

"I think not." He ran his hands over the roundness of her buttocks, caressed her linen-clad bottom, and then gently spread her legs apart, opening wider the split between the legs of the drawers.

"Gideon?"

"Hmm?" He could have unbuttoned her drawers and removed them altogether but there was something about her backside and legs covered in fabric, framing her womanhood, that was most erotic. His arousal hardened. He slipped his hand between her legs and she gasped. She was already wet and slick with desire.

"This isn't at all civilized of you." Her voice had that delightful breathless quality he had come to recognize. She wanted him as much as he wanted her.

"Do you think so?" He knew what she liked, what she wanted, and what drove her mad. He stroked the heated flesh between her legs in a slow, almost methodical manner. It still amazed him how merely touching her brought him to a state of intense arousal. His voice was low. "I should think the room alone would make this quite civilized."

"Yes . . . well . . ." Her breath came in short little gasps and he knew she was trying to maintain control, trying to resist surrender. Excellent. It would make their joining that much sweeter. And watching her was almost as exciting as touching her. He stroked her with one hand and with the other undid the buttons of his trousers.

"An English gentleman's billiards room . . ." He guided himself into her, sheathed himself in her soft heat. She sucked in a hard breath and he felt her tighten around him. He closed his eyes for a moment and summoned his own control. "Is as much a symbol of his position in the world . . ." He withdrew slowly, almost completely, then thrust into her just as slowly, deeply, and she throbbed around him. "As his library." He pulled out. "Or his title." And plunged again.

"His position?" Her voice was strangled, as if she could barely form the words.

"And an excellent position it is," he murmured. He grasped her hips and increased his rhythm. Her hands splayed out on the top of the table and she made those delightful little whimpering sounds that only increased his ardor. He thrust into her harder and faster and she rocked against him until his control failed. He moaned and thrust once more and exploded within her. Exquisite delight shot through him, intensified, no doubt, by the inappropriateness of their surroundings.

"No, Gideon, I . . ." Her voice was high-pitched and he knew what she wanted. He reached his hand between them and caressed her and almost at once she gasped. She clamped hard around him and the intensity of her release shuddered against him and radiated from her body into his.

For a long moment, neither moved. It struck him that there might not be anything quite as satisfying as spontaneous lovemaking in completely inappropriate and slightly dangerous locations. Perhaps they could try this again.

"Gideon?" Judith giggled.

He felt somewhat compelled to giggle himself. "Yes, Judith?"

"Do you have a billiards table?"

He laughed, found his handkerchief, and used it to assist himself in withdrawing from her in as civilized a way as possible. "I do indeed." Gideon folded the handkerchief carefully, buttoned his trousers, then pulled her petticoats up and retied them. "We should play sometime."

Judith snorted. "I believe we already have."

"I feel not unlike a ladies' maid." He arranged her skirts and found it was difficult to do so without thinking about what they covered. Without wanting her again. "And a damn fine job I have done too."

"I'm sure you have." Judith straightened, leaned back against him. "Oh my, that was . . . and I feel quite, quite . . ." She sighed. "It's rather difficult to stand at the moment, you know."

"I do know." He wrapped his arms around her and chuckled. "I make your knees weak."

"That's not all you do to me," she said softly.

"Oh?" His heart thudded in his chest. "What do I do to you, Judith? How do I make you feel?" He held his breath.

She was silent for a long moment. At last he felt her draw a deep breath. "I don't know how or maybe what to say." She shook her head. "I'm not sure this is wise—"

"Wisdom does not seem to be a prerequisite for us." He turned her around and stared into her eyes. "Tell me, Judith, tell me how you feel."

Faint voices sounded in the corridor, and at once Judith stepped out of his arms.

"Damnation. Not now." Gideon strode to the door, quietly removed the chair, then stepped aside. "Bloody poor timing."

"It could have been worse."

"It could have been better," he muttered.

Her eyes twinkled with amusement. "It's the price one pays for clandestine assignations."

He adjusted his cuffs and glanced at her. "Do you think every moment of potential embarrassment is amusing?"

"Probably." She smiled wickedly and patted her hair. "Now, do I look presentable?"

"You look delicious." He straightened his cravat.

"Now who isn't being serious?"

"My apologies, although I was being serious. However." He studied her critically. "Your hair isn't the least bit out of place. Nor is your gown. One of the benefits, I'd say, of improvisation—"

"Gideon!" She choked back a laugh. "It's going to be awkward enough to be discovered in here alone without people thinking—"

"That we've had a grand time in activities of an illicit nature involving you bent over the billiards—"

The door swung open. Gideon continued without pause. "So you see, Lady Chester, billiards is a very old, distinguished game and it is indeed a shame for a table of this quality to be allowed to lie here"—his gaze caught hers—"unused."

Judith snorted then coughed.

"I knew they were in here." Violet swept into the room, followed closely by Lord Mountford.

Gideon raised a brow. "And how did you know that?"

"I know how much you like"—Violet's gaze slipped to Judith, then back to Gideon—"billiards," she said brightly.

"I thought it was because we had looked everywhere else," Mountford murmured.

Gideon snorted. "You know nothing of the sort."

"Very well then." Violet shrugged. "I assumed you liked billiards because men generally do."

"I like billiards," Mountford offered.

"I knew it." Violet beamed at the man.

Mountford smiled back, then turned to Judith. "Judith, Lady Chester, I thought you were going to wait for me."

"I am sorry, Harry. I'm afraid I misled you. I had no intention of waiting for you. Now." Judith drew a deep breath. "Or ever."

Gideon winced. Mountford's expression fell. "But I thought—"

"I know what you thought and you have my sincerest apologies for that too. I believe it was a"—she slanted a quick glance at Violet—"a misunderstanding on the part of Lady Braxton."

"A misunderstanding?" Mountford stared at Judith for a moment, then blew a long breath. "I feel like something of an idiot."

"Don't be absurd, Harry. You have no reason to feel like an idiot." Judith laid a hand on his arm and favored him with an affectionate smile. "And I am most flattered."

"That's something, I suppose," Mountford said wryly. "Judith." He took her hands and gazed into her eyes. "It was lovely to see you again and I very much regret . . ." He shook his head. "If I have caused you any discomfort whatsoever." He released her hand and nodded at Gideon. "Good evening, Lord Warton." Mountford turned and took his leave.

"What extraordinarily bad manners." Indignation sounded in Violet's voice. "He didn't bid me a good evening."

Judith's eyes narrowed. "You're lucky he didn't strangle you with his bare hands."

"I have no idea what you're talking about."

"Judith," Gideon said slowly. "All Violet did was invite him here tonight. Granted, her motives were questionable."

"Questionable?" Judith glared at Violet. "I don't think there's any question at all about her motives. And she did far more than merely invite the man."

"I am not to blame if he misunderstood." Violet lifted a shoulder in a dismissive shrug. "You said it yourself that it was a misunderstanding."

"Lord Mountford understood exactly what you wanted him to think. Fortunately Lord Nottingdon saw through your scheme."

"What scheme?" Gideon asked.

"Yes, well, I did not give Nottingdon enough credit." Violet narrowed her eyes. "I swear that man has gone out of his way to annoy me since he was a child."

"With good reason, no doubt," Judith said.

"What scheme?" Gideon asked again.

"Nottingdon has never liked me, which has worked out nicely as I have never liked him." Violet's lips quirked upward in a knowing smile. "But he likes you. Quite a lot I should say."

Judith's chin rose the tiniest bit. "I like him as well. I consider him a friend. He has all the attributes one wishes for in a friend. Loyal, trustworthy—"

Violet smirked. "And good in—"

"Violet!" Gideon snapped.

Judith smiled. "Are you jealous, Lady Braxton?"

Violet's face flushed. "Don't be silly. I could have had him or any man I've wanted any time I've wanted. But until recent years, I have devoted my life to being a good and loyal wife. Whereas you . . ."

Judith's eyes were cold. "Whereas I what?"

This had gone on long enough. "Would one of you please explain to me what the two of you are talking about." He looked at Judith. "What scheme?"

Violet rolled her eyes toward the ceiling. "It's a trifle really."

"Yes, I suppose you would see it that way, but then manipulating the emotions of honorable men probably doesn't strike you as especially significant." Judith's voice was cold. "Do you want to tell him or shall I?"

"Very well." Violet sighed in resignation. "When I invited Nottingdon and Mountford I might have implied Lady Chester was interested in renewing their . . . friendship."

"What?" Gideon stared.

"One never knows." Violet shrugged. "I thought I was doing them all a favor."

"A favor?" Judith's voice rose. "A favor? You led Samuel and poor Harry to believe I still had feelings for them."

"You apparently did once, you might still." Violet smirked. "And if you do, Gideon should know."

"I suspect Gideon can take care of himself," Judith said sharply.

Violet scoffed. "Gideon has always been rather trusting when it comes to women."

"You would know." Judith snapped.

"And you—"

"That's quite enough, Violet." Gideon glared.

"No, Gideon, it's not nearly enough." Violet turned toward him and her voice softened. "Are you aware of this woman's reputation?"

"Reputations, like anything based on gossip, are often exaggerated," he said coolly and slanted a supportive glance at Judith. She stared back at him in an expressionless manner, and he realized his words now might be the most important he ever said.

"Hers isn't." Violet's eyes gleamed. "Why, at this very party there are at least three—"

"And you went to great pains to make sure they were in attendance. Good God." He stared in disbelief. "Did you pull the same trick with Helmsley as you did with the others?"

"Don't be absurd." Violet shook her head. "He's newly married. He probably would not have come at all, although one can never be too sure when it comes to men."

"So it was enough simply to have Helmsley present?" Gideon studied her. "And the others?"

"For goodness' sakes, Gideon, all of London is talking about you and"—Violet threw Judith a scathing glance—"this woman. It's one thing to talk about someone's reputation and quite another to come face to face with it."

"What did you expect would happen here tonight, Violet?" Gideon stared at her. "Did you think I would be shocked? Outraged? Fly into a jealous rage and berate her publicly for her past?"

"I thought you would come to your senses," Violet snapped. "I thought you would see how very wrong this woman is for you. How continuing this liaison is a dreadful mistake and is destroying your reputation as well. Besides, she could never make you the kind of proper wife you deserve."

"And if I don't want a proper wife?" he said sharply.

Violet gasped. "You can't possibly be thinking of marrying this creature?"

"My plans are no concern of yours!" He glared at her. "You forfeited that right years ago. I shall be with whomever I please and if that includes marriage, frankly, Violet, your opinion matters not at all."

Violet's eyes widened. "Come now, Gideon, you can't—"

"I can do whatever I damn well please." His jaw clenched. "As for Judith's reputation, what she has or hasn't done in the past is of no concern to me. Indeed, I have quite forgiven her her indiscretions and there's nothing more to be said on the matter."

"There's a great deal more to be said," Violet began. "I think—"

"I think we've all said far too much and I for one have had quite enough." Judith's voice was hard. "My dear Lady Braxton, you may talk about my reputation all you wish but I have never misused or misled a gentleman in any way. Nor have I ever exploited their affection for me to my own ends." Judith's smile was pleasant but the look in her blue eyes was cold. "Can you say the same?"

Violet's eyes widened in fury. "If you're referring to what happened years ago—"

"And given your recent behavior it appears nothing has changed." Judith turned to Gideon. "I should like to leave now."

"As should I." He nodded and they started toward the door.

"Gideon, you cannot simply leave," Violet huffed. "We still have things to discuss."

He stood aside and allowed Judith to pass through the door before him, then glanced back at Violet. "I thought I made myself clear, Violet, there is nothing left to say. Good evening." He closed the door firmly in his wake, leaving Violet sputtering alone, and realized as well he might just have shut the door on his past. The realization brought a sense of elation and, yes, even freedom.

Judith was remarkably quiet in the carriage on the return to her house and Gideon thought it wise to leave her to her thoughts. Just as he had thought, the evening had been a disaster. Still, it hadn't been a total loss. There had been that exhilarating interlude in the billiards room. He grinned to himself.

By God, he'd never done anything like that before. It was most uncivilized of him and he relished the memory. Beyond that he had defended her to Violet, and quite ably too, he thought, and had more than likely put his past firmly behind him. In addition, he had not allowed jealousy to rule his head although it had not been especially easy. But damn it all, he'd meant what he'd said to her. He was jealous of anyone she'd ever loved before him.

Which only begged the question: did she love him now?

Chapter 13

It was perhaps the longest carriage ride she had ever taken, and yet it took no time at all. Before tonight Judith had started to think, even perhaps to believe, there could be a future with Gideon. It was madness of course. Her own failings made certain of that. If she'd had any hopes at all they'd been dashed this evening.

They reached her house and he escorted her inside. She murmured something appropriate to the servants and a moment later couldn't recall her words. She wandered into the parlor and wondered exactly what she would say to Gideon now. He followed her, closed the door behind him, and leaned against it. "I have missed you, Judith."

She forced a smile. "You said that earlier."

"It bears repeating." He grinned, crossed the room to her, and took her hands in his. "I am sorry about tonight. I should have known Violet had something unpleasant planned."

She pulled her hands from his. "And yet we went anyway."

"I thought she had a valid point in that my appearance would alleviate any gossip about ill will between us."

"And she made that point when you spoke with her and did not mention that to me?"

"I explained that," he said slowly. "It was the day I left for the country. I had no opportunity to tell you."

"Did you have no opportunity to tell me you and she spoke at Lady Dinsmore's ball as well?" Her words were measured.

"I had the opportunity, it simply slipped my mind." He considered her carefully. "I did not consider it important."

She raised a brow. "Should I be jealous?"

"No, of course not. There is nothing to be jealous about."

"She is a part of your past."

"The important word there is *past*," he said firmly.

"Isn't it though," she murmured and moved away from him to study a Fragonard depicting French nobility frolicking in a parklike setting, the frolicking a form of flirtation and a prelude to seduction. "Have you been with a great many women, Gideon?" She glanced at him. "In the past, that is?"

He drew his brows together. "I was never with Violet in that sense."

"But you did love her."

"I thought so at the time. What has all this—"

"Let's disregard Lady Braxton then." She shrugged in a casual manner. "What of the other women?"

"The other women?" Caution sounded in his voice.

"How many other women have you been with?"

"I'm not sure—"

She raised a brow. "That many?"

He shook his head. "No, not that many."

"Well, how many?"

"I don't—"

"Allow me to assist you." She turned toward him and folded her arms over her chest. "More than a dozen? More than a hundred?" She widened her eyes. "Surely not more than a thousand?"

He stared at her. "You're being absurd."

"You're being evasive."

"Very well then, more than a dozen, less than a hundred." He glared. "Are you happy now?"

"Blissful."

He stared in confusion. "Why on earth does it matter? Why did you want to know?"

"It really doesn't matter, Gideon, whether it was a hundred or, oh, say, three. The fact is that you had other women, there were other women in your life before you met me. Before we became involved with one another. Before you even knew I existed." She clasped her hands together before her in a prim manner and smiled pleasantly. "And

I wanted to know so that I would know precisely what I was forgiving you for when I forgave you for all your past indiscretions."

"When you forgave me for my . . ." At once understanding dawned on his face. "Judith, I didn't mean that the way it might have sounded."

"Oh dear." She sighed. "You don't forgive me then?"

"Of course I do but . . ." He shook his head. "You're twisting my words."

"My apologies. Please forgive me for that too."

"I don't think so." He stepped toward her. "You're not being fair, Judith. You're taking my words in a manner I did not intend."

"How did you intend them?" she said in a tone sharper than she had expected.

He chose his words with care. "I intended to convey that I can overlook your past—"

"You can overlook my past?" She fairly spit the words. "How very gracious of you."

"I wouldn't call it gracious but . . . See here, Judith, this is not . . ." He huffed. "Damn it all, I was defending you."

"I need no defense, my lord. I have been a widow, not a wife, these past ten years. I have had no one to answer to save myself." Anger clenched her fists. "It is exceedingly difficult to spend one's life completely alone with no family. No one to care for, no one to care for you."

"That's why it's entirely understandable that you would not have conformed to certain standards of behavior," he said quickly.

"Conformed to certain standards of behavior?" Fury swelled within her. "As you have conformed to certain standards of behavior?"

"Don't be absurd. That's entirely different. I'm a—"

"Man?" She said the word as if it left a nasty taste in her mouth, and in many ways it did.

"Well, yes. Society looks at these things differently."

"I am not especially concerned about society. My only concern is with you."

"Then there is nothing to be concerned about." Again he moved toward her. "Your past is—"

"Forgiven?" She thrust out her hand to stop him and shook her head. "My adventures pale in comparison with yours, yet you are above reproach and I am to be forgiven?"

"No, damnation, not forgiven," he snapped. "That's not the right word. I don't know what the right word is."

"Would you have been happier if I had waited, then, on the off chance that you would come into my life? Sat in this house alone? Perhaps doing fine embroidery or—wait." She widened her eyes and gasped. "I could have thrown myself into charitable endeavors. Rescuing orphans, women of ill repute, that sort of thing. Oh, I could have been useful and really most acceptable."

The muscles on the side of his jaw clenched. "You're being irrational, you know."

"Yes, I do know!" She cast him a scathing glance. "One tends to be irrational when one realizes—"

"When one realizes what?" he said slowly.

"Gideon." She drew a calming breath. "You cannot get over my past. I could tell you that nothing meant anything before you. I could tell you as well that I have shared your bed more often than all the other men put together. I could tell you that there have only been three in the past ten years although I suspect you already know that. But I won't." Her voice hardened. "I make no excuses for what I have done and the decisions I have made. Nor do I regret them."

"I am not asking you to," he said quietly. "What are you asking of me?"

"I don't know!" She shook her head. "Perhaps I am asking that you accept me as I am."

"Why?" He studied her. "You show no willingness to accept me as I am."

She stared at him. "Now *you're* being ridiculous."

"No more so than you. You want the truth from me, Judith, well here it is." His tone was cool. "I can forgive, overlook, ignore—whatever word you would prefer that I use—your past but I cannot forget it altogether." He shook his head. "My character is not that strong."

She shrugged. "Then we have nothing to talk about."

"We have a great deal to talk about. This—whatever it is between us—is on your terms, it has been from the start, and I have had enough."

"What do you mean?" she said, although she knew full well what he meant. Hadn't Susanna warned her about this very thing at the beginning?

"You set the boundaries, expectations, limitations, rules, or whatever you bloody well want to call them. I had no say in the matter and I am tired of them." Anger sparked in his dark eyes.

"It didn't seem to bother you at the time," she snapped.

"It didn't at the time. However." His eyes narrowed. "It does now."

"Why?"

"Because nothing is as it was in the beginning. Bloody hell, Judith, whatever this between us was supposed to be, it's entirely different now. The expectations, *my expectations*, my desires if you will, have changed and I have no intention of abiding by your arbitrary rules."

"I don't know what you mean."

"Don't you?" He snorted in disbelief. "For one thing, I am apparently not supposed to be jealous of the men who came before me."

"I never said—"

"No, Lady Dinsmore told me that and I am damn grateful to her that she did." He grabbed her wrist and raised her hand up. "Is this why?"

"Let me go." She tried to pull away but he held fast.

"There's a crook in your little finger so slight I doubt anyone who hasn't kissed that finger would notice it, but I did. I've seen that before on people who have broken a finger. Or rather have had a finger broken." He trapped her gaze with his. "Who did this to you?"

"No one," she lied. "It was an accident."

"Hardly." He shook his head. "You were a protected, spoiled little girl in your childhood. Spoiled little girls rarely break fingers. If it had been an accident it would have been set properly. This wasn't."

"It was an accident," she said through clenched teeth.

He ignored her. "It couldn't have been Helmsley. I've never seen him show anger of this sort. He's not the type of man who would hurt a woman, even inadvertently." Gideon was speaking more to himself than to her. As if he were working out a puzzle in his head. Panic rose within her. "And unless I am a terrible judge of character, nor is Mountford or Nottingdon. Besides, you would not still be cordial to them if they were."

"Let me go." She gritted out the words.

"Good God, it was your husband, wasn't it?" Realization dawned in his eyes, and her stomach twisted. "Was he jealous? Was that it?"

"Stop it!"

"What else did he do to you?" Gideon's voice was hard.

"Nothing!" She wrenched free and backed away. "He was my soul mate, the love of my life!"

"You were seventeen years old!" Gideon stared. "What did you know of love?"

"He loved me! I loved him!"

"It doesn't ring true, Judith, it never has." He shook his head. "It makes perfect sense now. Why you never speak of him. Of your marriage. I should have seen it before."

"Nonetheless—"

"Who are you trying to convince?" His eyes were dark with unidentifiable emotion. Anger perhaps or pity or both. She didn't want his pity and at the moment she certainly didn't care about his anger. "Me or yourself?"

Without thinking she drew her hand back and let it fly. He caught it and yanked her into his arms. "I will not play by your rules anymore."

"Then we shall not play at all!" She glared at him.

"Oh no, it's not going to be that easy for you. You cannot walk away from me as you did the others. You cannot end this *without recrimination* because it has become more than you expected. Or wanted. More than is safe." His gaze bored into hers. "I will not permit it."

"You have no choice!" She met his gaze in an unyielding and defiant manner of her own. "You agreed!"

"We also agreed to honesty and you have not been honest."

"I most certainly—"

"Then be honest now." He stared into her eyes. "Do you love me?"

Her breath caught. *Yes!* "No."

"You're lying." He released her, his voice abruptly calm, cool, and remote. "And you do not do it well."

I do it very well. She drew a calming breath. "I think it's best if you leave now."

"Probably." Gideon studied her for a long moment. "It's convenient though, isn't it, Judith?"

"What?"

"This irrational argument. Your excessive anger."

"I see nothing irrational or excessive. You were condescending and arrogant and superior in your"—she paused to emphasize the word—*"forgiveness."*

"You're right, of course. The fact that I did not intend it as such, that indeed my intent was your defense, as well as my apology, does not negate its offense. Still, your ire strikes me as remarkably clever." He chuckled in a humorless manner that sent chills skating down her spine. "It serves as a legitimate and expedient way to get me out of your house, perhaps out of your life."

She sucked in a sharp breath.

"Know this though, Judith. Regardless of the circumstances or jealousy or anything else." His gaze met hers. "I would not hurt you for the world. Ever."

Her heart caught and a lump formed in the back of her throat. She wanted nothing more than to throw herself into his arms. Instead, she nodded. "You should go."

"I will for now but, mark my words, you will not be rid of me this easily." He stalked toward the door, pulled it open, then looked back at her. "Regardless of what you might think at the moment, through all that has happened tonight, one truth strikes me with a clarity I have never before experienced."

"Oh?" She held her breath.

"I am not the one who cannot get over your

past, dear Judith." He shook his head. "You are." And then he was gone.

"What in the name of all that's holy are you doing here?" Helmsley glared at Gideon through bleary eyes and cinched his dressing gown tighter. "Do you have any idea what time it is?"

"Of course I do." Gideon waved off the question. "It's very late or quite early depending entirely on your point of view."

"I had no point of view. I was asleep." Helmsley yawned and shook his head. "Edwards said you insisted he wake me. I trust this is urgent."

"I assure you it is." Gideon led the way toward Helmsley's library. "It's imperative that I speak with you."

"Now?" Helmsley trailed behind him.

"I couldn't sleep." It was the truth as far as it went, although sleep was the last thing on Gideon's mind.

He'd left Judith hours ago with every intention of returning to his own house but instead found himself telling his driver to circle the city. He needed to think, to digest, even to analyze what had passed between them, and he certainly couldn't do so where Aunt Louisa's interference was not merely possible but probable. She had not been invited to Violet's soiree, and while she claimed she hadn't the least desire to attend and indeed would have turned down the invitation had it been issued, she would still no doubt be lying in wait to quiz him on the evening's events. She'd predicted his attendance would be a mistake and in that, for once, she was right.

"I could certainly sleep. Indeed I was sleeping, quite soundly too." Helmsley paused at the library door. "This couldn't wait until morning?"

"No." Gideon shook his head, then paused. "Well, yes, I suppose. I mean nothing of significance will change between now and morning. Although . . ." His gaze met Helmsley's. "I might well be mad by morning."

Helmsley studied his friend for a moment, then sighed. "I should have expected this, I suppose. Even if you have scarcely spoken to me of late, Norcroft has kept me informed. And you're here now, so we might as well get on with it." Helmsley called to his butler. "Edwards."

"Yes. My lord." The butler immediately appeared from the shadows.

"Brandy if you please, Edwards, or whisky or something else appropriately suited to the hour."

"I have placed decanters of both in the library, my lord," Edwards said as if it were the most natural thing in the world for Helmsley to be entertaining unexpected guests in the wee hours of the night. "Will there be anything else?"

"I do hope not." Helmsley glanced at his friend. "I daresay you have probably had enough to drink already by the look of you."

"I look that bad, do I?" Gideon smiled weakly. "In truth, I haven't had a drink at all since we left Lady Braxton's party."

"Oh, well that explains a great deal. If you had

indulged appropriately you would be past caring about anything by now and I would still be abed." Helmsley paused. "A rather interesting gathering, though, didn't you think?"

"It was certainly interesting. Particularly the guest list. And you needn't be so circumspect. I am fully aware of who was in attendance and why."

"Not a coincidence then?"

"No." Gideon blew a long breath. "Simply a misguided attempt on Lady Braxton's part to show me the error of my ways in regard to Judith."

"Misguided?" Helmsley snorted. "You're a kinder man than I am, Warton." He led the way into the library. "I did wonder why we had been invited in the first place. Neither Fiona nor I has ever met the woman. I simply assumed between my family and Lady Braxton's we had either crossed paths or someone in our respective families had."

"The only connection apparently is Judith. And me. At least your invitation didn't indicate Judith was interested in resuming your relationship."

"And Mountford's and Nottingdon's did?" Helmsley settled in one of two comfortable chairs positioned before a fireplace. Decanters and glasses sat on a tray placed on a table between the two chairs.

Gideon nodded and sank into the other chair. "You knew of Mountford and Nottingdon then?"

Helmsley selected a decanter and poured two glasses. "You must remember, Judith and I have been friends for a number of years." He chose his words with care. "Before and even during her other . . . well . . ."

"Adventures?"

Helmsley grimaced at the word and handed him a glass. "Yes."

"Nottingdon was not fooled by Violet's manipulations but I felt rather sorry for Mountford, who was more than willing to take up with Judith where they had left off." Gideon sipped his drink, pleased to discover Helmsley had appropriately enough chosen the whisky.

Helmsley raised a brow. "And you call this action of Lady Braxton's merely misguided?"

"Given my past experience with Violet, tonight's plot was relatively minor. I should think . . ." Gideon paused and gazed around the room, his brow furrowed in confusion. "Is this your library?"

Helmsley chuckled. "It's a remarkable transformation, isn't it?"

"*Remarkable* isn't the word for it." Gideon stared. He'd been far too preoccupied to pay heed to the room at first although he had vaguely noticed something was different.

When Helmsley had bought this house shortly before his marriage, it had come filled with the often bizarre possessions of one of the previous owners. In this room alone, among the riot of color and texture occupying every inch of space, Gideon recalled stuffed and mounted animals, intricate carvings from exotic lands, bronze and stone statuary depicting gods and mythical creatures, and bits and pieces of long-lost civilizations. He had never understood how Helmsley could abide the chaos, let alone like it. But apparently he had and apparently his new wife did not. Now Helmsley's library looked, well, like a library, with accessible books neatly shelved as well as a desk, chairs, and a visible carpet, all of which might well have been in the room all along. "I don't believe I saw a fireplace the last time I was here."

"You probably didn't. The last time you were here I wasn't married to a woman who considered it her duty in life to organize my life." Helmsley nodded at two statues flanking the doorway, life-sized Nubians with crossed spears. "She allowed me to keep those. I must admit I have grown rather fond of them."

"Very nice," Gideon murmured.

"I am finding that marriage is an odd and unique state. Probably because it's between men and women." Helmsley sipped his drink thoughtfully. "In many ways our two minds are very much alike, yet we view the world from completely different perspectives."

"Even I could have told you that."

"You could have, but observation is not at all the same as experience." Helmsley shrugged in a sage manner that a man wearing a dressing gown should never attempt. "I can tell you it's a far cry from the simple observance of marriage to being in the thick of it."

Gideon stared. "So you've become an expert in—what? Six weeks now since you were joined in the bonds of wedded bliss?"

"It's the not quantity of time," Helmsley said in a lofty manner, "but the quality of the hours together."

"Then put that newfound wisdom to use." Gideon drew a deep breath. "Help me, Jonathon. I don't know what to do."

At once the atmosphere in the room sobered.

"About Judith, you mean?"

"Yes, about Judith." Gideon got to his feet and paced the room. "Who else would I be talking about?"

"Well, Lady Braxton is—"

Gideon shot him a sharp glance.

"Yes, of course. Stupid of me." Helmsley grimaced. "Sorry."

"You know Judith better than anyone except perhaps Lady Dinsmore."

"Possibly." Helmsley blew a long breath. "And yet, in spite of our long acquaintance, I daresay I don't know her at all." He paused. "But I know you."

Gideon narrowed his eyes. "And?"

"And I am curious as to what happened between the two of you tonight, especially given your presence here now. I saw nothing untoward at the party, nor did I hear anything, therefore I assume Lady Braxton's plan did not succeed."

"Not really."

Helmsley raised a brow.

"At least not in the way she had intended it. It did however prompt me to make a comment that ultimately triggered a nasty disagreement between Judith and myself." Even now Gideon couldn't believe the sheer stupidity and, yes, arrogance of what he had said. "I said I had forgiven her her past indiscretions."

Helmsley stared in obvious disbelief. "You didn't?"

"I did and you needn't look at me like that," Gideon said sharply. "I have already chastised myself quite enough, thank you. I did try to explain to her that I didn't mean it the way it sounded. That I didn't mean *forgive* so much as I meant *overlook*."

Helmsley choked.

"Yes, yes, I know. That's almost as stupid but I didn't know what to say." Gideon struggled to pull his thoughts together. "I was trying to explain that her past doesn't matter to me, and it doesn't for all intents and purposes, but it is there. It does exist as much as anything else about her exists and as such it cannot be completely ignored or entirely forgotten. But . . ."

"But?"

"But I don't condemn her for it. It doesn't mean I think any less of her. I don't. Not at all. I think she's . . ." Gideon shook his head. "I think she's quite wonderful. She's clever, she's lovely, she's amusing. I think she's everything any man could ever want."

"Did you tell her all that?"

"I'm not sure although I would wager that I didn't. Everything was rather out of control after that." He ran his hand through his hair and tried to recall exactly what was said between Judith and him. The more he'd gone over it in the carriage, the more confused he'd become. "She was very angry and I might have called her irrational."

"You called her irrational after you'd forgiven her her sins?" Helmsley said with barely concealed amusement.

"Tempers were lost on both sides at that point."

"I would have liked to have seen that," Helmsley murmured,

"I assure you it was not a pretty scene. And it went well beyond Judith's adventures during her widowhood." Gideon met his friend's gaze. "You once said you thought there was something wrong regarding Judith's marriage." He paused to gather his thoughts. "I believe Judith's husband was a jealous sort. Unreasonably so, I suspect."

"I can't imagine Judith ever giving a husband cause for jealousy," Helmsley said staunchly. "She's one of the most honorable people I know. Her word is as important to her as it is to any man."

"Don't make that comparison to her."

Helmsley frowned. "It's a compliment."

"She won't see it as such. As I was saying . . ." Even now Gideon found it hard to believe, but nothing else made sense. "I think he hurt her." Judith never spoke of her husband or her marriage and when she did it had the sound of recitation. She was adamant about not marrying again. Regardless of her stated reasons—her independence and wealth and all that—it did not ring true. Nor did her insistence that the breaking of her finger had been an accident. In spite of the anger between them at that moment, Judith would have laughed off his charge if he'd been wrong. Instead there'd been a look in her eyes he never wished to see again. Gideon drew a deep breath. "Physically, that is."

"She's told you this?"

"Don't be absurd. She'd never tell me anything of the sort. But I am convinced nonetheless." Gideon drained the last whisky in his glass, stepped to the decanter, and refilled it. "If he wasn't already dead I would have to kill him myself."

"And I would be compelled to assist you." Helmsley's jaw tightened. "No man should be allowed to hurt a woman, especially one under his protection."

Gideon was under no illusions. This sort of thing happened all the time. Women, especially wives, had few rights under the law. Still, he had never come face to face with it, and the very thought made him ill. Perhaps it was because those ancient ideals of gallantry and chivalry and the protection of those weaker than oneself, even in this day and age, still ruled his actions. Or perhaps it was because the lady in question was Judith, but the very idea that her husband, the man she swore loved her, the man she claimed to have loved, could have hurt her twisted his insides in a manner that made him want to retch. He nodded. "No man for whatever reason."

"And because you wish to protect her."

"Absolutely."

Helmsely nodded. "You would never allow anyone to hurt her."

"No, don't be absurd."

"Because you love her."

"Of course," Gideon said without thinking. "No. Possibly." He shook his head. "In truth, I don't know. How would I know if I loved her? I loved Violet or at least I thought I did at the time. How do I know if this isn't as dreadful a mistake as Violet was?"

"I suppose," Helmsley said slowly, "you don't."

Gideon glared. "You're not being much help."

Helmsley shrugged. "My apologies. Perhaps this will help." He paused for a long moment. "It seems to me you're hiding behind your past, behind Violet's skirts, as it were, to avoid your feelings for Judith."

"That's absurd. Ridiculous." Gideon blew a long breath. "But probably true." He shook his head. "I don't want to be in the position ever again of offering my heart to a woman who does not want it. If I am therefore overly cautious"—he shrugged— "it is to be expected."

"What of Judith's feelings? Does she love you?"

"She says she doesn't but"—Gideon shook his head—"I don't believe her."

"Why not?"

"Because I don't. Because there's something in the way she says it." He glanced at his friend. "Because I don't want to believe it."

"Whether you want to admit it or not, that in itself says a great deal." Helmsley thought for a moment. "It strikes me as well that Judith might be using her past, be it her marriage or her adventures or simply your feelings about her past, as an excuse to avoid anything permanent. She's allowed you to get closer to her than any man before. It may well be that she has the same difficulties accepting her feelings because of her past that you do."

"Perhaps what she needs, what we both need, is time."

"I thought you'd been out of town for the last week?"

"More time then." Gideon blew a long breath and sank back into his chair. "A few days maybe to consider all that we said to one another. To decide what we want. What we do now."

"And when you have reached this momentous decision, will you go to her?"

"Perhaps she'll come to me."

Helmsley choked back a laugh. "I'd like to see that."

"Regardless, I have never felt so helpless in my life." Gideon heaved a resigned sigh. "Or so stupid."

Helmsley chuckled. "Sure signs of love."

"I wish I knew."

"You can't always know, at least in my experience. It would make it entirely too easy, and there is nothing about love that is easy." Helmsley lifted his glass. "Love, old friend, is very much a leap of faith."

"And if you are too cautious or too frightened to leap?"

"Then you remain where you are. Trapped." Helmsley caught Gideon's gaze. "And alone."

Judith had no idea how long she stood and stared at the door Gideon had snapped closed behind him. She had no knowledge of the moment she finally sank down into a chair and continued to stare unseeing at the door. She didn't know at what point her butler had inquired as to whether she would be needing anything else and had then bid her a good night. For a very long time after Gideon's departure, the passing minutes, the passing hours, had had no meaning. Indeed, she'd felt quite numb, as if she'd stayed too long out of doors in bitter cold. In the back of her mind she was grateful for the void, for the emptiness, for feeling nothing at all, and wondered, or hoped, that perhaps, if she didn't move, all would be well. She would never have to feel anything again.

And just when she'd thought it was safe to breathe once more, with care and caution, the pain swept in, its intensity catching her unawares, sucking the very air from the room itself. It was somewhat like the pain she'd known when she'd discovered Lucian was unfaithful. And much more like that which had gripped her when he had died. Still, if truth were told, wasn't that tempered the tiniest bit by relief? Although relief had only brought about more guilt. It was a wicked cycle of pain and relief, guilt and recrimination. And it was entirely her fault, then and now.

Gideon was right, but then she'd always known the truth. She hadn't put her past behind her. Oh, not her adventures. As pleasant as they'd been, as nice as Jonathon and Harry and Samuel all were, her moments with them were not the least bit important. She hadn't allowed them to be. Susanna's observation was accurate as well. Any one of her adventures could have become so much more if she had not ended them before they could evolve into something serious. Something permanent.

Why then had she allowed Gideon to become something special, something precious, something unexpected? It was entirely possible she simply hadn't been on guard against him. After all, she had known him as an acquaintance for years. Who ever would have imagined that one day you would gaze into a near stranger's dark eyes, eyes you had never especially noticed, and be swept away by desire and passion and emotions you thought you would never feel again if indeed you had ever felt them before. *Le coup de foudre.* Gaze into those eyes and without warning see the mate to your very soul even if you didn't recognize it until later when you knew the sound of his laughter and the touch of his hand and the warmth of his character. And if Gideon was her soul mate, what did that make Lucian? A dreadful mistake?

She had always known that as well, somewhere deep down inside. But it had always been so much easier not to think about it, not to face the truth. If their marriage hadn't been a mistake, if she had been the wife he should have had, the wife he had needed to save his soul, *the wife she should have been*, he wouldn't have taken his own life. If she hadn't defended herself, if she hadn't locked him out of her rooms, if she hadn't threatened to leave him, then perhaps . . . But what she'd done was part and parcel of who she was. She could no more change that than she could change the past.

Lucian's death was on her hands. There was a price to be paid for that, a penance to be exacted. Not merely that she would not remarry, that she would live her life alone, but now apparently that she would live it with the knowledge that she could not share it with the one man who had captured her soul.

It was past time to end this particular adventure. The very thought tore at her heart, and she longed for the numbness of a few moments ago. It was obvious that Gideon would not let her go easily. She would simply give him no choice. It was part of their agreement, after all. And while he might refuse to abide by her terms, he had agreed that either of them could end it without reproach. Regardless of what he now said, she would hold him to that.

And then she would leave, vanish from his life altogether. She had told Samuel she would not flee, but fleeing with Gideon was a far cry from fleeing without him. Flight now seemed an excellent idea. Far better than to cross paths with Gideon again and again as they surely would if she remained in London. She had no desire to see him as the years went on. To see the woman, young, virginal, perfect, that he would inevitably wed. The children he would have who would surely bear their father's slightly wicked, altogether wonderful smile. And she had no desire to have him see her through the years. To watch her age and go from lovely to handsome to "she was considered quite a beauty in her youth." And worse yet, to see the look in his eyes change every time their gazes met in passing.

Fade from whatever affection he now felt for her to a vague acknowledgment that perhaps once, long ago, they had known each other. That was a penance too great for even her sins.

But she would go on with her life. And if there was an emptiness in her heart where Gideon had been, if her adventure with him was now the past she could not put behind her, she would nonetheless survive. She had survived the death of her parents, infidelity and rape by her husband, his death at his own hand, and a decade of guilt and blame and hatred from his sister. Why, a mere broken heart paled in comparison.

The pain, however, was another matter entirely.

Chapter 14

" Lady Chester has arrived, my lord," Wells said in a nondescript manner that belied the fact that he, and every other servant in Gideon's household, had been alerted to the possibility that Lady Chester might indeed pay a call on Lord Warton at any moment.

"Excellent." Gideon released a breath he had quite possibly held since he'd last seen Judith three days ago. Or more precisely, three days, fifteen hours, and twenty-seven minutes ago, give or take a minute. He had planned to wait one more day before storming over to her house, taking her in his arms, and declaring that he never wanted to spend another day without her. "Show her in."

Wells nodded and took his leave.

Gideon rose to his feet and started toward the

door. He stopped, moved to the front of the desk, and leaned against it in a casual manner. He glanced at the fireplace and wondered if perhaps that might not be a better place to stand. Blast it all. He blew a frustrated breath. This was ridiculous. What was he doing? Certainly he was unusually anxious and even a bit apprehensive but surely that was to be expected. The only reason he had waited any time at all was that he and Helmsley had agreed that Judith needed to make up her own mind about her own life. It was damn hard to be patient and allow her to do so, but Gideon knew there could be no future between them if she didn't come to terms with her past.

Now, thank God, apparently she had.

"Good day, Lord Warton." Judith sailed into the room as if she hadn't a care in the world. It was a good sign.

"Good day, Lady Chester." He stifled a grin and nodded at Wells, who discreetly stepped out of the library and closed the door quietly behind him. "Judith." He stepped toward her with every intention of taking her in his arms.

She held out her hand. "Gideon."

Her hand was not at all what he wanted. Still, he took it and raised it to his lips. "I have missed you more than you can ever know."

She smiled and pulled her hand away. "How very kind of you to say."

"Is it?" He narrowed his eyes and studied her. Her lighthearted manner might not be a good sign after all. "We have a great deal to talk about."

"Then perhaps you should have come to me," she said pleasantly and moved away from him as if she wished to put distance between them.

"I thought it would be best if you—if we—took a few days to consider all that we had said to one another."

"Excellent idea. I thought precisely the same thing myself. And now here I am." She beamed at him. "However, I cannot stay long. I have a number of errands to run but I did wish to speak with you."

Her tone was polite, cordial, and distinctly impersonal. A heavy weight settled in the pit of his stomach. "Did you?"

"I believe I owe you an apology, my lord."

"Oh?" He raised a brow. "For what precisely?"

"Any number of things." She laughed lightly. "You were right, you know. My behavior was somewhat irrational."

"With good reason," he said slowly.

"Perhaps. Still." She shrugged, "I should not have lost my temper. It was inexcusable. I don't know what I was thinking."

"I lost my temper as well and for that you have my apologies."

"Accepted." She cast him a brilliant smile.

"Judith—"

"You were entirely right as well about my . . . difficulties, as it were, in regard to my past." Her smile faltered for no more than a fraction of a moment. "I have given it a great deal of consideration in recent days, and it now seems to me that I have been doing little more than marking time in the last decade. Oh, I have walked and breathed and had my little adventures but I haven't allowed myself to truly live. It's past time that I did."

Hope flickered within him, and he stepped toward her. "Judith—"

"Please, Gideon." She moved away. "Do me the courtesy of allowing me to say what I have come to say. I do need to put the past behind me. And you, well"—she met his gaze firmly—"you are part of that past."

"What?" Shock coursed through him and he stared in disbelief.

"I need to start my life anew. Surely you can see that."

"What about us?" he said without thinking.

"Gideon, dear, there really isn't any *us*. Oh, we've had a lovely time together, truly the grandest of all my adventures, but we knew from the start it was not to be permanent."

"What if I now wish it to be permanent?"

Her eyes widened. "I do hope you are not speaking of marriage."

"And if I am?"

"You and I both know what kind of woman you should marry, and we know as well I do not fit the requirements you seek. Besides." She shook her head. "I've told you I have no desire to marry again."

"That can certainly change."

"I suppose it can." She paused as if to consider the possibility, then lifted a shoulder in a casual shrug. "But it hasn't."

"Because of him? Because of your husband?"

She hesitated for a long moment, then drew a deep breath. "Yes."

"I would never hurt you."

"I know that. But I might well hurt you and I would not wish for that to happen." She shook her head. "Some of us are simply not meant for marriage and permanence and—"

"Love?"

"Perhaps. But love has nothing to do with it, really. You and I have both experienced love in the past—"

"What I *thought* was love. This is entirely different."

"Yes, of course it is because we are far older and hopefully a bit wiser. And like civilized people we set certain rules—"

"Such as honesty?"

"A certain amount of honesty, yes." She paused and chose her words with care. "We also agreed that when either one of us decided it was time to go our separate ways we could do so without recrimination and . . ."

"And?"

"And that time has come."

He stared in disbelief. "That's what you came here to say?"

"I considered writing a note but it seemed rather cowardly."

"I thought you came to . . . to . . ."

"To what?"

"Certainly not to tell me you were ending it," he snapped.

"I am sorry if this comes as a surprise." Her tone was surprisingly casual, as if her words were of no significance at all. "After the other night I thought surely you would expect this."

"I expected nothing of the sort. What I expected was that you would have realized—"

"What?"

"That there is more to what we have shared than a mere adventure!" He glared at her.

She stared at him for a long moment, then shook her head. "But there can't be. One's fate is preordained. One's destiny is already determined."

"That's ridiculous and you well know it. One shapes one's own fate by the decisions one makes. The idea that there is no choice in life is nothing more than an excuse for—"

"For what?" Her chin snapped up.

"Cowardly behavior." He moved toward her. "Can you deny that you feel something for me?"

"Don't be absurd, of course I feel something for you." She turned away and glanced at the window, avoiding his gaze. He suspected she wished to look anywhere but at him. Because she wanted to end it? Or because she didn't? "We shall always be good, good friends."

"Friends?" He fairly spat the word. "Friends?"

"Yes," she said firmly, "friends." She drew a deep breath and smiled. "Now, if you will forgive me, I should be on my way." She turned away from him and started toward the door.

He couldn't let her go. "Wait." Not like this. She paused, her hand on the door handle, her back to him. Not at all. "What did you feel, Judith, the first time you looked into my eyes?"

Her shoulders straightened. "I felt you had very nice eyes."

He stepped toward her. "Nothing more than that?"

"No," she said firmly. "Nothing more."

"Do you want to know what I felt?" He moved closer.

"I don't think that is—"

He was right behind her now. Close enough to kiss the back of her neck. To pull her into his arms. And keep her there. "I felt excitement. Anticipation. Magic."

"Don't be—"

"When I gazed into the blue of your eyes, I felt something quite remarkable. As though I wasn't merely looking into your eyes but peering into your very soul. And it touched mine." His breath caught. "And made me whole."

"Stop it." She rested her forehead against the door. "Please."

"I felt as if I'd been struck." He leaned forward and spoke low beside her ear. "*Le coup de foudre*, Judith, bolt of lightning. That's what I felt the first time I looked into your eyes. And every time thereafter."

For a long moment she was silent, and he held his breath.

"Sometimes, Gideon." There was the slightest tremble in her voice, as if she was fighting back tears or struggling with emotions too intense to control. "The light lasts only for a moment. And no more." She yanked the door open and was gone before he could say another word.

Shock froze him in place and stole his breath. How could she simply waltz out of his life as if he—as if they—didn't matter? Damn it all, he loved her. Certainly he hadn't actually said it but surely she knew. Just as he knew she loved him. As much as she tried to hide it, he could hear it in her voice, see it in her eyes.

He wasn't sure why she'd decided to leave him now unless she was still angry with him. But that would indeed be irrational, and for the most part Judith was not an irrational woman. It all had to do with her late husband, he was certain of that. And, damnation, when he'd told her she still held on to her past, her husband was what he'd meant. Gideon certainly hadn't intended for her to decide he was part of the past she needed to put behind her. Not bloody likely.

Blast it all, he was her present and her future even if he hadn't fully realized it until right now. Admittedly he'd been slow to come to the realization that he did indeed love her, that they belonged together, but his own past had taught him to be cautious when it came to matters of the heart. He was willing now, even eager, to take that leap of faith that love required. Regardless of the repercussions, he could not live his life without her. He moved toward the door, and it swung open abruptly.

"My lord," Wells started.

"You needn't bother to announce me." Violet

pushed past the butler. "I am here now." She fixed Wells with a commanding eye. "Although tea would be nice." She turned to Gideon and cast him her most potent smile. "Good day, Gideon."

Gideon's jaw tensed. The last thing he needed or wanted right now was anything having to do with Violet. He forced a civil note to his voice. "I am on my way out so if you would be so kind as to—"

"But I've come to apologize and give you another chance."

If he hurried, he might still be able to catch Judith's carriage. "Violet, I don't have time for any more of your nonsense."

"It's not nonsense and you do have time. She's already gone." She raised a brow. "I assume you're running after Lady Chester."

"You saw her then?"

"I could scarcely miss her." Violet sniffed. "The woman practically knocked me over in her hurry to get to her carriage."

"I see." Violet was right. It was pointless to run after Judith now. He would find her later. No matter what she'd said, this was far from over. "What do you want?"

"I told you. I wish to apologize if I upset you in any way by my choice of guests."

He snorted. "I am not the one to whom you owe an apology. Perhaps you should have apologized to Lady Chester on your way in."

Violet shrugged. "I'm fairly certain she didn't even see me. She was in rather a hurry." She studied him curiously. "You must have had a nasty argument."

"It was nothing of significance." Unless, of course, Judith had noted Violet's arrival and took it entirely the wrong way. He groaned to himself. That was an additional complication he didn't need. "Very well then, your apology is acknowledged."

"Not accepted?"

"No. Is that all?"

"No." She huffed. "Gideon." A contrite smile curved her lips. "I should very much like to have another chance."

"Another chance for what," he said absently. On the other hand, a tiny bit of jealousy on Judith's part might be useful.

"For you and me."

"What?" His attention snapped to Violet.

"I thought you'd like that." She smiled in an overly smug manner.

He stared in horror. "Why on earth would you think I'd like that? I thought I had made myself perfectly clear."

"You might have indicated a certain lack of interest, but that was before you and Lady Chester went your separate ways."

"We have not gone our separate ways."

"She looked very much like a woman who was going her separate way."

He gritted his teeth and prayed for the strength to keep from strangling Violet with his bare hands. "Regardless of what it looked like—"

"Come now, Gideon." She waved away his comment. "This pretense of yours that you no longer have feelings for me is becoming tiresome. You are simply trying to make me earn your affection. I understand that, truly I do. I was quite vile to you, and I realize you can never completely forgive me, but I am willing to spend the rest of my life making amends."

"Violet!" What on earth had come over the woman?

She moved toward him. "You loved me once, and even if you don't completely love me at the moment, surely you can love me again."

She couldn't possibly be serious. He backed away. "I am sorry, Violet, but I have put all of that— I have put you—behind me."

"I make an excellent wife." She stepped closer.

"Nonetheless—"

"Can't you find it in your heart to give me the opportunity to redeem myself?" She moved to within an inch of him and gazed into his eyes. "To earn back your love."

He stared. "I don't know what to say."

"Gideon. I . . ." Her violet eyes widened. "I need you."

Without warning the years vanished. It was another day, another time. And another Gideon altogether. He shook his head. "Violet, I—"

"Gideon." A catch sounded in her voice, and she trailed her fingers over the lapels of his coat. "I have always loved you in my fashion. Now we can be together. And I want to be yours forever."

Surely she didn't mean it. Violet couldn't possibly love him. And even if she did, he didn't love her. If indeed she was sincere, she had his sympathy but nothing beyond that.

"Well?" A faint note of impatience sounded in Violet's voice. "Aren't you going to say something?"

At once, he realized the truth. Whatever she was up to, it was clear that Violet loved him no more now than she had nine years ago. Relief washed through him. He had no desire to hurt her as she had hurt him. And that too was a relief. "You nearly had me there for a moment." He chuckled and moved away. "I was starting to feel . . . well, something for you. I was starting to believe that you had changed. That you were sincere, even honest. For a moment I thought there was a possibility that you did indeed care for me."

"I do care for you," she said staunchly.

He raised a brow.

"Well, I do." She huffed, swiveled on her heel, and retreated to the nearest chair. She sank into it like a deflated sail. "We could be quite wonderful together."

He studied her carefully. "What do you really want?"

"Aside from you?" she said brightly.

He ignored her.

"I want what any woman wants. Home, family, security." She toyed with the arm of the chair. "Money."

"Money?" He grinned. "So that's what this is about."

"Don't be crude, Gideon. One doesn't discuss money. I would much prefer to discuss love, affection, that sort of thing."

His grin widened even though he knew he

shouldn't find this the least bit amusing. "Violet, are you—"

"I am a bit short on funds at the moment," she said loftily. "Nothing significant."

"Violet?"

"Very well. I need money. A great deal of money really, my expenses are considerable." She heaved a heartfelt sigh. "And I haven't a feather to fly with." She narrowed her eyes. "There, now are you happy?"

"Not at all," he said and tried to wipe the smile from his face. "How on earth did this happen? I thought Lord Braxton had quite a tidy fortune."

"William wasn't very good with money. I had no idea we were living well above our means. He was sheltering me. It was quite dear of him really. Pity he had to die," she murmured.

"Damn inconvenient of him."

She sighed. "Wasn't it though?"

"What about your family?"

"There's nothing there either. My father's title, of course, along with his country holdings, went to a cousin. My mother was left with the house in town and an insignificant fortune which she managed to squander before her death. And now the house is mine although it's a terrible expense. I might have to sell it and I should hate to do so. It's been in my family for generations." She glanced up at him in a mournful manner. "Did you know I was an orphan now? A widow and an orphan? With children." She sighed dramatically. "I am all alone in this cruel, cruel world."

"Except for the children."

She narrowed her eyes. "Yes, of course."

"And your husband's family is of no help?"

"Up to now, I have been dependent upon his family for support. They have done so for the sake of the children, after all, my son is the next title holder. Indeed they are paying for my house here in London. But they have grown weary of my expenses." She blew a resigned breath. "They are urging me to marry. To that end, they have selected a potential husband who is apparently quite amenable to the match."

"Old and wealthy, I imagine."

"Scandalously rich but not much older than you. He's not a bad sort really but, dear Lord, Gideon." She rose to her feet and paced the room, wringing her hands together. "He is nearly a foot shorter than I am. Do you have any idea what it's like to dance with a man nearly a foot shorter than you? Why, his nose is practically nestled in my bosom."

Gideon choked back a laugh.

"It's not at all funny. When I gaze down upon him I have an excellent view of his balding head. Gideon, do marry me, save me from an unwanted marriage."

He laughed. "Violet, you must come up with a new script. I have seen this play before."

"It could have a much happier ending for you this time," she said hopefully.

"I eloped with you once to try to save you from an unwanted marriage. Even if now the marriage truly is unwanted"—he shook his head—"I have no intention of doing it again."

"Are you certain? There is no dishonor in changing your mind, you know." She smiled in an enticing manner. "We could have a lovely life together."

He chose his words carefully. "There was a time when I would have given a great deal to hear those words, but even then, Violet . . ." His gaze met hers firmly. "It would have been a mistake."

"You're probably right." She cast him a disappointed glance. "I had no idea you were so sanctimonious. I am not fond of sanctimony."

"Understandable."

"I should be off then." She started toward the door. "Apparently I have a wedding to arrange. Pity it isn't ours." She glanced back at him. "Do you have any wealthy, unmarried friends who might be suitable for me? Preferably tall, with hair?"

He laughed. "You haven't changed in the least, Violet. You're still trying to use me to get what you want."

"Yes, I suppose you're right. I probably haven't changed. But then neither have you. Nine years later, and once again you are in love with a woman who doesn't want you." She smiled in a knowing manner. "Good day, Gideon."

"Good day, Violet." He kept a pleasant smile on his face until the door was safely closed behind her, then allowed it to fade. He walked slowly to his desk and sat down behind it.

Once again you are in love with a woman who doesn't want you.

No, Violet was wrong. She had no idea what she

was talking about. Violet knew nothing whatsoever of the relationship between Judith and him. Beyond that, Violet didn't know him at all and, in truth, never really had.

Still, what if he was wrong about Judith's feelings? He'd been wrong once before, and it had left him shattered even if he now realized what he'd felt for Violet was a pale imitation of what he felt for Judith. And his heart hadn't been broken as much as his pride and his illusions. It wasn't love at all. His feelings for Judith were entirely different. Deeper, richer . . . more. How much worse would it be now?

Your arrogance will be your downfall.

Was it arrogance that made him think that Judith loved him as he loved her? Arrogance that made him refuse to believe that she truly wished to end their relationship? Arrogance that fueled his certainty that her decision had more to do with her past than with him?

He rested his elbows on the desk and buried his face in his hands. Was he wrong? Was he as mired in his past as she was in hers? Doomed to repeat his mistakes again? And this time lose his soul forever?

"Gideon?" Aunt Louisa's voice sounded from the doorway.

He drew a deep breath, composed himself, and raised his head. "Yes?"

"I saw Lady Braxton leave and I understand Lady Chester was here before her." Aunt Louisa approached the desk, genuine concern on her face. "Are you all right, my boy?"

"Am I all right?" *I have just decided to honor the wishes of the love of my life, the other half of my soul, and allow her to walk out of my life. And I already feel her loss with an ache so intense, death would not be as painful.* "Yes, of course." He got to his feet. "I am quite well, thank you." He adopted a polite smile and started for the door. "I may be found at my club later if you have need of me."

"Gideon?" Aunt Louisa drew her brows together. "I know you have no feelings for Lady Braxton, therefore I assume it is Lady Chester who has put that devastated look in your eye."

"There is no look in my eye, devastated or otherwise. However." He forced an unemotional tone to his voice. "You have no further need to worry about my involvement with Lady Chester. We have agreed to stop seeing one another."

"I see," she murmured.

"She—we—thought it would be for the best."

"No doubt." She studied him intently as if she was trying to read his thoughts or his heart. "And you are . . . pleased about it? Happy with this decision?"

"Happiness is of no particular concern." He nodded and again turned toward the door. A great deal of alcohol would not make him feel better, but with luck it would make him feel nothing at all. And that was preferable to feeling entirely too much. He paused and turned back to his aunt. "Oh, and if your list of suitable prospective brides is available, I should like to have a look at it. It's past time I get on with my life. Fulfill my duties, live up to my responsibilities, that sort of thing."

"Yes, of course," she said faintly.

"Excellent." He nodded and left the room. He called for his carriage, then decided instead to walk the distance to his club. Gideon did like walking. It helped if one wanted to think or provided a distraction if one didn't.

If Judith was determined to put him in the past, so be it. He had meant what he'd said to Helmsley. He would never again offer his heart to a woman who did not want it. Still, Judith would own his heart always. Whether she wanted it or not.

Chapter 15

"What on earth is going on here?"

Judith looked up from the notebook in her hand and stared across the packing crates stacked throughout her parlor. *Dear Lord, what is she doing here?* Judith drew a deep breath. "Good day, Lady Radbury. I must say this is a surprise."

"The surprise, Lady Chester, is mine." The older woman's gaze skimmed the room. "Whatever are you up to?"

"I should think it would be rather obvious." Judith smiled pleasantly. "I am packing."

"Indeed it is obvious," Gideon's aunt said sharply. "The question is where are you going and why."

"I am going to Paris, and there I hope to join an expedition forming to collect orchids in Colombia."

Lady Radbury stared in disbelief. "Are you insane?"

Judith shook her head. "Not at all."

"You're going to South America to pick flowers?"

"I am going to Colombia to hunt orchids," Judith said firmly.

Lady Radbury sniffed. "Well, it's the maddest thing I have ever heard." She drew her brows together. "You do realize you're a woman, don't you?"

"I am aware of that fact. But I shall not be the first woman to join such an expedition, and I daresay I will not be the last."

"I don't know what the world is coming to," Lady Radbury said under her breath and picked her way around the crates. "When did you decide this?"

"A few days ago, but I have considered it for years."

"When are you leaving?" Lady Radbury stopped and peered into a crate.

"As soon as arrangements can be made."

"I see." Lady Radbury glanced at her. "Rather an extreme means of escape, don't you think?"

"It's not a means of escape at all. It's something I've always wanted to do," Judith said slowly. "The opportunity has arisen to do so and—"

Lady Radbury pulled a Meissen shepherdess from a nest of wood shavings and studied it. "And what about Gideon?"

"What about Gideon?"

Lady Radbury raised a brow. "We're going to

play that game, are we? Very well then." She carefully replaced the figurine in the crate, made her way to the sofa, and sat down. "Come join me, Judith, we need to talk."

"I should love to chat with you, Louisa, but I have a great deal to accomplish here and not a lot of time in which to do it." Judith waved at the sea of crates. "This room alone will take another day or so. I need to meet with my solicitor and arrange for a friend to keep my dog."

"You're planning on being gone a long time then?"

"At least six months, possibly a year." *Maybe forever.* "I am considering leasing the house in my absence, therefore I plan to store the furnishings until I return."

"As you will be gone such a long time, surely you can take a few moments now." Louisa patted the sofa beside her.

Judith hesitated. She had no desire to hear whatever it was that Gideon's aunt wished to say. She had no desire to speak of him at all. It was enough that he was in her mind every minute, enough that everything she saw or touched reminded her of him and reminded her as well of what she could never have.

Louisa rolled her gaze toward the ceiling. "Please."

"As you wish." Judith placed the notebook on the edge of the nearest crate and signaled to the maids packing crates near the windows to leave. She skirted a precarious stack of still empty containers and settled in a chair near the sofa. She folded her hands in her lap and waited for the other woman to begin.

"I was"—Louisa closed her eyes for a moment as if praying for divine guidance—"wrong. I thought I should say that before I go any further."

"You were?" Judith stared. "I must say you have taken me by surprise. We scarcely know one another at all, but the admission that you might have been incorrect about something strikes me as completely out of character."

"My dear Judith, it is. You have no idea how much it pains me to admit I might have been wrong about anything, let alone anything important." Louisa heaved a dramatic sigh. "But there you have it. I was wrong."

Judith chose her words carefully. "Dare I ask what you were wrong about?"

"Gideon. You. You and Gideon together." Louisa gestured in an aimless manner. "But mostly Gideon."

"You think I am not the wrong woman for him after all?"

Louisa snorted. "Oh no, I think you're utterly wrong for him. You're not at all what he needs in a wife. You're completely unsuitable."

"I believe we've had this discussion before," Judith said coolly. "And you have nothing to concern yourself with now because Lord Warton and I have agreed to end our—"

"What I was wrong about, my dear Judith, is declaring that I didn't care about his happiness. I do care." She fixed Judith with a firm stare. "Very much so."

Judith shook her head. "I fail to see what Lord Warton's happiness has to do with me."

"Then I was wrong about you as well," Louisa snapped. "You're not nearly as intelligent as I thought."

"That's a distinct possibility," Judith said sharply, then forced a note of calm. "Louisa, I—"

"He's miserable, you know. He has been for the last few days, but today, after you left . . ." Louisa shook her head. "There's a look in his eyes today as if he has lost something he treasured more than life itself."

An ache formed in the back of Judith's throat.

"If you don't know already, he is in love with you, and I strongly suspect you are in love with him as well. Especially now that I see the lengths you are willing to go to to put him out of your life."

"Louisa, I—"

"Judith, through these weeks that you and he have been together I have seen my nephew in a way I have never seen him before. For the first time since I have shared his house he has been, well . . ." She sighed in resignation. "Happy. Truly happy. If being with you makes him happy, then it's nothing short of sheer stupidity for the two of you not to be together."

"You don't understand." Judith shook her head. "I have no desire to marry again."

"That is stupid." Louisa huffed. "You do realize my only objections to you were age and your independence, and then there is your somewhat exaggerated reputation. But I also think you are a . . . a good person and you are certainly good for him." She narrowed her eyes. "Why don't you wish to marry again? Most women do. Even I would probably marry again given the right gentleman."

"For the very reasons you mentioned. I value my independence." Judith shrugged. "Marriage once was enough."

Louisa studied her for a thoughtful moment. "Gideon would never hurt you."

"Did he say something to you?" Judith said without thinking.

"No. Not a word." Louisa stared in an assessing manner. "The apple does not fall far from the tree, you know."

"I don't know what you mean," Judith said slowly.

"I knew your late husband's mother before her marriage although she was little more than an acquaintance. I saw her on rare occasions after her marriage as well. She was a timid thing and quite clumsy. Always falling down stairs or out of carriages, absurd little accidents. Insignificant incidents, really, unless one took them as a whole. It was yet another accident that took her life." Her gaze met Judith's directly. "Her husband was a violent man. I didn't know him but I knew of him. No one, save perhaps his children, mourned at his death."

Judith drew a steadying breath. "I loved my husband and he loved me."

"And Gideon loves you now. And you love him."

Judith chose her words with care. "Have you ever considered, Louisa, the possibility that he might not hurt me but that I will hurt him?"

Louisa stared for a long moment, then smiled. "No." She rose to her feet. "But he is hurting now."

Judith stood. "I never wanted that."

"Then go to him, Judith, tell him of your feelings. For goodness' sakes, marry the man. Unless . . ." Louisa paused thoughtfully. "Unless I'm wrong. You do love him, don't you?"

"No, I don't," Judith said quickly but not quickly enough.

"I knew it. I am never wrong."

Judith scoffed.

Louisa ignored her. "You do not lie well, my dear, we shall have to work on that. One should never be too honest with men, especially husbands. Once you and Gideon are married—"

"I am not going to marry Lord Warton." Judith stared at the other woman. "Why won't you believe me?"

"Because it was recently pointed out to me that nothing is as important in one's life as happiness." Louisa smiled in a satisfied manner. "I intend to see my nephew happy. And you make him happy. And if you are happy as well, I shall be, if not precisely happy, then content."

"You do understand he has never spoken of love and he has not asked me to marry him?"

"Mere trifles." Louisa waved dismissively. "Men

are usually slow to commit to either love or marriage. But mark my words, he will."

"I am going to South America," Judith said firmly.

"I doubt that. However, if you are going"—Louisa grinned—"I would wager you are not going alone. Did you know when Gideon was a little boy he wished to be an explorer?" She chuckled. "He will love the jungle."

"He would hate the jungle." Judith stared.

"He will love it because you are there." Louisa moved toward the door, deftly skirting the open crates and stacked containers. "You should know that I am not above manipulating people's lives. In fact I rather enjoy it." She cast Judith a triumphant smile. "Welcome to the family. Good day."

"Good day," Judith murmured and sank back into the chair.

Gideon loved her? She had suspected, maybe even hoped, but knowing only made matters worse. She loved him and he loved her and it didn't matter. She had failed one man she'd thought she'd loved. She would not fail the one she truly did. If Louisa was right, if Gideon did love her, all the more reason for her to get out of his life. And spend the rest of her days alone.

No. Determination swept through her, and she got to her feet. She was tired of living her life alone and she refused to do it any longer.

And there was only one person more alone in the world than she was.

Chester House never failed to provoke feelings of unease in Judith. Even on the brightest days the house maintained an air of gloom and the shadows stretched endlessly. Through the years she had lived here she had never been able to consider it home. She had, on occasion, even wondered if there were unseen creatures inhabiting the house beyond those of the mortal world.

"Whatever are you doing here?" Alexandra stepped cautiously into the parlor.

"I have come to see you." Judith smiled brightly. "Sister, dear."

Alexandra's eyes narrowed. "Why?"

"I wished to tell you of my plans." Judith clasped her hands together and braced herself. "I've decided to travel to Colombia to hunt for orchids."

Alexandra stared at her. "Where?"

"Colombia." Judith shrugged. "It's in South America."

"I know where it is," Alexandra said slowly, "I didn't mean *where* so much as I meant *why.*"

"Why?" *Because I need to get as far away from Gideon as I possibly can.* "Because it's time. Past time, really. I should have done this years ago."

"Boring lectures and that glass house of yours aren't enough for you? You want to tramp through a jungle as well?"

"It shall be a grand adventure, and like any grand adventure it shall be even better when shared with someone."

Alexandra raised a brow. "Your Lord Warton is going with you?"

"No." Judith casually moved to the nearest sofa and seated herself. "You are."

"Me?" Alexandra fairly squeaked the word. It would have been most amusing under other circumstances. "Me?"

"Yes, you." Judith nodded. "I have decided ten years—thirteen really if you consider . . . never mind. It scarcely matters. It's far too long a time for two people to hate one another, especially two people who have no one else in the world but each other." She paused. "Although I never actually hated you."

Alexandra stared.

"Oh, I disliked you intensely but I never hated you. At any rate." Judith drew a deep breath. "I should like for us to become friends."

"But *I* have hated *you*! Sincerely and unequivocally and not to be confused for a moment with mere dislike. Hating you has been the great passion of my life." Alexandra sank onto the sofa and stared at Judith. "I certainly don't want to be your friend now and I have no desire to travel to the ends of the earth with you!"

Judith waved away the comment. "Come now, it's not quite the ends of the earth."

"It's far closer than I would ever wish to get, thank you!"

"I didn't think you would appreciate the idea at first but you'll come around."

"Why on earth would you think that?"

"I could say it's because I am your only means of support but I would prefer not to." Judith met the other woman's gaze directly. "Eventually you will realize that this makes perfect sense because we have no one else, Alexandra, and I, for one, am tired of being alone. We have no family save each other and we have let this rift between us go on for far too long. Besides, there's really nothing left for us here."

"Dear Lord," Alexandra muttered.

"I know this comes as a shock to you. I was rather shocked myself when the idea occurred to me scarcely more than an hour ago—"

"You might need to give it more time." Alexandra's voice had a slightly strangled, high-pitched sound to it.

"Nonsense, it's brilliant. I should have thought of this years ago. However, I do understand the idea of us becoming friends, even sisters—"

"Sisters!" Alexandra choked out the word.

"—is not something you've so much as considered. Therefore we needn't leap into it with both feet, so to speak. We can proceed in a more leisurely fashion." She paused to give Alexandra a moment to catch her breath. The poor woman did not look at all well. "I know it will take you a bit of time to adjust to the idea of South America and you shall have it. The expedition I wish to join leaves from Paris in six weeks. As you were already going to Paris I thought I would accompany you as your traveling companion. It will be an excellent way for the two of us to begin to know one another better. Besides, you need a traveling companion, and as I am a widow, I really am perfect for—"

"I'm not going to Paris," Alexandra blurted.

"Why on earth not?" Judith's voice rose. "London is boring. You said so yourself."

"It's become less boring of late."

Judith narrowed her eyes. "What are you talking about?"

"Well." Alexandra grimaced. "I've decided to marry Nigel Howard after all."

Judith stared in disbelief. "The penniless poet?"

"Yes. No." Alexandra shook her head. "Not exactly. That is to say, Nigel has not been entirely truthful with me."

"Oh?"

"He is a poet but he's not exactly penniless. It seems he is second in line for a title and is already heir to a tidy fortune. He has never acknowledged his money because he felt money would hinder his creative muse. The man might well be madder than I am. Still." Alexandra smiled, a true smile. Judith had never seen such a smile on her before. "He is a very nice man."

"You're getting married?" Judith still couldn't quite believe it.

Alexandra wrinkled her nose. "You're shocked, aren't you? You probably think it's a dreadful idea. That I shall surely ruin the man's life."

"No. Not at all." Judith shook her head slowly. "I think it's quite lovely."

"Do you really?" Alexandra stared suspiciously. "Why?"

"Because you seem . . ." Judith never thought she'd say such a thing in regard to her sister-in-law. "Happy, I think."

"Happy?" Alexandra thought for a moment, then nodded. "Yes, I believe I am. I don't think

I've ever been happy before. It's really quite nice. So." She drew a deep breath. "You can see why I won't be going to Paris or anywhere else."

"Nor should you," Judith murmured. "I shall speak to my solicitors at once about transferring ownership of the house to Mr. Howard."

"No." A firm tone rang in Alexandra's voice. "We don't need this house and I don't want it." She looked around and shuddered. "It's a dark, wicked place, and the only reason I ever wanted it at all was because you had it and it should have been mine. I am quite looking forward to leaving it forever."

"Then I shall sell it and add it to the rest of the money Lucian left as a wedding gift or dowry, whatever you prefer." Judith raised a brow. "Unless you don't want the money either?"

"Oh, I'll take the money," Alexandra said with a grin.

"Good." Judith smiled. "Well, that's that then." If anyone had told Judith even a day ago that she would be disappointed that she would not be traveling with Alexandra and struggling to become her friend, or indeed that it would be her idea to do so in the first place, she would have laughed aloud. Now disappointment washed through her. "I shall simply have to go by myself."

Alexandra studied her. "What of your Lord Warton?"

"He is not my Lord Warton." Judith blew a long breath. "Nor will he ever be."

"Why not?"

"Because it's not possible."

Alexandra snorted. "If it's possible for me to find happiness and a respectable marriage, anything at all is possible. Why can't your Lord Warton be your Lord Warton?"

"Because I am afraid," Judith said without thinking and wondered that she had said it at all. And wondered as well if Alexandra was the only one in the world she could have said it to.

"Yes, I suppose you would be," Alexandra said more to herself than to Judith, then sighed. "I've been somewhat unfair to you all these years, I know that."

Judith shrugged. "I understood."

Alexandra rolled her gaze toward the ceiling. "Dear Lord, I do so detest when you're noble."

"I'm not the least bit noble. I understood because I more than likely would have acted the same way had I been in your position."

"I doubt that. For as long as I have known you, you have always been kinder than people have deserved. Probably because you have never seemed the least bit unsure as to your place in the world. In the lives of your parents. In Lucian's heart."

"And yet it was not enough was it?" Judith shook her head. "At least not in respect to my husband. I failed him when he needed me."

Alexandra studied her for a long moment. "Perhaps you're right, perhaps it is time for us to become . . . well, to put aside our differences at least. Indeed, in my weaker moments I find I am tired of hating you, Judith. And we do have much in common. I too have always sworn I would never marry. The madness, you know."

Judith scoffed. "Nonsense, you're not mad. You never have been."

"No." Alexandra chose her words with care. "I'm not."

"Lucian wasn't mad," Judith said quickly.

Alexandra blew a long breath. "Not yet."

A voice in the back of Judith's head urged caution. She wasn't at all sure she wished to hear what her sister-in-law had to say. Still, it was past time. "What do you mean?"

Alexandra got to her feet, folded her arms across her chest, and walked to the window overlooking the terrace. "Did he ever speak to you about our parents?"

Judith shook her head. "Not that I can recall." In truth, she'd learned more from Lady Radbury today than she ever had from Lucian. "I made some assumptions about your father given the stipulations in his will but Lucian never spoke of your father or your mother."

"Our mother died when we were very young. Neither of us remembered much of her." Alexandra stared out the window. "What sort of man was your father?"

"My father?" The question struck Judith as odd. She thought for a moment. "He was a good man, I think. Reserved in his manner, at least regarding affection, but I always knew he cared for me. And I shall always miss him." She smiled softly at the memory of the tall, fair-haired man with the sober expression and the smile in his eyes. "I know he must have been disappointed that I was his only child, that he'd had a daughter instead of sons, but he never made me feel that was in any way my fault."

"For that alone I could hate you," Alexandra murmured. She stared out the window in silence. Finally she drew a deep breath. "I shall not bore you with tales of my father. Suffice it to say, neither Lucian nor I missed him. He was not a . . . a pleasant man. His wife and his children were his possessions, not his family."

"I see."

Alexandra snorted. "No you don't. You can't possibly. My brother lived in fear that he would become like my father one day."

Judith held her breath. "I don't understand."

"My father was cruel for the sake of being cruel. He was violent and brutal with a vicious nature . . ." She shook her head. "Odd, when you grow up with a man like that you think that's how everyone is. Somehow, you made Lucian, and me as well, realize that was not entirely true."

Judith should have been surprised by Alexandra's admission. But even before Lady Radbury's revelations Judith had suspected Lucian's father had not been a kind or loving man. The dark, grim nature of the house alone proclaimed that there had been little happiness here.

"He thought you were his savior."

Judith gasped.

Alexandra glanced at her. "Don't look so stricken. He was wrong. You were far too young and entirely too naïve to be anyone's savior. I knew it from the beginning and I think he did as well. Still he hoped." She turned back to the window. "I am sorry, Judith." She shook her head. "All these years I have allowed you to think Lucian's death was your fault. Indeed, I have encouraged you to believe that you drove him to it because of your actions on that one night."

Judith drew a shaky breath. "Perhaps if I had not been so—"

"You had nothing to do with it." A weary note sounded in Alexandra's voice. "Do you believe in fate? Destiny?"

Judith started to say yes, then shook her head. "I'm not sure."

"I am. Lucian always feared he was destined to become the man our father was. He swore he would not allow that to happen. That night, the night he died—"

Judith stood, moved to Alexandra's side, and realized her sister-in-law's gaze was fixed on the spot on the terrace where Lucian's body had been found.

"After he hurt you. After you refused to allow him into your rooms—"

"I should never have—"

"No." Alexandra shook her head. "Only a fool would have let him in. And you had no idea what would happen next."

The back of Judith's throat ached. "It was my fault."

"If it was anyone's fault, it was mine. And his. We had both watched his temper grow shorter, his actions become more violent, and we did nothing. Not that there was anything we could do.

That night, he was shocked by his behavior, but more, he was terrified. He was convinced he was turning into our father and he would not allow that. He threw himself off the roof because of what he did to you, not because of anything you did to him."

Judith swallowed hard. "Alexandra, you can't know that."

"I do know it, Judith." Alexandra drew a deep breath. "Because I was there."

Shock slammed Judith and stole her breath.

"I knew that night, indeed, everyone in the household knew, something dreadful had happened between the two of you. I saw Lucian pounding on your door, and when he went up to the roof, I followed him." Alexandra's brow furrowed with memory and regret. "I tried to talk to him but he wouldn't listen. And I didn't know what to say." She paused to collect herself. "He told me I should tell you how very sorry he was."

"Alexandra." Judith couldn't get out the words.

"I tried to stop him. I distinctly remember reaching for him, trying to grab him." There was a haunted note in Alexandra's voice. "And then he was gone. Over the side of the house. Into the night. I couldn't bring myself to look over the edge of the roof." She shook her head. "I didn't want to look down on him like that. See him small, at a distance. Like a broken doll, tossed aside." She blew a long breath. "I knew he couldn't survive but I hoped, for a moment anyway. I ran down to the terrace but he was . . . it was . . ."

"But he wasn't found until the next morning,"

Judith said quietly. She remembered that morning distinctly. The cries of the servants who found Lucian's body. The pain of his death and the sheer horror of realizing it was her fault.

"I didn't want everyone to think—to *know*—the truth. I thought it would seem more like an accident if someone else found him. So I stayed with him until dawn, then hid and waited until he was found." She shook her head. "For a long time I wondered how my heart could continue to beat if his didn't. After all, our hearts had beat in unison since before we were born.

"I should have told you then that it wasn't your fault but"—she shrugged—"my pain was such that I had no desire to ease yours. And as the years passed, and I was dependent on you for my home and my support and your life seemed so carefree—"

"Did it?"

"Wasn't it?"

"In many ways I suppose it was but only because I had no one to care for. No," Judith corrected herself. "Because I refused to allow myself to care for someone or allow someone to care for me."

"Because you thought you were to blame for Lucian's death? Because you felt somehow you had failed him? And if you failed him, you could certainly fail someone else, and the consequences might be just as tragic?"

"Something like that," Judith murmured.

"Well, you were wrong."

Judith stared.

The corners of Alexandra's mouth quirked upward. "Is it so hard to believe? That you were wrong?"

"About this?" Judith nodded. "Yes."

"He was on this path his entire life. You were . . . incidental." Alexandra's gaze met hers. "If it hadn't been you it would have been someone else. Or something else. I think now death by his own hand was inevitable once he believed he was becoming our father. There was nothing you could have done to save him. "

"Surely, if I had known—"

"But you didn't know. You didn't know about his demons and his fears. And even if you had, it wouldn't have made any difference." Alexandra blew a resigned breath and turned back to gaze out the window. "I knew him better than anyone. His demons were mine and I couldn't help him."

Judith's gaze followed Alexandra's, and for a silent moment they shared a bond forged from a common tragedy, a union ten years in the making. Judith tried to gather her thoughts, her emotions, and found them scattered and confused.

One disclosure from Alexandra was not enough to counter a decade of guilt and remorse. Still, Judith was gripped by a relief so intense, she wanted to weep with the sheer force of it. It was as if a huge weight had been lifted from her shoulders. Or her heart. With it came a sense of freedom of being, a lightness of her soul. And she could breathe.

"Why are you telling me all this now?"

"I don't know." Alexandra was silent for a long moment. "Perhaps because I no longer feel the need to punish you for my own failings. Or because my bitterness has faded in the wake of new and unexpected feelings."

Judith smiled. "My gratitude to the penniless poet."

Alexandra shook her head as if she could not believe her own words. "So you see, sister dear, there's no reason at all why your Lord Warton shouldn't be your Lord Warton."

For a moment Judith's spirits rose, then plummeted, and she grimaced. "I fear it's too late for that."

"Why? Because you've made your plans for picking flowers in the jungle?"

"Because I've ended it with him." Her heart ached with the words.

"You ended it with him?" Alexandra raised a brow. "Not the other way around?"

"Yes."

"Then tell him you've changed your mind. Tell him"—Alexandra grinned—"you were wrong."

"I don't think that will matter." Judith shook her head. "I've caused him a great deal of pain and I can't imagine he can ever forgive me."

Alexandra stared at her. "Don't disillusion me now, Judith. I have always thought you were the most courageous woman I have ever known. Look at your life. You would not allow Lucian to hurt you again. You did not crawl into a hole after his death but instead you've made a rather interesting life for yourself."

"A life alone," Judith said wryly.

"Yes, well." Alexandra sighed. "I take some measure of responsibility for that." She rolled her gaze toward the ceiling. "Judith, do you love this man?"

Judith hesitated then shrugged. "Yes."

"Does he love you?"

"I think so."

"Then do something about it. You said you were tired of being alone. I certainly don't want to have anything to do with you. It seems to me if you don't wish to live the rest of your days alone, you need to get this Lord Warton back."

Judith thought for a moment. The only reason at all she had ended it with Gideon was her fears. Now Alexandra had eliminated those for the most part. Even Susanna and Lady Radbury had given their approval. If she went to Gideon and he wanted nothing to do with her, she would be no worse off than she was now. And if he did . . .

"Well?"

"You're wrong, Alexandra. He's not *this* Lord Warton." Judith squared her shoulders. "He is my Lord Warton and it's past time I let him know."

Chapter 16

"It is a fact one cannot deny that, on occasion, the more one drinks the more lucid one becomes." Gideon frowned at the nearly empty glass in his hand. "That only applies, of course, if one's fondest desire is not to be the least bit lucid."

"I should think he's accomplishing that," Cavendish said under his breath.

"No." Norcroft studied Gideon with a practiced eye. "He's remarkably sober. More's the pity."

"It was the food," Sinclair said, and shook his head. "We never should have allowed him anything to eat."

"I wasn't even hungry," Gideon muttered.

"I was," Cavendish murmured.

"Perhaps," Norcroft began, "as you are still coherent in spite of your best efforts—"

"In spite of *our* best efforts," Sinclair interrupted.

Cavendish chuckled. "We are nothing if not helpful."

"—you would care to share with us exactly what brought about this desire of yours for oblivion." Norcroft studied him closely. "Or do you plan to continue without pause until it is left to us to carry you home?"

"I have no plans." Gideon shrugged. His only plan when he had arrived at his club a few hours ago was to drink until he could no longer see Judith's face when he closed his eyes. Or hear her voice. Or feel her touch. It would have worked quite nicely too, except one by one his friends had arrived to share in his misery or provide comfort. He wasn't entirely sure which since he hadn't had the slightest desire to talk about Judith or what had transpired between them. Still and all, when one's world had shattered into a thousand pieces it was rather nice to have friends. He glanced around the circle of men. "Actually, I do have a plan."

Norcroft nodded. "Excellent."

"I plan to peruse the list of eligible young women that my aunt has compiled and I have ignored up to now, and from that choose a suitable bride." Gideon raised a glass to his friends. "That is my plan."

Cavendish stared. "That's not much of a plan in my opinion."

"I don't even know his aunt and it doesn't sound like a very good plan to me," Sinclair said under his breath.

Norcroft stared. "What about Lady Chester?"

"Lady Chester is no longer my concern," Gideon

said in a lofty manner, and noted the alcohol must have had some effect. Why, the pain he felt at the mention of Judith's name was scarcely worse than if he'd had a leg cut off or an arm torn away or his still-beating heart ripped from his chest.

The other men exchanged wary glances.

"That explains a great deal," Sinclair murmured.

"Why isn't Lady Chester your concern?" Norcroft said slowly.

"She doesn't want me," Gideon said simply.

Cavendish frowned. "Not at all?"

"Not even a tiny bit." Gideon caught the attention of a waiter and gestured for a refill. "I thought she did. I thought she loved me."

"And?" Norcroft said.

"She says she doesn't."

Sinclair raised a brow. "She came right out and said that?"

"Yes."

"And you believed her?" Cavendish asked.

"No, but ..." Gideon shook his head. "We agreed that either of us could end it whenever we wished to do and she so wishes."

"It's never good when they end it," Cavendish said in a sage manner. "Not the natural order of things."

Gideon shrugged. "All she wants is to remain friends."

Sinclair raised a brow. "And you've agreed to that?"

"Not exactly." Gideon's voice hardened. "I have no desire to be her friend."

"You're just going to let her go then?" Norcroft asked.

"I will not pursue a woman who does not want me." Gideon drained the last tiny drop from his glass. "I've done that once and once was quite enough."

A murmur of assent waved around the circle.

"Unless of course," Norcroft said thoughtfully, "you still want her."

"Oh, it's an entirely different matter if you want her." Sinclair nodded. "It wouldn't do at all to let a woman you wanted get away."

Cavendish's brow furrowed. "When we say *want*, what precisely are we talking about?"

"I thought she wanted me as much as I wanted her. Now . . ." Gideon shook his head. "I don't know. I don't wish to be seen as a fool and certainly don't want to feel like a fool."

"Is it *want* in the carnal sense?" A hopeful note sounded in Cavendish's voice.

"I believe we're speaking of love," Sinclair said to Cavendish.

Cavendish shook his head in a mournful manner. "I was afraid of that."

"I don't want to make another mistake. What if I'm wrong about her feelings? What if she doesn't love me?" Gideon's jaw tightened. "I will not chase after a woman who does not want me."

"You've said that already." Sinclair studied him curiously. "It's your pride, then, rather than your heart that's at stake here."

"Not at all." Gideon stared at the American in annoyance. "It's definitely my heart."

"Then I should think looking a fool or feeling a fool or even being a fool is worth the risk." Sinclair paused. "If indeed your heart is involved."

"You should probably fight for her," Cavendish said in an offhand manner.

"Fight for her?" Gideon crossed his arms over his chest. "And who precisely am I supposed to fight with?"

"You're fighting with Lady Chester for Lady Chester of course," Cavendish scoffed as if what he'd said actually made sense. "She says she doesn't love you. You don't believe her. You simply have to make her accept the truth."

Gideon raised a brow. "Is that all?"

"Warton." Norcroft leaned closer. "It seems to me if you love her . . ." He paused. "Do you love her?"

Gideon huffed. "Yes."

"Have you told her?" Sinclair asked.

Gideon blew a long breath. "Not exactly."

Cavendish snorted.

"Well then, before you let her walk out of your life you should tell her how you feel," Norcroft said. "It all depends on which is more important to you. Your pride or your heart."

"My arrogance will be my undoing," Gideon said under his breath. Bloody hell they were right. Even Cavendish. It scarcely mattered whether he looked like a fool for chasing after a woman who didn't want him. If she did love him and he didn't do all in his power to keep her, that would indeed make him a fool. "You're right," he said slowly. "All of you."

Cavendish grinned. "I knew we were."

A throat cleared behind Gideon. He glanced over his shoulder to find a club steward with a sour expression on his face standing behind him. "Yes?"

"My lord, we have something of a problem." The man's usually serene demeanor was distinctly nonplussed.

"Yes?"

"There is a"—the steward's lips pressed together in a disapproving line—"*lady* in the foyer who insists on speaking to you at once. She says it's urgent."

Judith? Gideon's heart leaped in his chest and he stood. "Of course."

"There he is." Aunt Louisa's voice rang out across the room. The other men jumped to their feet out of respect or to get a better view, Gideon wasn't sure which.

"Good God." Cavendish stared in disbelief.

Sinclair choked back a laugh.

Norcroft shot Gideon a quick look of support.

Gideon knew he should do something, but shock and the most perverse sense of amusement rooted him to the spot. His aunt swept through the hallowed room toward him.

"My lord." Sheer horror sounded in the steward's voice. "I must insist that you do something immediately. A lady has never set foot in this room before."

"I shall do what I can but I can make no guarantees," Gideon said mildly, realizing in the back of his head his days at this particular club were probably numbered. "That lady is a force of nature unto herself and has, to my knowledge, rarely been deterred from her goal. Which, at the moment seems to be me."

Aunt Louisa made her way toward Gideon with a single-minded determination, scattering club members in her wake. "Gideon, I must speak with you at once."

"Apparently," Cavendish muttered.

Aunt Louisa cast him a quelling glance. Cavendish smiled weakly and stepped back.

"You do understand, women are not allowed in this club," Gideon said coolly.

She waved off his comment. "Of course I do, although now that I am here I don't see why." She glanced around the room. "It's not nearly as grand as I thought it would be."

The steward gasped. "Madame, I must insist—"

Aunt Louisa ignored him. "Gideon, you must do something at once. It's Lady Chester."

His breath caught. "What about Lady Chester?"

"She's leaving London," Aunt Louisa said. "She's going off to the jungle to look for orchids."

Gideon clenched his jaw. "With Lord Thornecroft no doubt?"

Aunt Louisa's eyes widened. "Is Frederick going as well?"

"I don't know." Gideon glared. "You just told me."

"I certainly wouldn't put it past the old goat but I have no idea if he's part of this or not. And it scarcely matters." Her gaze met her nephew's. "Your Lady Chester is about to flee your life and if you don't act immediately, you might well lose her forever."

Gideon studied his aunt. "You said she was wrong for me."

"She is." Aunt Louisa heaved a resigned sigh. "But there are worse things in life than choosing the wrong woman if that particular wrong woman is the one who makes you happy."

Gideon raised a brow. "You wish me to be happy then?"

Aunt Louisa huffed. "Apparently. Gideon." She placed her hand on his arm. "If this woman is the one woman who will make you happy, then"—she squared her shoulders—"you would be a fool to let her go."

"You would hate to be a fool," Norcroft murmured.

"Indeed I would." Gideon gazed down at his aunt. He should probably tell her he had already decided not to let Judith go but he was rather enjoying this change of heart on the part of his aunt. "What of my responsibilities? Continuation of the family name? Children and that sort of thing?"

"You're still a young man, Gideon, and please God, you have a long life ahead of you. As much as duty is important, I hate the idea of you being unhappy for the rest of your days. As for children"—she gestured dismissively—"they are not a complete impossibility. One never knows after all. Odder things have happened." Aunt Louisa sighed. "And your cousins will be thrilled."

"Are you certain about this?"

"I am always right." Aunt Louisa drew a deep

breath. "She's only leaving because she thinks it's what is best for you. She loves you, nephew. She as much as admitted to me." She gazed into her nephew's eyes. "Go to her, Gideon. Tell her how you feel. Stop her. Marry her."

"Very well then, you've convinced me." Gideon bit back a grin. "When is she leaving?"

"Today," Aunt Louisa said without hesitation. "Any minute now."

"Then I should go." He started toward the door. "I should hate to have to follow her all the way to South America."

"Paris," Aunt Louisa called. "She's going to Paris first."

"Very well. France it is, then." He glanced back over his shoulder at his friends. "Would you be good enough to escort my aunt out of the premises before you are all asked to leave and not ever return?"

"It would be an honor," Norcroft said.

"Although now that I am here," Aunt Louisa's voice trailed behind him, "I should think a small glass of whisky would not . . ."

Gideon grinned to himself and ignored the indignant glares of club members as he made his way to the door. Bless his aunt's interference. As much as he had already decided not to give up on Judith without a fight, now that he knew she loved him as he loved her, exhilaration had vanquished the vestiges of melancholy. Determination filled him. He would not let her go. Not now, not ever. He should have known he was right about her feelings. He'd never been the kind of man to allow doubt to color his thinking. It was obviously an underrated benefit of arrogance. She had done this to him, or rather love had done this to him.

He exited the building and paused at the top of the steps leading to the front walk. If he missed her at her house he would go to the docks and then all the way to France if he had to. He was not about to let this woman out of his life. Not now. Not ever.

Hours later, Gideon stalked through his front entry and continued without pause into his library.

"My lord," Wells called after him, "you have—"

"Not now, Wells." Gideon shut the library door behind him, strode across the room, and poured a glass of brandy. Damn the woman anyway. Where in the hell was she? An awful gnawing sensation in the pit of his stomach had been growing ever since his first stop at Judith's house. Her butler had sworn she had not yet left for Paris and claimed he had no idea where she was. But the servant was decidedly evasive and Gideon wasn't at all sure if that was at Judith's instruction or if the man was protecting his mistress or simply giving her time to put distance between them. Gideon had inquired at a shipping agent's and determined there were no ships leaving for France today. He had then stopped at both Lady Dinsmore's and Lord Thornecroft's. Lady Dinsmore had had no idea of Judith's plans nor did Lord Thornecroft, although he was annoyingly amused at Gideon's obvious frustration.

It scarcely mattered. Gideon tossed back the glass of brandy. If he didn't find her today he would find her tomorrow or the day after. If he had to travel to the streets of Paris or the jungles of South America or hell itself—

"Have I come at a bad time?" Judith's voice sounded behind him.

His heart caught and he turned and stared at her. "What are you doing here?"

"I . . ." She wrinkled her nose. "I'm not entirely sure."

She was here and that was all that mattered. Still . . . "Have you come to say goodbye?"

She paused for a moment. "No."

He raised a brow. "You're going off to hunt orchids without saying goodbye then?"

"No." She shook her head. "Yes. That is, I'm not entirely sure what I'm doing or where I'm going." She drew a deep breath. "I thought there were things you should know before I leave."

"Oh?" He propped his hip on the corner of his desk and studied her. "In the interest of honesty?"

"If you wish." Judith chose her words with care. "As you know, I have long felt that I was not destined for permanence . . . for marriage. My husband—"

"He hurt you, I know that." Gideon shook his head. "How can you think that I would ever hurt you?"

Her eyes widened. "I don't. Not for a moment." She drew a deep breath. "My fear was that I would hurt you."

"Go on."

"My husband's death was not an accident." Her gaze met his. "He took his own life."

"Judith." This was not at all what he had expected. He straightened and stepped toward her.

"No, please." She held out her hand to stop him. "I need to say this. You need to understand."

"Very well."

"The night he died, he had been in a jealous rage for no reasons save those in his own head. He hit me. He forced me to my knees. He broke my finger. He . . ." Her voice caught. "I have never spoken of this to anyone. I never thought I would. But then I never thought . . ."

He wanted to take her in his arms, comfort her, assure her that no one would ever hurt her again. Instead he couldn't seem to move. "What?"

"I never thought there would be anyone I could tell." She wrapped her arms around herself and gazed into a past he could not see. "Afterward, I locked myself in my rooms. He pounded on the door. I was terrified and worse, I was angry. I told him I was leaving him and I meant it. He begged me to open the door and I wouldn't. He pleaded for my forgiveness and I refused."

"Nor should you have forgiven him," Gideon said under his breath. Anger surged through him at what this man she had loved had done to her.

"A short time later, he . . ." She paused as if the words were too painful to say aloud. "He threw himself off the roof."

The horror of her words echoed in the room.

"And I blamed myself." Her voice was calm, matter-of-fact. She looked at him. "Until today."

His heart twisted for her. "Judith."

"Today, I learned that my husband took his own life because he thought he was becoming the type of cruel, brutal man his father was." She blew a long breath. "I had no idea. I didn't know anything about his father, nor did I know about the demons that haunted Lucian. And even if I had, his sister believes it wouldn't have mattered."

His brows drew together. "She knew this? All these years and she didn't tell you?"

"Alexandra has her own demons and a great deal of bitterness."

"Even so—"

"For ten years, I thought it was my fault." Her voice trembled. "That I was a terrible wife, a vile person. That I was not somehow . . . *enough*, good enough, I suppose. That I drove him to his death." She paused for a long moment. "And all these years, I have not allowed myself to care for anyone in anything other than a temporary, frivolous way." Her chin lifted and her gaze met his. "Until now."

His heart sped up. "Oh?"

"I have always thought that I would spend the rest of my days alone. Without family or affection. A penance of sorts. I was resigned to it. Now . . ."

"Now?" He held his breath.

"Now, I find I don't wish to live another day, another hour"—her voice broke—"without you."

He stared at her in silence. A myriad of thoughts

and emotions filled his head but the right words eluded him.

"Well?" She gestured in a nervous manner. "Say something. Anything. Tell me that your aunt was right and you do love me or that she was right and I am wrong for you. Tell me that I'm a dreadful person and you could never possibly care for me, or tell me to go away, or . . . or something. Gideon, I am presenting you with my heart and if you don't want it, I need to—"

"Judith," he said slowly. "Do you remember at Lady Dinsmore's ball when you looked at her grandmother and said how wonderful it must be to reach advanced age"—without conscious thought he moved toward her—"and be surrounded by family and people who love you?"

She swallowed hard. "Yes."

"People who will miss you when you're gone?"

She nodded.

"At the end of your days, Judith . . ." He stared down at her, his gaze bored into hers. "You will be missed."

An odd sob broke from her and he took her in his arms.

"You will be missed by the husband who will love you for the rest of his life. And if we are fortunate enough to have children, you will be missed by our children and our children's children."

"Gideon." She sobbed. "I do love you."

"And I love you. And if you want to hunt orchids in jungles or lounge under the sun in the south of Spain, you will not do it without me." He gazed into the blue of her eyes and saw love and joy and everything he'd ever wanted and hadn't known he'd wanted until her. "And I promise you every day will be an adventure."

His lips met hers, and for a long moment she clung to him and he held her and he knew, as he had never known anything before, that this, *that she*, was what he had waited his entire life for. She was the missing half of his soul. And whether he'd admit it or not, he'd known it from the moment her gaze had met his. The moment lightning had struck and fused the two of them together. Forever. *Le coup de foudre.*

He raised his head and smiled down at her.

"And sometimes, dear Judith, *this time*, the light lasts forever."

Epilogue

"Where are they again?" Sinclair said idly, swirling the brandy in his glass.

"South somewhere, I think," Cavendish murmured. "South America?"

"No, the south of Spain." Oliver signaled to a passing waiter and was, as he had been for the past three weeks, grateful that he was still able to do so.

There had been some discussion among the club hierarchy about whether Warton, as well as Oliver and Cavendish, guilty simply by association, would be allowed to maintain their membership. Sinclair, as an American, was not technically a member at all but had the privileges of membership thanks to the sponsorship of the other men. Warton had apologized profusely, sworn his aunt would never again step foot in the club, although privately all wondered how anyone could prevent that from happening should she take it in her head to do so, and had as well made a sizable contribution to the club's refurbishment fund. And all now was as it had been.

Except, of course, now there were only three.

Sinclair frowned. "I thought they were going to South America?"

"Lady Chester, or rather Lady Warton now, had apparently planned to go to Paris and then on to Colombia to hunt for orchids," Oliver said. "Her new husband convinced her otherwise. For the moment at least."

"I would wager the man will be in the jungle before the year is out." Sinclair grinned.

"I never imagined Warton would be the first to fall." Cavendish shook his head mournfully. "If it can happen to him, there's scant hope for the rest of us."

"Who did you think would be first?" Sinclair asked.

"Well." Cavendish's gaze slid from Sinclair to Oliver and back. "I would have put my money on you."

"Me?" Sinclair scoffed. "I am not the least bit inclined toward marriage."

"No, but your father has already attempted to arrange one match for you. A father determined to see his son well married is nearly as bad as a mother." Cavendish grimaced. "I can attest to that personally."

Oliver grinned. "Then I would have thought you would have been next."

"Fortunately"—Cavendish grinned—"I am far more clever than anyone suspects."

"You do hide it well," Sinclair murmured.

"One never expects too much from a man who is interested in little more than a good time. Someday I shall emerge from my cocoon of frivolity fully mature and ready for the responsibility of title and family and wife. Until then"—Cavendish raised his glass pointedly—"I intend to enjoy myself."

"Personally, I would have wagered on you to be the first." Sinclair's gaze met Oliver's. "You do seem the marriage sort."

"I might have wagered on myself as well. I have no particular aversion toward marriage." Oliver shrugged.

"And yet," Cavendish said, "you are not actively seeking it."

"Absolutely not," Oliver said staunchly. "There are, after all, four shillings and a fine bottle of Cognac at stake."

"Still, one does have to wonder who the true winners are in this game of ours," Sinclair said idly. "And the ultimate loser."

The men fell silent for a long moment. Oliver wondered if the other two weren't the least bit envious of Warton. He hadn't expected it, and might well only admit it to himself, but he was a touch jealous of their now-married friend. Not specifically because of Lady Chester, although she was indeed something special, but of what Warton had found that the others had not.

"In the years we've known him, I don't think I've ever seen Warton quite so . . ." Cavendish looked at Oliver. "What is the word I'm thinking of?"

Oliver raised a brow. "Happy?"

"Yes, that's it. The man is happy. Annoyingly happy." Cavendish shuddered. "But at what price?"

"Marriage to Lady Warton?" Oliver chuckled. "I daresay that is not as much a price as a prize."

"To the happy couple then." Sinclair got to his feet and raised his glass. The other men followed suit. "To Lord and Lady Warton. Wherever they are."

"And to the next among us to fall." Cavendish shook his head. "God help him."

"And as always, gentlemen." Oliver raised his glass. "To the last man standing, whoever he may be."

In the following pages
you are cordially invited to a tea party
in which the author has invited six characters
and discusses all sorts of things . . .

Guests for *afternoon tea*

∞

Name *Pandora, Countess of Trent*
Address *c/o The Wedding Bargain*

Name *Gillian, Countess of Shelbrooke*
Address *c/o The Husband List*

Name *Marianne, Marchioness of Helmsley*
Address *c/o The Marriage Lesson*

Name *Jocelyn, Viscountess Beaumont*
Address *c/o The Prince's Bride*

Name *Rebecca*
Address *Undetermined*

Name *Elizabeth, Lady Collingsworth*
Address *c/o A Visit From Sir Nicholas*

"So," I said in as casual a manner as possible, given I had never before actually poured tea from the pot that matched my mother's silver coffee service. Frankly, my oversized cup from a family visit to the Baseball Hall of Fame zapped in the microwave with a tea bag—Lady Grey, if you please—tossed in, was about as far as I went when it came to tea.

Not only was I using the aforementioned never-before-used teapot, but I was serving experts in the art of tea pouring. Women who could probably pour tea in their sleep while engaging in scintillating conversation, serious flirtation, even ruling their worlds. They could be charming, clever, amusing, and never spill so much as a drop. Talk about multitasking.

I knew this about these women because, well,

I had invented them. The six pairs of eyes studying my every move belonged to six of my favorite heroines: Pandora Effington Wells (Countess of Trent); Gillian Effington Marley Shelton (Countess of Shelbrooke); Marianne Shelton Effington (Marchioness of Helmsley); Jocelyn Shelton Beaumont (Viscountess Beaumont); their sister Rebecca; and Marianne's daughter, Elizabeth Effington Langley (Lady Collingsworth). "Favorite" being somewhat inaccurate, because I like every heroine I've ever written.

Of course I'd never had six of them staring at me before.

"So," I said again with a short little laugh. You know, one of those odd, high-pitched sounds that's more like embarrassment, even panic, than anything close to amusement.

"May I?" Marianne Effington smiled in a polite manner, gently but firmly pried the teapot from my grasp, and proceeded to fill the cups of the other ladies with all the skill and grace of the perfect Regency heroine. "You don't mind do you?"

"Not at all. Works for me." I smiled gratefully, although I did mind a little. It was hard not to. After all, I was a twenty-first-century woman. I had mastered computers, programming a VCR (still working on the DVD recorder), and parallel parking. It grated that I could be undone by something as simple as pouring tea.

"Perhaps," Jocelyn craned her neck and peered around me, "if your servants were about . . ."

"Oh, I don't have servants," I said, and immediately wished I had kept my mouth shut. All the ladies stared at me in wide-eyed shock. "Well," I gestured feebly, "it's a small house." At least it was small in comparison to Effington Hall or Shelbrooke Manor or Beaumont Abbey.

Gillian stared. "Do you mean to say there is no butler? No footmen?"

"No underfootmen? No housekeeper?" Pandora's eyes widened. "No maids?"

"Are you trying to tell us that you actually clean your house yourself?" Elizabeth gestured at the room. "Floors and windows and such?"

"Of course." I shrugged as if it were no big deal and hoped none of them would notice that my windows and floors and such hadn't been seriously cleaned in a very long time, as evidenced by the unrepentant dust bunnies lingering in the corners of the living room.

A voice in the back of my mind asked why, if I was inviting imaginary people for tea in the first place, didn't I simply invent make-believe servants to clean the house and serve the tea. Or better yet, why didn't I just make up a fantasy mansion in the very best part of London and, while I was at it, might as well do something about those extra pounds—

I firmly squelched the voice and refused to listen to another word. For one thing, I already had my hands too full with my imaginary guests to listen to a voice that only existed in my head. That would be really crazy. And for another, somehow it didn't seem fair to make up servants and a different house, not to mention that weight business. The whole idea of this tea was to invite some of my heroines to visit my world. After all, I lived in theirs periodically.

"Surely you have a cook though?" Rebecca said faintly, as if the very thought of not having a cook was too much to bear.

"I wouldn't wager on it." Pandora glanced at the cakes and tarts I had bought at a very frou-frou bakery. "Although those do look tasty."

"Thank you." I grinned. "I picked them out myself."

"And an excellent choice." Gillian delicately wiped a crumb from the corner of her mouth and cast me an affectionate smile. "I, for one, think it's quite lovely for you to have invited us. I haven't done anything even remotely exciting in a very long time."

"It's an adventure I would say." Marianne beamed. "Completely unexpected and therefore quite grand."

"Grand?" Jocelyn drew her brows together. "I'm not at all sure I'd call it grand." She leaned toward her older sister and spoke under her breath. *"She has no servants."*

"Nonetheless, I find it all most exhilarating," Marianne said firmly.

Gillian nodded. "As do I."

"I don't know." Becky shook her head. "I feel rather vague and indecisive about it all myself."

Jocelyn studied her. "You do look rather odd. Not pale so much as—"

"Indistinct. No, transparent." Elizabeth nodded. "Yes that's it. Transparent. As if one could see right through you."

Pandora winced. "I hadn't wanted to mention it; it seemed rather rude. But, well, now that it's been said aloud." She cast Rebecca a sympathetic glance. "I must admit I can see right through her."

"Oh dear," Rebecca murmured. "I don't feel transparent, but somehow I can't quite decide."

Jocelyn huffed and glared at me. "This is all your fault you know."

"Mine?" I gasped indignantly. "How is this my fault?"

Marianne looked at me as if I had an IQ too low to support life. "You haven't, oh, *done* anything with her, you know. She hasn't been fleshed out, as it were."

"She's little more than an outline." Gillian thought for a moment. "Waiting for color, definition, that sort of thing."

Elizabeth stared in admiration. "That's very good."

"It's simply what comes of being married to an artist," Gillian said in a knowing manner. "One finds oneself looking at all sorts of things in an entirely different way."

"Please, whatever you do, don't get her started on the effects of light at various times of the year." Pandora grimaced.

"Light is scarcely an issue, we're discussing Rebecca," Marianne said firmly. "Besides, the light is shining right through her."

I looked from one woman to the next. "I'm really sorry about this." I nodded toward the rapidly fading Rebecca. "But I don't get it. How is this my fault?"

"Oh for goodness' sakes." Jocelyn rolled her gaze toward the ceiling. "It's your fault because you haven't written her story yet."

"She has no substance. No texture. No solidity." Marianne rested her hand on the ever more translucent hand of her youngest sister. "She's never been more than a minor character."

"She's popped up in three books." I tried not to sound defensive.

"Four," Rebecca said faintly.

"Are you sure?" I thought for a moment. They were right. But of course they would be. They were usually right. I had written them that way. "Sorry, you're right. Three as a teenager and one as an adult."

"A happily married adult with children of her own, as I recall." Gillian's cool gaze pinned mine, and I realized she was the daughter of a duke. I had written her well. "Although you've never mentioned who she married."

"I'm not feeling at all well," Rebecca murmured.

"But whatever you do"—Pandora's gaze narrowed—"do not marry her to a man named Charles."

"We all know what happens when you name a man Charles." Marianne sipped her tea in a resigned manner.

Gillian and Elizabeth traded glances.

I probably should have expected this. Whenever I need a dead husband in a book I usually name him Charles because my husband's name is Charles. It's a joke. Really. Admittedly, sometimes Charles dies slowly and with a great deal of pain, but even the real-life Charles sees the humor in it—most of the time. I drew a deep breath. "My husband thinks it's funny."

"My first husband," Gillian began, "my *dead* first husband wouldn't think it was the least bit amusing. Knowing his fate was sealed simply because of his name."

"Nor would mine," Elizabeth added.

"Although he'd be just as dead if she had called him Ralph or Edwin." Jocelyn nodded in my direction. "If it suited her purposes to have him dead, he'd be dead. She'd write him that way." Her gaze met mine and she grinned. "And I, for one, rather like your Charles joke."

"Thank you," I said.

She leaned toward me. "I daresay it keeps your husband on his toes."

I choked back a laugh. "Yeah, it's kind of fun."

Marianne cleared her throat and nodded toward Rebecca. "About Rebecca."

"Perhaps I should go." Rebecca's voice had little more substance than her appearance.

Marianne glanced down at her hand. A minute ago it had rested on top of Rebecca's. Now it went through her sister's hand. It was very creepy, especially for afternoon tea. "That might be best, dear."

Rebecca sighed, forced a brave, if vague, smile and silently faded away.

It was more than a little unnerving, even for me.

"That was certainly odd," Gillian said under her breath.

"Still, it's not as if we aren't just as imaginary as

Rebecca. Even if we're not quite as," Jocelyn grimaced, "transparent."

"True enough, I suppose." Pandora sighed. "We are simply products of a fertile imagination."

"Or not," Gillian murmured.

All eyes turned pointedly toward the now-empty spot on the sofa, where not even a dent in the cushions indicated where Rebecca had been.

I wondered it if was too early in the day for a Cosmopolitan. I'd bet my guests would love Cosmos. Or a lemon drop. Or one of those mango martinis . . .

"As odd as that was, it cannot be compared with being at tea with your mother and your aunts and realizing at this very moment"—Elizabeth wrinkled her nose—"they are younger than you are."

"I thought that might be a problem," I said more to myself than to them. But hey, what was I supposed to do? I had invited each heroine at the point where I knew her best, which was the end of whatever book was about her. Unfortunately, that meant that a twenty-one-year-old Marianne was sitting in my living room beside her twenty-nine-year-old daughter.

"That is awkward," Gillian said sympathetically, but you could tell she enjoyed being thirty again.

"I quite like it." Marianne beamed at her daughter.

"What was that you said earlier?" Jocelyn thought for a moment. "Ah yes, 'works for me.'"

The other women laughed, although Elizabeth was definitely less amused than my other guests.

But laughter eased whatever tension there might have been, and the gathering broke into animated conversation. They spoke to one another the way sisters or friends did who hadn't seen each other for a while. I wondered what happened in their worlds when I wasn't writing about them. Did it continue as I had set it up? Were there huge changes and events, triumphs and tragedies, in their lives that I would never know anything about because they weren't pertinent to the next book? Or did everything stop? Did they just stand still waiting to be resurrected for another book in which they'd be thirty years older?

Interesting thought. A little weird but interesting. Maybe we could talk about that.

I looked expectantly at my little group of chattering heroines. I hated to interrupt, but this was my tea party and I had vacuumed and bought tarts and everything. I cleared my throat.

No one noticed.

"Excuse me," I said politely.

With an absent glance, Marianne refilled my cup and continued talking to Pandora. Other than that, they ignored me.

"Pardon me," I said once more with more force.

Again, it was as if I didn't exist. If it wasn't so annoying it would have been pretty ironic.

"Hey! Ladies! Yo!" I glared at the assembly. "I didn't invite you all here so that you could chat amongst yourselves. This isn't what I had in mind."

Pandora raised a brow. "What did you have in mind?"

"Well, I don't know exactly. I just thought it would be . . . fun. You know, to hang out together."

"Hang out?" Gillian's brows drew together in confusion.

"Spend time together." I really had to watch my language. I met the gaze of each woman in turn. "In one way or another, each of you represents the best of me and the worst of me. Some of you have the characteristics of my closest friends. Good"—I met Jocelyn's gaze—"and bad."

Jocelyn's eyes narrowed. "Why did you look at me?"

I ignored her. It felt good. "In many ways, each and every one of you is who I would like to be. I know you better than I know my best friends and I want to talk to you. Not watch you talk to one another."

"Of course you don't." Marianne reached over and patted my hand. "We've been horribly rude. Do accept our apologies."

"No problem," I muttered. It was hard to stay annoyed at them. They were so charmingly written.

"Now then," Pandora said brightly. "What shall we talk about?"

"Family? Friends? The latest fashions?" Elizabeth frowned. "Although it might be somewhat difficult to agree on what constitutes latest."

"We could talk about art or literature or politics," Gillian suggested.

"Or men," Jocelyn said casually.

"Men?" I wasn't sure this was a good idea. Who

knew what they might say? On second thought, it probably wasn't a *bad* idea.

"Excellent idea." Marianne beamed. "Are we agreed then?"

"Men it is." Gillian grinned.

Pandora laughed. "Men."

Elizabeth hesitated then sighed. "Men."

Everyone looked at me as if they expected me to lead the discussion. Like I was a counselor and they were waiting for group therapy. Please. In spite of their imaginary nature they were probably far more stable than I was at the moment.

"Okay then. The topic of discussion," I braced myself, "is men."

To be continued . . .